THE TROUBLEMAKERS

MAREN HILL

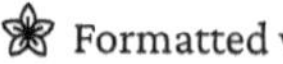 Formatted with Vellum

All that is necessary for the triumph of evil is that good men do nothing.

— EDMUND BURKE

COCOON

The piercing scream of a siren was not uncommon in the city. What was concerning was how abruptly it stopped—right outside the college. For a few seconds, the sudden silence suspended life on campus, turning surprise into suspense.

As classes changed, the halls filled with the sounds of hurrying feet, clipped conversations, and slamming doors. Verity stepped out of the staffroom just in time to see uniformed ambulance attendants rush toward the front office, a stretcher between them.

Curious onlookers hovered, drawn by the commotion but hesitant to get too close. The bell rang again, nudging them toward their next class.

"Okay, let's give them some breathing room," Verity called out. "Clear the area. Classes have begun." She scanned the hallway for loiterers.

As students drifted off, Verity moved closer, approaching Ethel—Kendra's secretary, who stood away from her desk, visibly shaken.

"What happened?" Verity asked softly.

Ethel's face was pale, her voice trembling. "I—I don't know.

Kendra rushed out and told me to call an ambulance. She said Nicole had collapsed—just like that."

In the office doorway, Kendra emerged. Her gaze avoided them, focused on the floor as she crossed to the washroom. Her expression was closed, unreadable.

A moment later, the attendants returned, guiding the stretcher out. Nicole's body was motionless, wrapped in a gray blanket. Her face, deathly white, was eerily still, frown softened, eyes closed.

Verity did well to hide her shock. Her life so far had been relatively untouched by trauma, and seeing Nicole like that was a shock she wasn't prepared for. Verity's mind raced, desperate for answers —but there were none to be found. The silence that followed felt heavier than the siren's scream, like the calm before a storm.

ROOTS

*L*ong before that terrible morning at the college, Verity's life had followed a gentler rhythm.

By the time Verity started dating Charlie in July 1972, she had already graduated from Toronto Teachers' College. She'd been lucky enough to land a teaching position at the local community college soon after. It was a surprise to her that she loved teaching adults, even more than younger students, because discipline problems were not even on the agenda.

Charlie had gained three years of work experience in a downtown Toronto legal firm, but he longed to return to the West Coast, where he'd vacationed during his undergraduate years. When the opportunity to join the prestigious firm of Michelson and Ellis as an associate lawyer arose, Charlie grabbed it.

Even though Verity loved her job, she loved Charlie even more, and as soon as her contract ended on April 30, 1973, they moved 3,000 miles west, landing in Vancouver, B.C.

IT WAS Saturday morning in mid-June, and Charlie welcomed the weekend break from his work at the new law firm. His work was challenging, as expected, but he felt comfortable one month in and liked his associate lawyers. Raising the Venetian blinds on the south-facing windows, Charlie glanced back at Verity, who was approaching from the kitchen.

"We're so lucky to get a view of False Creek and, look, it's going to be a nice day."

Verity joined Charlie at the window, a steaming cup of coffee in her hand.

"No kidding, Charlie; I can't say that I miss living among the towering high-rises on the edge of Cabbage town, with only a hint of the natural world."

Charlie smiled and placed his arm across Verity's shoulders.

"Toronto was great in many ways, but I think we're going to love being west-coasters now."

They chose a color scheme of gold, brown, and orange hues, figuring that would help warm the expected damp and rainy days typical of Vancouver's fall and winter weather. Verity arranged a group of six tangerine-colored pillows across the back of the brown leather sofa, a welcoming splash of orange against a chocolate background.

A yucca tree with three trunks accented one side of the sofa, while a fantail palm graced the side of Charlie's favorite lounge chair. In the kitchen, a large Boston fern hung close to the sink for easy watering.

In the entryway, Verity displayed her best nature photographs in matching black frames, dramatic against the red pepper walls. A jade sculpture of a polar bear sat on the living room mantel, a wedding gift from Charlie's parents.

Their bedroom was serene and luxurious, and they agreed to keep the bedside tables clear of anything but a lamp and a clock radio. A down duvet with a silk cover and matching pillowcases in a teal green invited them to bed each night, often after a shared candlelit bath gently scented by a blue-tinted bubble bath called "ocean spray".

Glancing around the room, Charlie turned to Verity and gave her a gentle hug.

"Verity, you have a flair for decorating. All those fine details really make a difference."

"Aw, thanks, babe; it was a team effort."

She returned the hug and intended to make a grocery list for the next day, but Charlie held on.

"Now, maybe you could pay some attention to some of my fine details before you launch into another project."

The intense look in his eyes and the sweet smile on his handsome face lured Verity to an early night under the billows of the teal-green duvet.

Flipping through the classifieds one Saturday morning in early July, Verity's attention was captured by a job opening at Everton Community College. She couldn't believe her eyes.

"Charlie, this is unreal. There's an instructor position available at Everton, and it's right up my alley."

Verity danced with excitement, waving her arms and swaying her hips. Charlie looked up from his share of the Vancouver Sun, peering over the rim of his reading glasses.

"No way! Talk about perfect timing. I hope you get it, hon. I know how much it'd mean to you."

Verity stopped dancing.

"These positions rarely crop up because teachers are like Pit Bulls. Once they get in, they don't let go."

Verity stiffened her bent fingers and interlaced them, mimicking the clasping jaws of a Pit Bull.

"But how could I possibly get it? There'll inevitably be tons of people applying for that job."

Charlie frowned. "C'mon, Verity; you're an excellent candidate. Go for it."

He jutted his chin forward as if catapulting her into the position.

Verity let out a deep sigh and was silent for a few seconds.

"I mean, I have recent experience at the community college level and actual teaching credentials, which, by the way, aren't required for community college teachers. And my degree and prior work experience are in the exact subject area."

"Well, there you go. I'd hire yuh, babe, no question."

Charlie winked, and Verity chose to think of his gesture as an affectionate kiss rather than any minimization of the opportunity before her.

"Charlie, I want this job so, so much, you don't even know."

Verity set about unpacking her resume, teaching credentials, reference letters, and anything else she could think of to make her application shine.

This would be the perfect job for me.

A MYSTERIOUS PROPOSAL

*I*t happened to be her birthday—Monday, July 16—when Verity received the phone call.

"Mrs. Child, are you available for an interview for the instructor position you applied for in our Business Office Training Division?"

Verity's heart fluttered. "Oh yes, I'd be delighted to attend an interview."

'Delighted' doesn't come close to what I feel—more like ecstatic.

After the call, Verity jotted down the details on the kitchen notepad. Jared's secretary had made sure to remind her: the interview would take place at the Everton campus, not Hillside, where the business office programs were taught.

VERITY ARRIVED at the main campus of Everton College, impressed with how well-kept the grounds were. Her horticulturalist parents taught her the names of many plants, including their botanical names, at a young age, and she recognized nearly every species growing on the college grounds.

Sweeping green lawns surrounded the old brick building, intersected by a wide walkway leading up to the main entrance. The concrete slabs of the walkway were bordered on each side by a row of poplars; their gently flickering, heart-shaped leaves reminded Verity of her hometown, where long laneways bordered by majestic poplars often led to stone mansions shrouded in secrets that people only whispered about.

Mock Orange. A misleading scent. Just to the left of the main stairs, Verity spotted a shrub with delicate white flowers that mimicked orange blossoms. But Verity remembered her parents telling her that those so-called orange blossoms were deceptive. The sweet smell of citrus would attract insects, but not bear fruit.

Ascending the limestone steps toward the front door, Verity looked up at the clock tower. The Canadian flag fluttered in the gentle breeze of the warm summer day.

The air inside the building was stale and smelled of wood varnish melting in the blistering sun. Verity guessed that none of the old, multi-paned windows opened to the fresh air outside. No one else was in sight, although she heard the echo of footsteps and mumbled voices in some far-away hall. The campus directory, immediately visible upon entry, sent her to the third floor.

Wide steps would accommodate crowds of students as they changed classes. Grasping the brass stair rail, Verity felt a nervous excitement as the sound of her footsteps echoed up the stairwell.

Down the hall and to the right, Verity found an open door with a sign that announced "BUSINESS DIVISION" in bold black letters. She took a deep breath as she approached the desk and announced her arrival to the receptionist.

"Hello. I'm Verity Child. I have an appointment with Jared..."

"Oh yes, Jared will be with you in a moment."

Before Verity could sit down in the waiting area, a door swung open.

"Verity Child? I'm Jared Sinclair, Director of the Business Division." He greeted her with a handshake and a smile, then stepped aside to let her enter first.

As she passed him, Verity noticed the brass nameplate on the door bearing his name and title.

Jared was tall and slender, around fifty, his salt-and-pepper hair giving him a distinguished air. A wide sea-green tie complemented his crisp white shirt with its long collar. Shiny shoes and pressed slacks completed his professional look.

"Please, have a seat," he said, gesturing toward the chair opposite his desk.

Verity sat down, setting her purse neatly on the floor, as Jared settled into his leather high-back chair, leaning away from the sturdy oak desk. She sensed him subtly sizing her up while she looked at him with calm anticipation. To steady herself, she let her gaze drift briefly to the window, identifying the Weeping Fig near it—*Ficus benjamina* sprang to mind without effort, a small mental anchor in the moment.

Jared began, "Your résumé is impressive."

"Thank you," Verity said with a polite smile, listening closely for what would come next.

"As you know, this position involves teaching Typing and Business English, or Communications."

Verity gave a quick, attentive nod, keeping her expression neutral.

"It's a three-month substitute position at our Hillside campus, not here at the main campus," Jared added.

"Yes, that would be perfect for me, Jared. I'd love to teach here, and those subject areas are exactly my specialty." She hoped she didn't sound too eager.

But Jared remained overly serious—and to Verity's dismay, he didn't acknowledge her enthusiasm.

"One thing we're looking for is an instructor who has strong class management skills. Would you mind outlining any specific techniques you use to manage a class of unruly students?"

Verity blinked, caught off guard. She couldn't recall ever teaching an entire class of *unruly students*. This was a community college, not grade school. She paused, thinking carefully before she answered.

"I'd say my number one technique for classroom management is maintaining a positive attitude," Verity began. "I don't expect negative behavior—I go in assuming everything will go smoothly. I follow my lesson plan as if we're a team working through a project, and more often than not, that's exactly how it plays out."

Jared chuckled quietly, glancing to the side.

Verity felt a flicker of insult but stayed composed, determined to keep things professional. She clarified gently, hoping he'd understand.

"The key is engagement. If students are interested, there's less room for disruption. I try to understand what motivates them. For example, one of my most successful activities with Grade 12 students was role-playing job interviews—it made them feel prepared and involved."

Jared squinted slightly, as though weighing her response. He reached for a pen beside his desk phone, rolling it between his fingers as if to anchor his thoughts.

Then, his tone shifted. His next words surprised her.

"As you may know..."

He leaned back in his chair, as if to put more distance between them. Studying her face, he continued.

"The main mandate at our Hillside campus is to train adult students for business office careers. But there've been ongoing issues in the Business Office Training Division—serious ones."

Jared tilted his chin upward slightly, his brow furrowing as if he'd just caught a whiff of something unpleasant.

"What kind of issues?" Verity asked carefully.

He raised one eyebrow. "We're not entirely sure. But whatever it is, it's been going on for too long. We need someone who can help us figure it out."

He tapped his pen against the desktop.

Verity hesitated, unsure how much to probe. Still, she offered a polite response.

"I'm sorry to hear that. Are the concerns isolated to the Business Office Training Division, or do they involve the broader Hillside campus?"

Jared paused before replying. "These problems affect everyone, Verity. And they seem to be getting worse, not better."

He glanced down at the desktop and let out a heavy sigh.

"I see."

Verity felt she wasn't making progress—and yet, she also sensed she wasn't meant to dig deeper.

An awkward silence hung in the air.

Jared cleared his throat. "You see, when the team isn't cohesive, it becomes harder to move forward."

"Yes, I understand."

Verity wanted to keep the conversation going, show engagement, but the vagueness of his comments left her unsure of what to say next.

"And when you have colleagues plotting to disrupt things, to undermine you..." He trailed off, staring at the desk and slowly shaking his head.

Verity leaned forward slightly. "Just so I'm clear—you believe some members of the teaching staff are working against the Division's best interests?"

"We don't know if it's one person or more," he said, his voice quiet.

"I see. Can you give me an example of how they're trying to upend things?"

Jared paused. "If I knew exactly how they were operating, I could probably figure out who's behind it."

Verity shifted in her chair, her patience thinning. "Do you know who's behind it?"

"We have our suspicions."

So now he thinks it's just one person.

Verity sat still, hopeful that more information was coming, while still wondering how all of this involved her. She waited for Jared to continue.

This time, his demeanor shifted. His eyes looked brighter, and he seemed more present, more engaged.

"We're looking for someone who can blend in, keep their ear to the ground, identify the troublemakers, and report back to us."

He paused, as if measuring her response.

So now we're back to the idea of more than one 'troublemaker'.

"Is that something you think you could do?" Jared looked her straight in the eye.

Verity paused, looking away. The tone of the interview had shifted. Barely five minutes had passed, and she suddenly felt ambushed.

Her gaze dropped to her purse on the floor, and for a moment, she pictured herself grabbing it and bolting for the door.

This wasn't what she'd expected—not after her interview at Toronto Community College, nor after the many others she'd experienced along the way.

The morning had begun with her meticulous plan in motion: clean, pressed clothes laid out neatly on the bed, faux pearl earrings in the classic Chanel style—long enough to be noticed, not so small they'd disappear into her hair.

She'd set her alarm early, building in extra time in case anything unexpected arose. She could barely contain her excitement as she'd walked toward Jared's office, full of hope that this might finally be the job of her dreams.

And now this.

Ambushed.

A profound sense of disappointment replaced Verity's nervous excitement. Her teeth clenched as resentment welled inside, making it hard to respond.

Trying to mask her discomfort but still appear interested in the position, Verity glanced at the weeping fig, then the floor, and back again.

She wondered what she could say in the next few seconds to stay in the running, without committing to something she found unpalatable.

Deep down, Verity still wanted the job. Maybe her characteristic optimism could help her navigate this unexpected obstacle.

There was a time I wondered what it would be like to be a detective. Maybe this is my chance.

Verity's unfiltered reply slipped out before she could stop it.

"So, you're looking for a spy of sorts."

Jared shifted in his chair, discomfort crossing his face. "Well, I wouldn't call it that." He twisted slightly away from Verity and crossed his legs. "We just thought a newcomer without alliances among the teachers might be the best person to figure out which ones seem determined to block progress at every turn."

Verity didn't bother asking who "we" referred to.

When the interview began, Jared talked about troublesome students; now it was troublesome teachers.

"Yes, that must be very discouraging. And I can see how a neutral newcomer might have a good chance at solving the mystery."

Her words felt distant, disconnected from what she truly thought. Yet if she wanted to keep her chances alive, she had to sound on board.

But deep down, she wasn't so sure.

Verity knew better than to throw away her chance to work at the college level without giving it careful thought, but her deepest honesty wouldn't allow her to agree to play the role of a spy.

Is that even ethical? Legal?

She struggled with how to respond.

"And when you mention not developing alliances, I suppose you mean hiring someone who acts like a sort of sponge, soaking up information to report back to you. Is that right?"

Verity sensed the delicacy of the situation and worried she might blow the interview at any moment.

"Unbiased information is key. That would give us something to work with."

"Yes. And would this information come in written reports?"

"We can figure out those details later."

Jared tapped his pen impatiently on a pad of paper on his desk, but Verity didn't want to feel pressured into something she wasn't sure about.

At this stage, it seemed to Verity that Jared hadn't looked at his plan through a realistic lens.

"If you don't mind, I'd like some time to consider this further. I want you to know how much I want this job, but since this is new information that wasn't initially shared, I hope you'll understand my need to reflect on it."

"Of course. Do you think you can get back to me by tomorrow? I have other applicants to consider."

Verity bent forward and retrieved her purse from the floor. Pushing her chair out of the way as she rose, she took a few steps away before looking at Jared again.

"Yes, I'll be in touch soon, definitely by tomorrow." Verity tried to manage a smile, masking the concern she felt.

Jared raised his eyebrows as if to say, *What do you think?* But Verity steered away from any further conversation.

Verity left his office feeling confused and disappointed, wondering if other candidates were being considered.

Passing the reception desk, Verity could hear the receptionist on the phone.

"Yes, Nicole, I'll relay that message to Jared. Six o'clock at the Boondocks. Okay."

"Yes, Nicole, I'll relay that message to Jared. Six o'clock at the Boondocks. Okay."

As she descended the stairs, Verity felt conflicted. What she had hoped would be the gateway to her ideal job now felt shadowed by the request to act as an informant. The unexpected turn left her feeling tainted, unsure how to reconcile her ambition with this new reality.

Stepping into her old, light metallic green Cadillac felt like returning to something familiar. People often marveled at how easily she could parallel park the long beast, but Verity appreciated the square design of the hood and trunk—they gave her clear, reliable markers.

She felt an affinity with the car. It was like her: old-fashioned and dependable. Before turning her key in the ignition, she took a moment to collect herself. She reminded herself that life had been good to her, especially when she played by the rules.

She reflected on her professional journey until now. And she realized that her professional training, field experience, and credentials —none of that prepared her for the decision Jared had asked her to make today.

CALL THEM UP!

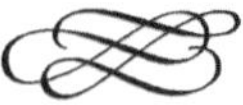

Back in their apartment, Verity had waited until Charlie got home from work to recount the details of her unusual interview.

She smiled when she heard the front door open.

"Hey," she called from her spot on the living room sofa. "How was work? Have you had dinner?"

"Work was busy." Charlie's keys clanked onto the hall table as he walked in. "And yeah, I grabbed a bite on the way home. You?"

He leaned down to give Verity a quick kiss, then dropped onto the leather sofa, jostling her slightly.

"So," he said, settling in. "How was the interview?"

"I'll just say it was the strangest interview I've ever had. It seemed unbelievable even as it was happening—and now that I've had time to think about it, it feels even more strange."

"How so?"

"Jared Sinclair wanted to hire me to be an informant." Verity turned to look at Charlie, waiting for his reaction. "I kid you not," she said, raising her eyebrows. "He wants someone to spy on the other teachers and find out who's causing problems over there."

Charlie stared straight ahead, silent. Verity touched his arm, prompting him to look at her.

"Get this—he wouldn't even tell me what the problems were. He was incredibly vague about the whole thing."

"Interesting job description," Charlie said. "What did you say to him?"

"I told him I wanted the job, but I needed time to think about this unexpected part of the role. It was completely new information."

"Uh-huh. How did that go over?"

"I suppose my response surprised him as much as his request surprised me. I mean, people *covet* these jobs; they don't turn them down. Most would leap at the chance."

Charlie rested his head against the back of the sofa. "And may I remind you just how much you wanted this position?"

"Yes, I'm aware," Verity said. "But beyond wanting to continue my teaching career in a field I love, with the students I love, there's another reason I *need* this job."

Charlie turned to give her his full attention.

"I need something to balance out your workaholic ways, Charlie." She leaned in, pressing her forehead to his, her gaze mock-stern.

"We make a good pair, then, Verity," he said with a grin. "Because we both know when you're working, you go at it full steam ahead, too."

They smiled at each other, a shared understanding passing between them.

"But listen, Verity, you just listed three very compelling reasons to take this job. If you want my advice, call them first thing tomorrow and say yes. You can figure out the rest later."

"I hear you, Charlie, I do. But what if I can't meet Jared's expectations?"

"You're worthy, Verity. And so much more. Have faith in yourself." Charlie stood and walked over to the liquor cabinet. "And I get that you have your ideals—most of us do, especially starting out. But then reality comes along, and sometimes those ideals... well, they don't all survive the ride."

VERITY CALLED Jared Sinclair's line at 8:00 a.m. sharp. His recorded voice invited her to leave a message.

"Oh, hello, Jared, it's Verity Child. I wanted to let you know I'd be delighted to accept the position as you described, if it's still available. You can reach me at 675-3434. I look forward to hearing from you. Thank you so much."

Aarrggghhhh. Did I just accept a job that wasn't officially offered? And delighted? Am I delighted? Why is this so confusing?

BY MIDWEEK, Jared's secretary called with an invitation to a second interview the following Monday—with Kendra Howard, the Program Coordinator at the Hillside campus.

After planning her outfit and reviewing her notes, Verity stood at the kitchen sink, staring at the cluster of bamboo on the windowsill. "*Dracaena braunii,*" she said aloud. "Lucky bamboo—the epitome of good fortune and happiness."

Okay, she thought. *I'll take that as a sign.*

She chose her interview clothes with care and made sure to get out for her morning run. The night before, she set her alarm extra early to allow time for any last-minute surprises. Mentally preparing for a positive experience, she hoped this second interview would be more straightforward than the first.

DESPITE HER CAREFUL PREPARATIONS—INCLUDING a relaxing bath on

Sunday night that sent her into a deep sleep beside Charlie by 10:00 p.m.—their night turned out far different than planned.

In her dream, it was a windy afternoon. Verity stood in a wide field, long grass whipping against her bare legs. Overhead, a parasailer floated higher into the sky, his cheerful yellow-and-red-striped parachute rising toward a canopy of billowing white clouds.

Then, the mood shifted. A thick cover of gray clouds rolled in, darkening the sky. Instead of beginning his descent, the parasailer kept climbing, disappearing completely into the cloud bank.

Verity stared upward, neck craned, holding her breath. Still no sign of him. Still nothing. No sound, no movement. She felt helpless and alone in the vast field, unsure of what to do.

At last, a burst of colour emerged from the clouds. Relief flooded her—until panic seized her.

He was falling. Fast.

Was there a hole in the parachute?

Whoosh. Whoosh. Whoosh.

He plummeted straight toward the earth, and the only possible landing zone was unforgiving ground.

Verity sprinted toward the spot where she guessed he might hit. She had only seconds to decide where to stand and not get hurt herself.

When he crash-landed, half of his body disappeared into the ground. He didn't cry out. There was no blood. No people. No one rushing to help.

Compelled forward, Verity crept closer, a cold weight settling in her stomach. When she reached him, she bent down and placed a hand on his shoulder.

He smiled. His eyes were wide and unnatural.

Then, in an instant, his head snapped around, revealing another face: one twisted and gruesome—pitch-black eyes, blood streaking across ghostly cheeks, lips purple and leathery like crocodile skin, teeth bared in a hideous grin.

A deafening roar split the air as the figure rose, now fully unburied. Unharmed. Unstoppable.

And he was coming for her.

Untangled from the wreckage, he chased her with inhuman speed. Verity ran, but she knew—

She didn't stand a chance.

Her terrified screams jolted Charlie from a deep sleep, snapping him bolt upright. He shook Verity's shoulder firmly, trying to pull her from whatever horrors she still imagined

"Verity, Verity, wake up; you're having a nightmare." She sat up in bed, bewildered and distraught, her body drenched in sweat. Charlie watched a bead of perspiration trickle from her eyelid onto her cheek.

But even awake, Verity couldn't shake the feeling that the nightmare wasn't over.

ONE MORE THING

The sickeningly sweet scent of cheap perfume assaulted Verity's senses as she pushed open the door to Kendra Howard's office. It reminded her of a piano teacher she'd had as a child—sitting beside Mrs. Helmsley on the piano bench for what felt like an eternity, the overpowering fragrance making the hour feel like punishment.

Inside, scrawny, broken stems and pale, wilted leaves of a spider plant dangled helplessly from the bookshelf, as neglected as the brand-new hardcover books resting beside it. The walls of the small, hole-in-the-wall office were an institutional off-white, bare of pictures or decoration. Kendra Howard herself was the only thing in the room that looked well-cared for.

Not one hair of Kendra's sleek, black page-boy hairstyle was out of place; paired with her thick, caterpillar-like eyebrows, it gave her a sharp, no-nonsense look. A silk scarf tied with meticulous precision perfectly complemented her plum suit. Verity guessed she was around forty-five.

As Kendra stepped forward from her desk, she greeted Verity with a wide smile and an outstretched hand.

"I'm Kendra Howard," she said, giving Verity a quick head-to-toe once-over, lingering just a moment longer, Verity thought, on the area around her bosom. It happened so fast that Verity wondered if she'd imagined it.

"Hello, Mrs. Howard, I'm..."

Kendra cut her off, exclaiming, "I know who you are; come on in," as if introductions were unnecessary. "And please, call me Kendra." She sat down, motioning for Verity to take the chair opposite her desk.

"Did Jared tell you anything about the position?" she asked, glancing up from the papers she was hastily organising on the desktop.

"He said I would teach Typing and Business Communications if I'm hired, and that it's a three-month substitute position."

"She stopped arranging the papers, folded her arms on the desk, and met Verity's gaze. Well, there've been a lot of problems in the Business Division—started long before I became Coordinator."

Oh, here we go again.

Verity noticed how quickly Kendra made it clear that the root of the problems wasn't her fault.

"My best advice to you, Verity, is to remain neutral in your relationships with the staff."

Verity sat up straight in her chair, absorbing Kendra's motherly counsel to steer clear of trouble.

How could a spy possibly uncover vital information if they didn't get involved?

Still, she kept her full attention on Kendra, hoping for any helpful insight.

"I practise neutrality in my role as coordinator, and it's worked out very well for me." Kendra nodded to herself as if affirming her wisdom, a satisfied smile spreading across her face.

"You see, my dear, you don't want to align yourself with the wrong people and risk jeopardizing your chances for advancement."

Verity offered a polite nod, her expression tinged with concern. As she sat back in her chair, Kendra's tone grew more serious.

"However, I think things will improve around here once Shirley — the instructor you'll be replacing — is gone. Her last day before going on sick leave happens to be the day you start, but you might do well to avoid her."

She paused, then added in a lower, more confiding voice, "She's not well, you know."

Composing her best look of empathy, Verity secretly revelled in excitement. Kendra spoke as though the job was already hers.

This could lead to a permanent position if I play my cards right. But she quickly reminded herself not to get ahead of things.

"Do you have office management experience?" Kendra asked, making it clear she hadn't even read Verity's résumé.

"Oh yes," Verity replied, eager to share her qualifications. "I have a B.A. in Office Management from the University of Mapleton," she said, pausing slightly, hoping the name might carry some weight.

Kendra looked blank and cut her off. "Credentials can get you in the door, but they don't guarantee a seat at the table." Verity caught the gleam in her eye—Kendra enjoyed her private joke.

Smiling, Kendra added, "As far as I'm concerned, you're hired... but it's up to Jared." She stood and moved toward the door. "Now, I really must run—I'm not supposed to be here at all. It's the first day of my vacation, and I'm catching a plane to Hawaii in an hour and a half."Kendra smiled broadly and said she would let Verity know if she got the job when she returned in two weeks. "Or, if I don't, Jared will." Verity felt a rush of air as Kendra swept open the door.

Returning the smile, Verity rose from her chair, thanked Kendra, and made her way to the open door. She was nearly in the reception area when Kendra called after her.

"Verity—just one more thing."

Verity turned, and Kendra stepped aside, motioning her back into the office, out of Ethel's earshot. In a lowered voice, she said, "You'll eventually meet an Irish woman named Stella. Steer clear of her. You strike me as clever, so I trust you'll see for yourself—she's not someone worth your time."

"Noted," Verity replied, and left promptly, feeling like she'd had enough weirdness in the last forty-eight hours to last a while. But asking Verity to avoid Stella was like asking a toddler to ignore a rack of freshly baked cookies left within reach.

DRIVING HOME, Verity couldn't help musing over how swiftly Kendra had chosen her as the top candidate, without even glancing at her résumé. There was something oddly eager, almost theatrical, about the woman. Excessively welcoming, like a carnival barker selling tickets to the House of Fun.

But more unsettling was her remark about Shirley. *"She isn't well, you know,"* suggested something more serious—perhaps a mental health issue, Verity thought. And then to imply that things would improve simply because Shirley was leaving? To say such things to a potential employee made Verity question what sort of boundaries were respected in this place.

Do I want to work in a place where that even crosses my mind?

One thing was clear: Kendra had been so eager to replace Shirley that she'd delayed her Hawaiian vacation to size up a possible replacement. What on earth had Shirley done to deserve such open denigration?

Despite herself, Verity already felt slightly tangled in staff politics. She awaited confirmation of her hiring with only a trace of doubt, though oddly, she wasn't as thrilled as she thought she'd be.

Strange not to feel more excited about landing the job I'd dreamed of... or is it?

CONTRACT

73-07-25

Dear Mrs. Child:

It is my pleasure, on behalf of the Everton College Council, to offer you a faculty position at the Hillside campus. The three-month, short-term contract would be from Monday, August 6, 1973, to Friday, November 2, 1973.

I trust your association with Everton College will be enjoyable and rewarding.

Dr. Farmer
Principal
Everton Community College

WITHIN TWO WEEKS, Verity had signed her contract, relieved to see there was no mention of the proposed role of informant.

"Charlie, which outfit do you think would look better on me for my first day at Hillside?"

Verity had laid out three options across their queen-sized bed. While she leaned toward classic styles, at home she preferred to go without makeup and wear natural fabrics whenever possible. Her favourite dress was a long, flowing cotton maxi.

With a bath towel wrapped around his waist, Charlie emerged from the shower that Saturday morning. "Oh, I don't know. They all look good on you." He paused, then pointed. "Maybe the navy-blue suit and white blouse. If you want to look businesslike, take it to the max."

Then, shifting gears, he added, "Hey, what say we go for a walk on the Seawall this morning? I could use some fresh air—maybe we can grab some lunch."

"Yeah, I always like that one too. On the other hand, I don't want to seem intimidating, especially to adult students who might not have been in school for years. Sure, I could use some exercise—maybe we could find something to eat in Stanley Park?"

"Right on!" said Charlie. "Can you be ready to leave in about half an hour?"

Verity was preoccupied. "What about the pink flowy skirt outfit? That's fun, don't you think?" Then, without waiting for an answer, she added, "I think I'll settle on the blue wrap dress—it seems like a good in-between."

She chose a short-sleeved, periwinkle blue dress. The sleeves were gently gathered at the shoulders, their narrow hems neatly pressed. Her thoughts returned to Charlie's question. "As far as lunch goes, if you've got the moolah, I've got the time. And yes, I can be ready in half an hour." Verity hung her clothes back in the closet as they continued the conversation.

"How's the teaching prep going?" Charlie asked as he slid into his blue jeans.

Verity took a moment to admire how handsome Charlie looked fresh out of the shower. Her eyes traced the strong lines from his broad shoulders and smooth, hairless chest down to his slim waist and narrow hips. As he buckled the leather belt on his blue jeans, she imagined undoing it and pulling him back onto the bed. He stayed surprisingly fit for someone with a desk job—and someone who ate out as much as he did, she thought.

"Here's the scoop," Verity said as Charlie grabbed a pair of socks. "Luckily, they use the same Business English and Communications textbook I used in Toronto. I still have all my old lesson plans, which I can tweak for this setup."

She added, "And typing's self-paced, so my main job is staying ahead of the keenest learners. I could teach all the basics with my eyes closed."

Her enthusiasm wavered. "I have to admit, I'm a bit apprehensive about that place. How do you build good relationships with colleagues when you're hiding an agenda?"

Charlie pulled a white T-shirt over his head and slid it onto his arms. "That sounds rough, Verity. If I were you, I'd try to forget about any agenda and do what any new employee would—be yourself."

"What if being myself isn't good enough?" Verity asked. Charlie rolled his eyes.

"Well, you know me—I make friends fast, always have. And here's the kicker: people have always told me their secrets without me even asking. Could come in handy if you're planning to be an informant... or if you're about to uncover something no one wants you to know."

NICOLE

*V*erity arrived for her first day of work at the Hillside campus feeling somewhat apprehensive. The college was about fifty years old. A drab place in need of an update, the walls were off-white, and the floor tiles were dark grey with light grey speckles. The stairs were rubberized to help prevent slipping.

Armed with a mental list of questions, Verity reminded herself this was an opportunity to gain experience and live up to the professional standards she valued as a teacher.

If the interview was strange, however, the first day of work was even stranger — and Verity had no idea just how much she was about to discover behind those dull walls.

She headed straight to Kendra's office, just as she'd been told. A slim, dark-haired woman was leaving, offering to bring muffins for break.

"Oh yes, please — banana nut," Kendra said, then paused. "Actually, no. Nicole will probably join us, and with her severe nut allergy, it's safer if I have a bran muffin instead."

The woman nodded. "I'll see what they have," she said, hurrying off.

"Good morning, Kendra," Verity greeted with a bright smile, feeling pleased to be part of the Hillside team.

Kendra appeared in the doorway with a welcoming smile, returning Verity's greeting.

"Ah, good morning, Verity; please come in."

She had a pleasant, outgoing manner, but Verity caught a hint of concern in her eyes—a slight crease between her brows, as if something was on her mind.

Does she dislike my dress? Or is there something stuck in my teeth? Did I forget deodorant?

Verity stepped into the tiny room, immediately hit by the sharp smell of cigarette smoke.

"I must apologize for the smoke. Jared was just here." Kendra smiled to herself, and Verity caught a strangely familiar tone in how she spoke of him. "If it were anyone else, I wouldn't allow it."

Thankfully, Verity wasn't invited to sit. Instead, Kendra led the way to the staffroom, the sharp click of her shiny patent-leather pumps echoing down the hallway. Verity would soon learn that Kendra's signature stomp made sneaking up on her nearly impossible—a built-in drum announcing every arrival.

Once inside, Kendra pointed toward a vacant cubicle at the far end, leaving Verity to navigate and make her own connections.

"That'll be your desk. Nicole's is just in front of you; you can wait there for her. If you have any questions, ask Nicole," Kendra instructed. "Oh, and in case you're wondering, the big open space in the middle is for staff meetings."

As Verity settled into the steno chair, she heard Kendra's heel stomp echoing down the hallway.

Glancing around the staffroom, Verity noticed how the bright fluorescent lights battled the natural light pouring in from the large east-facing windows. Each instructor's cubicle offered a small measure of privacy, with enough room to pin up timetables, memos, family photos, and perhaps a child's artwork.

To Verity, the large open space in the middle of the room offered a welcome contrast to the clutter of paperwork, office supplies, stacked books, and personal knick-knacks scattered throughout the cubicles. She could easily imagine teachers sliding their chairs into the open area for staff meetings.

Only two women were in the room when Verity arrived. One, seated in the third cubicle behind her own, didn't look up from the book she was reading, even though Verity was a newcomer. The other woman rose immediately and approached with a booming voice.

"Good morning. I'm Stella. You must be Verity." She bowed slightly as she spoke, a kind smile lighting her face.

"Yes, hello, Stella. Nice to meet you. And what do you teach?"

"I'm head of the English Department. What will you be teaching, Verity?"

"Typing and Business English and Communications—while Shirley is away."

Verity blinked. She was surprised that the head of the English Department didn't know she'd been hired to teach in that department.

"Filling in for Shirley, are you?" Stella's belly shook with a soundless laugh, her bright blue Irish eyes sparkling as she awaited Verity's response.

"Yes." Verity's voice softened. She wasn't sure what to make of Stella's reaction. Was the substitute position considered a joke?

"Have you taught at Everton College before?"

"No, I'm from out of province. What about you?" Verity, suddenly less confident, tried to shift the spotlight away from herself.

"Oh, I'm an old-timer here. If you need help settling in, just let me know." Stella adjusted the stack of textbooks she was carrying, then leaned in slightly, her tone dropping. "Just choose your friends wisely. It can make a big difference around here, you know."

Verity wasn't sure how to take that last remark. Coupled with similar warnings from both Jared and Kendra, Verity was beginning to think her new job might be less about teaching and more about navigating a minefield.

"I'm just waiting for Nicole to help me get started," she said, forcing a smile.

Stella's lips curled into a smirk. She raised her eyebrows and nodded slowly, as if Verity had confirmed something she already suspected.

"Oh, Nicole's going to help you out, is she? Well, good luck with that."

Still chuckling to herself, Stella turned and strode out the door.

Teachers came and went—some offering polite smiles, a few tossing out friendly hellos. Verity sat quietly at her desk, feeling a bit ridiculous, like someone who'd shown up to the wrong party. The rhythms of the place moved around her: the shuffle of papers, the low murmur of voices, the occasional clomp of heels in the hallway. Everything in motion—except her. She felt like an outsider looking in.

Waiting for Nicole felt endless. Verity wished someone had given her a school calendar, a timetable, anything to anchor her in this unfamiliar place. The growing sense of uselessness gnawed at her until finally, she stood and crossed the room.

"Hello, I'm Verity. I thought you might like to know who the newcomer is."

The woman glanced up and, chuckling softly in a deep voice, said, "I'm Angela. I teach Bank and Teller Training." Something in her manner seemed almost apologetic, and that hint of humility endeared her to Verity right away.

Angela's cubicle was flanked by a tall bookshelf crammed with volumes on public administration.

"I'm familiar with business administration," Verity said, nodding toward the collection. "But not public. You clearly have a strong interest in the subject."

"Yes, I'm working on my MPA," Angela replied, her tone modest but warm—enough to satisfy Verity's curiosity about her quiet, bookish colleague.

Back at her cubicle, Verity had barely settled into her chair when the staffroom door swung open. A stranger strode in and made a beeline for the cubicle marked out for Nicole, directly in front of Verity's. Without much more than a vague smile, the woman dropped a heavy load of books onto her desk, let out a long sigh, and plopped into the steno chair with an air of weariness.

Even after all that waiting, Verity had the distinct feeling she was about to be ignored. Still, she rolled her chair slightly forward, peeking around the edge of the cubicle wall, and ventured a hopeful introduction.

"Hi. I'm Verity Child. Kendra asked me to…"

Nicole glanced up at Verity but cut her off before she could finish.

"Yes, I know who you are. I'm Nicole, and I'll be with you in a minute," she said tersely, then turned back to the stack of papers on her desk. She stuck the end of a gold pen between her teeth, staring at a document as if Verity weren't there. After a moment, she marked something on the timetable pinned to her section of the cubicle wall.

Verity watched her closely. Nicole's busyness seemed more deliberate than necessary. *Was it shyness? Insecurity?* Verity had seen this kind of behaviour before—often in people who projected confidence but felt unsure inside.

Finally, Nicole turned and shoved a sheet of paper across the desk as though tossing a bone to a dog.

"Here's the class schedule," she said. "It shows what subjects you're teaching, where you'll be, and when."

"Thanks. It's good to have this; now I can get organised." Verity smiled appreciatively.

"Yes, you have everything you need to know right there on that piece of paper. The bell rings ten minutes before the hour to give students time to get to their next class. There's a ten-minute break in the morning and a one-hour lunch break. Since classes end at three, there's no afternoon break."

Sensing a slight irritation in Nicole's tone, Verity tried to add a positive note.

"It's nice to have an early finish to classes. That gives us time to prepare for the next day, right?"

Nicole didn't respond, letting Verity's effort drop. Instead, she carried on with her own rhythm.

"The filing cabinet in room 103 is shared between you and me; the top drawer is mine."

"Okay, so does that mean I can use the other drawers?"

"No. Well, sort of. The other two are shared but kept locked. We store tests in there—don't want those going missing. Completed exams are kept for a month after the student graduates in case of any disputes. After that, they go into long-term storage."

"Sounds like the bottom drawer is mine, then," Verity said, nodding in agreement.

"We follow a continuous intake system here, so students can start their program at the beginning of any month."

"Yes, I've worked with that system before. September seemed to be the biggest draw."

Nicole gazed out the window, leaning back in her chair and crossing her arms.

"Uh-huh. September is horrendous around here." She barely glanced at Verity, fulfilling her orientation duty with minimal enthusiasm.

"I've got the whole typing program laid out in an easy-to-follow manner." Nicole handed Verity a multi-page document titled *Course Outline: Typing 180 and 181*. Waving a hand toward the document, she said, "Just follow that and you'll be fine."

Nicole rolled her chair back from her desk, signalling the meeting was winding down.

Flipping through the document, Verity noticed a section labelled "Lesson Plans."

"Uh, do you mean you want me to follow your course outlines? Or the prepared lesson plans?"

"As I said," Nicole sighed deeply, giving the impression she could hardly be bothered.

"Just follow the program like everyone else, and you'll do fine."

Verity squared her shoulders and faced Nicole. "I'm an experienced teacher, Nicole, and this is my specialty. I enjoy preparing my own lesson plans." She smiled politely.

Nicole's upper lip curled in a sneer—no smile softened her expression. "You know, I don't have time for this." She stood abruptly. "Just follow me downstairs. I'll show you how things are done around here."

Verity would take over Nicole's Typing and Office Procedures classes—Typing 180—starting the next day. Any further questions, she figured, would have to wait... or perhaps go unanswered altogether.

Opening the rear door, they descended a long flight of stairs to reach the typing rooms on the lower floor. The overpowering smell of bleach in the stairwell marked their descent.

Once inside the classroom, Nicole went straight to her chair at the front and sank behind the solid oak, double-pedestal teacher's desk.

Verity wondered if Nicole was tired—she'd seen elderly or unwell people make a beeline for a seat as soon as they entered a room, as if it were a necessity.

Feeling somewhat like an outsider, Verity, who hadn't been introduced to the class, tried to follow Nicole's lead. She quickly scanned the room, then settled into an empty chair beside Nicole's desk.

Room 102 was a corner classroom with windows on both the north and east sides. Apart from that luxury, it looked like a typical typing room, with students seated one behind the other in rows of five and the teacher's desk centred at the front. A cluttered bookshelf stood at the back of the room, and Verity wondered why such a symbol of disorganization was allowed in a business office training classroom.

Nicole slid open the centre drawer of her desk and selected a red-ink marking pen. Raising her voice to be heard over the clatter of typewriter keys, she began, "A large part of your first week with the September intake of Typing 180 will be spent explaining and implementing the daily routine of typing drills to improve speed, accuracy, and technique; teaching them how to calculate timed writing scores; and showing them how to prepare assignments for submission. These students are mostly from previous intakes, so they are aware of the routines. The newest typists have only been here three days, because of the August long weekend."

Verity listened attentively as Nicole continued.

"Their final mark will be a combination of net typing speed, production score, and a subjective mark." Nicole paused, inviting Verity to contribute — a departure from the earlier part of their meeting.

"And by 'production', you mean assignments such as correspondence, meeting minutes, reports, memos, that sort of thing, right?"

Nicole turned her head to look at Verity. Her unblinking eyes suggested she had just witnessed a toddler yank her favourite flower from the garden. She glanced out toward the busy students, then back at Verity before continuing.

"Minutes of a meeting, reports for presentation, and book manuscripts are all part of Typing 181, obviously for our more advanced students. These Typing 180 students are working on their level of production now—letters and envelopes," Nicole said, waving her hand dismissively toward the students. "Just walk around and see if anyone's having any problems."

As Nicole returned to circling errors on timed writings or slashing a red diagonal line across the page, Verity waded into the classroom, walking up and down the rows of students, their eyes glued to the words they were copying or stopping to read the assignment. Verity tried to look comfortable, but felt anything but.

As she passed a student sitting toward the back of the first row, typing a business letter, Verity glanced at the work and noticed a common error.

"Excuse me," Verity said, smiling at the student. "I'm Verity, and I'll be taking over from Nicole starting tomorrow."

The student stopped typing and glanced up. "Oh, nice to meet you, Verity. I'm Fiona."

Verity smiled again and pointed to the Subject line on the page. "I just noticed something here. What style of letter is this?"

"Oh, it's modified block."

"In that case, as you may recall, the subject line needs to be centred, not aligned with the left margin."

"Ah, yes, I forgot about that. Thanks for the help. I'll have to start over."

Fiona removed the paper from her typewriter and began again.

Even with large windows on two sides, the room felt lifeless. The uninspiring view of the parking lot to the north didn't help, and the interior was equally bleak. Bare walls offered no pictures, posters, or colour to brighten the space or reflect the classroom's purpose.

A grey metal table, stocked with staplers, a hole punch, rulers, staple removers, a paper cutter, and a box of carbon paper, stood beside the beige metal filing cabinet next to Nicole's desk.

As Verity's walkabout brought her back toward Nicole's desk, Nicole noticed her studying the supply table.

"They put their timed writings and any other work to be proofread, checked for formatting accuracy, or credited for marks in those trays there." Nicole waved toward a three-tiered grey metal tray, each tier labelled. "The top tier is for timings, the second for production, and the bottom for work returned for credit."

Nicole continued, seemingly glued to her chair. "I leave their marked work in these two trays on my desk—one for timings, one for production."

"Okay, good to know," Verity replied as she resumed surveying the classroom.

Beside the messy bookshelf at the back of the room, Verity

spotted a stack of spiral-bound, paper-backed timed writing drill books and a pile of hardcover typing textbooks—the same ones she'd used back in college in Toronto.

She resumed walking the aisles, trying to look purposeful. Some of the adult students, mostly women, glanced up as she passed, a few offering brief smiles. One asked, "Are you going to be teaching here?"

"Yes," Verity replied. "I'll be taking over this class starting tomorrow. Meanwhile, do you have any questions about today's work?"

Realizing she hadn't officially introduced herself, Verity reminded a student to format the date as 08-07-73, then walked to the whiteboard behind Nicole's desk and wrote her name in large blue letters: *Verity Child.*

Nicole glanced briefly at the board, then at her watch, before returning to her marking.

Each desk was equipped with a stand to hold copy—whatever the student was following as they typed. The electric typewriters were a mix of Remington, Smith-Corona, Olympia, and Olivetti models. Only two of the coveted IBM Correcting Selectrics—the most modern machines—were available.

That day, one Selectric was covered with a plastic sheet, a piece of paper taped to the cover reading, "Reserved for the use of the instructor." The other was in use by a student.

Verity removed the plastic cover from the unused machine, revealing a heavy, burnt-red metal typewriter featuring the innovative golf-ball-shaped type element.

"Students aren't allowed to use the self-correcting feature on that one," Nicole called out from the front of the room.

Verity glanced at the key marked with an X just under the shift key on the right. When pressed, it would cover the error to be corrected. In a class where every typo needed to be visible, corrective features were not allowed.

She walked toward Nicole's desk. "I'm glad to see such a variety of machines here. It'll help the students adapt more easily to a real workplace."

Nicole kept proofreading, offering no reply.

Once again, Verity felt irritated by Nicole's lack of engagement, but she didn't give up.

"And it's so much better having a room full of electrics. Do you remember typing on manuals, when the typebars would jam?" Verity pictured those narrow metal typebars crashing together and hoped this shared memory might draw Nicole out.

"I like to leave the past in the past," Nicole said, eyes glued to her papers.

Verity stopped short, staring down at Nicole. They faced each other—Verity standing over Nicole's desk, Nicole's head bowed. Verity felt her molars clench as she crossed her arms. Leaning in slightly, she lowered her voice so only Nicole could hear.

"If you keep looking down, does that erase me from your mind, Nicole? Does it make it seem like you don't have to deal with me at all?"

Nicole looked up. This time, her expression had softened. In a low voice, she said, "Look, Verity, I don't mean to be rude, but to tell you the truth, I haven't been feeling well lately. It's been hard to get through the day."

Verity straightened, taking in the shift in Nicole's tone and the new information. "Okay, I'm sorry to hear that. I admit, I thought something was off, but not knowing you well, I wasn't sure."

"Yeah, I've just been extra tired lately. This job is taking its toll on me." Nicole's sadness was a stark contrast to her usual anger.

"Hopefully, you'll get some rest when I take over your class."

"Yeah. Let's hope so." Nicole didn't sound convinced. She glanced at her watch again. "Five more minutes to the bell."

Though Verity had nearly given up trying to build a good relationship with Nicole, her empathy kicked in. So far, it hadn't been the collegial atmosphere she'd hoped for—but maybe things would improve once Nicole got a break from teaching.

Verity turned her attention back to the students. Their focused, unassuming faces reminded her of students she'd taught at Toronto Community College, and she began to feel more at ease. She couldn't wait to take charge of her classroom the next day.

Nicole suggested Verity start marking the day's assignments to get familiar with the system. "Two marks off for incorrect line spacing, two for wrong indentation, and five for each typo. If there are more than five typos on any assignment, put a diagonal line through it and have them redo it. They get one more chance."

Verity rolled an extra steno chair over to the supply table. Nicole reached out with a red-ink pen.

"Oh, no thanks, Nicole. I never mark with red," Verity said, pulling a green-ink pen from her purse.

"Suit yourself. It's your class now. I'll be mostly upstairs managing the program. Between my classes and Shirley's, you'll have your hands full down here."

Nicole's tone reverted to that parental admonishment, and Verity felt like a child being scolded. She pushed a heavy metal cutting board aside and tried not to let her frustration show. She began proofreading, but her mind wasn't really on the words in front of her.

And then, Nicole's stern voice shouted above the clatter of electric typewriters, aimed at a middle-aged woman sitting in the second row.

"Annie, I need to talk to you about your assignment; come up to my desk, please."

Seeming embarrassed to be singled out, Annie slowly approached the desk, eyes fixed on the floor for as long as she dared. When she reached Nicole, her worried eyes and trembling hands revealed her fear. She listened attentively as Nicole frowned and pointed out various transgressions on the papers before them.

Although Annie was visibly shaking, Nicole didn't soften her tone. "Being a crybaby will get you nowhere in the work world, Annie, and you can be sure your attitude will be reflected in your final mark. I'll allow you to redo the assignment and hand it back to Verity at tomorrow's class. No later. Go ahead and take your seat."

Red-faced and with tears in her eyes, Annie hurried back to her seat.

Nicole noticed the concern on Verity's face but didn't expect what was coming next.

"Nicole, I need to speak with you. Now. Out in the hallway."

"If you must, Verity; the class is almost over."

"Trust me, this can't wait."

Nicole slowly rose from her chair, looking solemn, and followed Verity's lead.

Once in the hallway, Verity decided it was safer to step outside. She didn't want anyone overhearing their conversation—especially not Annie, who might return for her belongings. They slipped out the side door, finding the area empty.

Facing Nicole squarely, Verity struggled to contain her frustration. "Look, I don't know where you get off thinking it's okay to treat a student like that. What you did to Annie was unprofessional and completely uncalled for."

Nicole backed against the cement-block wall, hands behind her back for support, her gaze drifting to an open field to the right, away from Verity. After a brief pause, she turned back toward her.

Verity fired both barrels. "It takes a lot for an adult student to come back to school after all these years. You have no idea the kind of horrendous living situations some of them endure every single day. And for you to sit there and shame Annie like that, so much that she had to leave the room in despair? Nicole, I'm here to tell you it's not only disrespectful and inappropriate, it's downright unprofessional."

Nicole stared out toward the parking lot, her face pale. Verity wondered if she might faint.

Her voice weakened. "I, uh… well, it was an important assignment."

"I don't care if it was an application to med school. If you can't understand how to support students, especially adults, then I don't know what you're doing here, pretending to be a teacher in adult education."

Verity wasn't used to seeing Nicole in such a weakened state, and even more surprising was the fact that she had caused it.

But Verity wasn't about to let it go. As the bell rang, signaling the end of the teaching block, she added one final warning.

"Don't you ever—and I mean ever—speak to one of my students that way. I won't tolerate it, and if you do, I'll report you to Jared and beyond."

She turned to open the door, holding it ajar for Nicole. Together, they returned to Room 102 to gather their belongings. As Nicole picked up a stack of papers, Verity thought she noticed a slight tremor in Nicole's right hand.

IDEALS

$\mathcal{B}$ack in her apartment that evening, with Charlie still at work, Verity drew a warm bubble bath and poured herself a cool glass of Chardonnay. She was determined to wash away the tension of the afternoon's encounter with Nicole.

Settling into the tub, she rested her head on the waterproof pillow and let the steam curl around her face. Her thoughts drifted—not to tomorrow's lesson plans or even to Annie—but back to her very first day of practice teaching at Teachers' College in Toronto. The memory of Mrs. King's classroom remained vivid: the layout, the lighting, and even the exact words spoken that day were all still remarkably clear.

The odour of dirty running shoes, freshly sharpened pencils, and half-eaten apples greeted Verity as she swung open the Grade 3 classroom door, ready to take over from Mrs. King that Monday morning. It was her first time stepping into a real classroom with real students, and she was buzzing with nervous excitement.

The room was a kaleidoscope of colour and creativity. Construction paper displays lined the walls, each carefully cut and printed to make learning feel playful and inviting. A monthly calendar, bordered with multicoloured puzzle pieces, hung beside a chart of the days of the week. The teaching circle carpet was a cheerful jumble of alphabet letters and numbered spots, worn slightly in the centre where little bodies had gathered day after day.

Verity could already picture her future classroom—styled in her way, full of warmth and wonder—the kind of place students would love to come back to each morning.

The students seemed to be settling in, perhaps having been told to tidy up in preparation for her arrival. Some sat quietly in their seats, but Verity sensed a general buzz and restlessness as they prepared for a change.

"Get the hell out of that cupboard and sit back down in your seat!"

Mrs. King's voice shattered the ordinary hum as she shouted across the classroom at a straggly-haired boy. In response, he tossed a game board onto the play area floor, then sauntered back to his desk, head bowed, hands in his pockets.

Verity stopped short, staring wide-eyed at the boy and the teacher, trying to grasp what she had just witnessed. In her world, teachers didn't swear at students. It felt deeply disrespectful—to that student and to the rest of the class. It set the wrong tone.

Verity was choked. Her long-awaited debut into the world of teaching had suddenly turned sour.

She felt embarrassed. The enthusiasm she'd poured into preparing her lesson plan dimmed in an instant. Struggling to mask her emotions, she forced herself to move forward, greeting Mrs. King with a quick nod and setting her teaching materials down on the desk. A cloud of discomfort settled over her, and she wasn't sure she'd be able to shake it off.

"Good morning, Verity. Are you ready to begin?" For Mrs. King, it seemed an effortless transition from yelling to civility.

"Yes, good morning, Mrs. King. I'm ready." Verity managed a smile, hoping she could find her footing in the next few seconds.

She cast a glance around the room. Twenty-six wide-eyed faces stared back at her, waiting, expectant, curious—for her to take command of the next fifty minutes of their lives.

"Good morning, class…"

Verity had chosen a topic she was certain would capture the attention of third graders. A story about a young girl who liked to spy on others immediately drew them in. To make it even more engaging, Verity had transformed a doll the size of an eight-year-old into the character, complete with a magnifying glass, notepad, and pen.

By the time the last student filed out of the room, Verity was still smiling. The lesson had gone well. But before she could leave, there was something she couldn't ignore. Her teaching ideals fuelled a quiet bravery, and in that moment, she didn't care if speaking up might affect her evaluation.

She approached Mrs. King's desk, heart thudding, and said evenly, "I have to admit—I was shocked when I heard you swear at Jarvis. That's not something I ever expected to hear in a Grade 3 classroom, especially from a teacher."

Mrs. King paused mid-motion, her hands full of papers she'd been stuffing into her briefcase. "I beg your pardon?" Her tone was sharp—more a challenge than a request for repetition.

Verity shifted her weight but didn't back down.

Peering over the top of her glasses, Mrs. King's voice hardened. "Until you've put in twenty-four years of teaching, I suggest you don't question the classroom management techniques of someone more experienced."

She paused, assessing Verity, who glanced at the floor, struggling to hold back what she really wanted to say.

Then Mrs. King added, as if it were the final word: "Understand, Verity—this is inner-city Toronto." She enunciated each word with exaggerated clarity, as though the setting itself justified her actions.

Verity held her breath, waiting—hoping—for some kind of clarification.

Mrs. King delivered it without hesitation. "This is the way their parents talk to them at home. It's the only language they understand."

Verity couldn't bring herself to respond. Her thoughts swirled with everything she wanted to say about role modelling, about dignity and respect—but she knew it would fall on deaf ears.

She picked up her teaching materials and offered a neutral, "Hmm. That's news to me, for sure. Well, I'll see you tomorrow, Mrs. King."

Without waiting for a reply, Verity stepped quickly out the door, determined not to leave room for further discussion.

One thing was certain: in her own classroom, she would do things differently.

Pulling the plug to drain the tub, Verity began to step out. Her mind returned to Nicole's shaming of the student named Annie — it had certainly struck a nerve. Reflecting on Mrs. King and her own practice teaching experience helped Verity understand why she'd reacted so strongly to Nicole's behaviour. From what she could see, even from that first day at Hillside, being a good role model was likely not high on Nicole's priority list.

And Verity knew she couldn't let that become the norm—not if she wanted to make a real difference.

HE LIKES RED HAIR

Verity's second day at Hillside dawned bright and clear—a warm August morning with not a cloud in the sky. Arriving half an hour early for her 8 a.m. class, she climbed the concrete steps to the main floor feeling a sense of happiness and importance. She made her way to the General Office to check her mailbox.

"Good morning," she greeted Ethel, Kendra's secretary, who was busy typing and only nodded in response without looking up. Kendra's office door was firmly shut, a bold DO NOT DISTURB sign fixed to its back. It wasn't the kind of sign you glaze over after seeing it a dozen times—those large black capital letters practically screamed their intention, leaving no room for excuses.

Verity continued down the hallway and pushed open the staffroom door. The room was empty except for the bookish woman she'd noticed the day before, sitting studiously at her desk as others buzzed in and out around her.

Verity sat down at her desk and began sorting through her books, papers, pens, and a timed writing clock. The staffroom door swung open and shut as teachers filtered in.

"Good morning, teachers and students," Ethel's tinny voice echoed over the PA system. "Just a reminder that our eight o'clock classes are cancelled this morning due to a student assembly at the main campus. Classes will resume on this campus at 11:00 a.m. sharp. Thank you."

With unexpected time on her hands, Verity decided to explore the lower floor to familiarize herself with the layout—this time without Nicole's shadow looming over her. Spotting an open door and an otherwise empty classroom, other than the woman she assumed was the teacher, Verity stepped inside and introduced herself.

"Hi there. Pardon the intrusion—I'm Verity Child, the new Typing and Communications instructor."

The woman looked up from the filing cabinet drawer and smiled warmly. "I'm Christie. It's nice to meet you. Just give me a minute—I don't want to forget something—and then we can chat, okay?" Her voice was a bit high-pitched, and Verity found it curious that she seemed to be asking permission to continue.

"That's more than okay; please, take your time."

Tall and slender, dressed in a flattering white pantsuit, Christie had gorgeous strawberry blonde hair—long, straight, and thick. Yet beneath her polished appearance, there was an undercurrent of insecurity that didn't quite match.

Verity sat down and began familiarizing herself with an old Remington typewriter. Noticing Christie had paused her work, she asked, "Where's the ratchet release on this one?"

Christie furrowed her brow. "The what?"

"You know—the release that lets the carriage move freely back and forth."

Christie still looked puzzled. A pink flush crept across her cheeks as she admitted, "I specialized in French and music at university. I've never taught typing before." After a brief pause, she added with a half-smile, "It's rumored Jared likes red hair."

Don't tell me Jared Sinclair is a philanderer. I'm starting to dislike that guy.

"Interesting. Anything else I should know about our discerning boss?"

Christie was quiet for a moment, then seemed to make a decision. She moved closer and took a seat beside Verity.

"Well, if you like juicy gossip..." She paused, watching Verity for any sign of interest.

Verity clasped the edge of her right ear between her thumb and forefinger and gave it a playful tug.

Christie leaned in and whispered, "He likes to play around. Rumour has it he keeps a swanky apartment downtown—specifically for one purpose." She bowed her head, as if ashamed to have said it out loud. Then she glanced up at Verity, her head still tilted downward.

"Is he married?"

"Eeeeyep." Christie raised her eyebrows meaningfully.

"Oh. Uh, I think I'll forget you ever told me that."

Verity had a knack for putting people at ease, and she was pleased to see Christie relax.

"Told you what?" Christie covered her mouth with her palm, eyes wide in mock innocence.

Changing the subject, Christie said, "Verity, if you'd like to join me and a couple of the other teachers for lunch, we'd love to have you. It's a nice change from eating on campus—we usually head across the road to the cafeteria at Riley's Department Store. We call ourselves *The Lunch Club*," she added with a grin.

Verity accepted gratefully, looking forward to spending time with Christie and meeting others, away from the halls of Hillside and the undercurrents she was already starting to feel. She welcomed the chance to form new connections that might offer a counterbalance to the Nicoles of the world.

❧

As Verity walked into Room 101 to meet her class of sixteen advanced Typing 181 students for the first time, the distinct odour of tuna sandwiches wafted up to her nostrils. She waited until all the students had assembled, then tapped the timed writing bell to get their attention. The room fell silent.

"Good morning, class. My name is Verity. And the first order of the day appears to be a reminder that this is a classroom, not a lunchroom—so please keep any food items under wraps until you leave. Some offices have strict policies about food in the workplace, so we want to set a good example here. Understood?"

A few smiled briefly, others nodded. With Verity's instruction to continue, the students struck typewriter keys, studied their copy, and resumed work.

The classroom was similar to Room 102, only without windows. Verity was already forming plans to make it feel more inviting.

Since advanced typists often worked independently, she turned her attention to the cluttered bookshelves, which had become a dusty repository for miscellaneous file folders, outdated textbooks, broken copyholders, boxes of carbon paper, and old typewriter ribbons.

So absorbed was Verity in the task of reorganizing that class time flew by. As the students packed up and filed out, Christie appeared in the doorway.

"Ready for lunch?"

They exited from the basement level and reached the small shopping mall across the road in no time. Just as they approached the front entrance of Riley's, another teacher joined them—Christie introduced her as Janet, head of the Legal Secretarial program.

Verity hadn't realized how hungry she was until the aroma of fried food and fresh coffee welcomed them into the bustling cafeteria. Her stomach growled as her thoughts turned to lunch.

The bookish Angela was already seated at a table, a cup of coffee in her hand. She waved to be seen amid the crowd, and the newcomers joined the queue, scanning the day's offerings. Riley's was known for its bountiful salads featuring crisp lettuce and flavourful add-ons.

"Oh, that shrimp salad looks yummy!" Christie said, eyes wide.

"I wonder what the soup is today—they make excellent soup. I order it even in summer," Janet added.

"I can't take my eyes off that chocolate cake," Verity said, eyeing the stacks of pretty pink cake boxes on the shelves behind the counter. "That and a cup of coffee would set me up nicely for the afternoon."

Janet noticed her looking. "Those are the signature bakery boxes from Riley's," she told Verity. "You can always tell where someone's been when you see them carrying one of those pink boxes."

Such was the easy banter among Verity and her colleagues. She settled on a roast turkey sandwich with a side salad. The clatter of heavy white dishes and the low murmur of patrons' voices lent a comforting familiarity. After paying the cashier, they joined Angela at their usual table.

Sunlight poured through the tall café windows as conversation flowed. "How was your weekend, Verity?" Angela asked.

"Oh, my husband Charlie and I went kayaking in Deep Cove. Perfect weather. The water was calm, and the views were gorgeous. If we'd known how beautiful Vancouver was, we might have come sooner."

Verity felt genuinely happy to be part of the group, and they seemed to enjoy her company. She was especially grateful to Christie for extending the invitation and hoped she'd be included the next time they went out for lunch.

But her comfort was short-lived.

DON'T GET TOO COMFORTABLE

*I*n her cubicle back in the staffroom, Verity prepared to instruct a class in Business English and Communications. Stella, who'd cordially introduced herself on Verity's first day, was talking to a woman she addressed as "Teresa." Verity observed Stella discreetly from across the room.

Stella's Irish blue eyes darted from side to side the entire time she talked, making her seem as if she was always on alert, ready to catch anyone who might overhear the highly secret, top-priority information she was about to share. Her white shoes looked like they were made of plastic, and their pointed toes reminded Verity of a leprechaun. Red and blue tassels dangled over the tops, which were punctured with a smattering of tiny holes. Short in stature, Stella wore wide-legged pants with an untucked shirt hanging down over her hips.

Noticing Verity looking her way, Stella headed over. "Verity, have you met Teresa yet?"

"No, I haven't."

"Well, she also teaches Communications, so let me introduce you," Stella said, leading the way back to Teresa's cubicle.

As soon as Stella introduced Teresa to Verity, she tucked her teaching materials under her arm, saying, "Cheerio, I have a class to teach," and hurried out the door.

Verity recognized Teresa as the young woman she'd seen exiting Kendra's office on her first morning, the one who'd offered to buy Kendra a muffin for break time.

"Teresa, hi there. I guess you and I already have something in common," Verity said.

Teresa's lips pulled back in a slight smile as she returned the greeting but seemed unable to manage anything more. Verity wondered if she'd been too forward with this seemingly introverted woman.

"You know, we used this Communications textbook at the college where I taught in Ontario. I quite liked it. What about you?"

Teresa nodded. "It's pretty easy to follow, lots of examples, which the students like and, I must admit, it helps me too." This time she smiled broadly.

Verity wondered if Teresa was one of those introverts who just needed a bit of warm-up time before diving into conversation.

Teresa's desk was a model of organisation. A picture of a little boy occupied the right corner, displayed in a small brass frame. It was the only decoration in her cubicle. On her brown coffee cup, written in large white letters, were the words, *Stay Grounded.*

"Who's this little boy?" Verity asked.

Her question brought a big smile to Teresa's face. "That's my son, Michael. He's seven now, five in that photo."

I guess that's the key that unlocks Teresa's heart—ask about her son.

Verity was excited about meeting her Communications classes that afternoon. Teaching grammar, punctuation, spelling, and effective business writing and speaking was always a tough sell, but she loved the challenge. Students who were reluctant often argued, "Who cares, as long as you get your meaning across?" Verity would agree with them. "Yes, we communicate every day, easily getting our message across, sometimes without much thought to so-called correctness. But," she'd add, "if you want to be formally educated, then you learn the rules." That usually ended the argument.

The classroom was arranged with long tables on each side of a middle aisle, and students sat in individual chairs. There was plenty of room to spread out their books and complete assignments. Verity was pleased to see the extra whiteboards lining the walls—she planned to provide examples of proper sentence structure, punctuation, and grammar.

"Good afternoon, class; my name is Verity, and I'm pleased to be your Communications instructor for this term." She smiled, looking from left to right, trying to connect with all the students in the room.

"Do you have any questions about your last assignment?"

No one raised a hand. "Okay, then—let me find out what you remember about the use of gerunds."

AT THE END of Verity's second day at Hillside, she sat at her desk at the back of Room 103, piecing together a lesson plan for the next day. A light tap on her arm made her look up.

A woman with warm brown eyes that seemed to pop out of their sockets bent forward slightly, her bright eyes fixed on Verity.

"I just wanted to thank you for taking my classes while I'm away, and to wish you good luck." Her words offered a timely note of support, but Verity noted she said, "my" classes. She recalled Kendra telling her at her second interview that she'd be "replacing" Shirley. Verity wasn't sure what this woman's intentions were.

Verity found it odd that the teacher she was replacing wanted to make clear that the position belonged to Shirley, not her. *Does Shirley know something I don't?*

"Oh, you must be Shirley." Verity smiled and offered her hand, masking her surprise at being suddenly drawn into conversation with one of the instructors she'd been told to avoid—the other being Stella.

Shirley returned the smile warmly, her softened eyes showing no trace of attitude, only sincerity. She leaned back against the edge of a student desk, resting her hands on the desktop for support. "I know it can be tough starting out in a place like this, especially right here." Shirley laughed, and Verity joined in, eager to be friendly.

Then the conversation stalled, casting an awkward shadow over their meeting. Shirley glanced around the room. Verity propped her elbow on the desk, supporting her head with her left hand as if to steady herself amid the unexpected encounter.

Shirley smiled again. "I was about to say, 'See you in a month.' I know you're new and probably don't understand why I hesitated."

She paused before adding, "It's just that you'll soon learn not to count on things going as planned around here. When things *do* go as expected, that's the real anomaly." She gave a breathy laugh as if trying to lighten the mood.

Verity considered Shirley's words, then ventured, "Sounds like there "Whether or not you're aware of the problems," Shirley said, "if Kendra and Jared—or even Nicole—decide something needs to change, then change *will* be on the horizon."

Verity sat in silence, turning over Shirley's words. She glanced away, resting her chin lightly on her hand, her gaze drifting toward the baseboards as she considered what she'd just heard.

Then she looked back at Shirley. "Mm-hmm. But is that really any different from most workplaces? Management calls the shots, isn't that right?"

"This isn't any ordinary workplace, Verity. That's my point." Shirley shook her head slowly. "But I'm not trying to discolour your experience here—truly, I'm not. You seem nice, and I hear you're well qualified." She raised her eyebrows and tilted her head. "I'm just saying: don't get too comfortable."

Again, Verity paused, contemplating Shirley's warning. She pressed her left index finger to her forehead, as if the gesture might help her absorb what she'd just heard. Across from her, Shirley straightened, as though preparing to leave.

Verity was ready for the conversation to end. "Okay, well, thank you for the warning, Shirley. I'll keep it in mind." Rising from her chair, she walked Shirley to the door. Her parting words were sincere. "Meanwhile, I hope to see you back when you're well—and let's hope there's enough room for both of us."

Once Shirley had gone, Verity returned to her classroom and began to pace, her thoughts spiralling in all directions.

Jared said my position was temporary, just like any substitute role. Kendra told me I'd be replacing Shirley—'she isn't well, you know'— which made it sound like she wouldn't be coming back. But Shirley seems to think otherwise.

Shirley's bulging eyes reminded Verity of her aunt, who suffered from Graves' disease. She wondered if that had anything to do with Shirley being on leave. And did Shirley have mental health issues, as Kendra had hinted? It sure didn't seem that way.

Why had Shirley included Nicole among the decision-makers? From the very beginning, Verity's experiences at Hillside had been strange. And now, in just her first week, instead of gaining clarity, things were growing murkier by the day.

Forget about staying neutral. I need to find out what's going on here.

Shirley's parting words—*don't get too comfortable*—echoed in her mind, leaving Verity with a lingering and undeniable sense of foreboding.

THE NEXT MORNING, Nicole approached Verity's cubicle. Without any greeting, she began, "Since you and I will be sharing certain students..." and proceeded to impose her personal opinions about students onto Verity before Verity had the chance to form her own impressions.

Consulting her class list, she launched into a string of opinions that left Verity cold.

"Ruby Jakesta has a chip on her shoulder, as most foreign students do. Eileen Smithers is a troublemaker," she warned.

Nicole proclaimed that the entire May intake was "rotten."

"Look, Nicole, I want you to know that I consider your comments to be both insensitive and unprofessional."

"So much for teamwork, Verity." Nicole spun around and returned to her desk, tossing the class list onto the desktop. Grabbing her coffee cup, she headed out the door.

THE CONVERSATION with Shirley lingered in Verity's mind that morning, so when she noticed a teacher named Joyce sitting at her cubicle, she decided to investigate further. Joyce was studying her class timetable, her brow furrowed in quiet concentration.

"Hi, Joyce. We haven't officially met, but I heard others call you by name," Verity said with a friendly smile. "I'm Verity."

Joyce looked up and returned the smile warmly. "Hello, Verity. Welcome to the henhouse." She chuckled at her comment. Joyce was the most senior of the teachers, clearly close to retirement age.

Verity eased into the conversation. "I just met Shirley downstairs —she seems like such a nice person."

Joyce's eyebrows lifted slightly. "Oh yes, dear, Shirley was well-liked by most of us here."

"Was?"

Joyce cleared her throat and picked a bit of lint off the sleeve of her pink cardigan. "She was just here temporarily, you know. And I remember Kendra flew to Hawaii for a week—came back just as Shirley went on sick leave. Some of us found that very telling."

"Oh, so Kendra didn't want to be around Shirley, then? Did they have a disagreement or something?"

Joyce gave a faint smile. "I think you'd have to have been here to begin to understand, dear. But I will say this—Shirley is smart, and she's not one to take things lying down."

"Yes, I got a sense of that in the short time I spoke with her," Verity said.

Joyce paused, thoughtful. "I believe Shirley has one more week left on her contract, then she's gone for good."

"Oh," Verity said slowly. "I didn't get the impression that she was aware of the 'gone for good' part."

"Not surprised, dear. And sad it all is—so sad and unnecessary." Joyce stood and gathered her things. "Now I have to get home and let my poor doggie out for a walk. See you tomorrow." And with that, she bustled off down the hall.

BACK HOME AGAIN, Verity found herself thinking about how much Joyce reminded her of her beloved Aunt Lucy—the person she knew she'd miss most when she and Charlie left Toronto. As it turned out, Verity had been so caught up with everything at Hillside that she'd barely had a chance to think of her. Now, she took a moment to reflect on her last day with her dear aunt.

They'd always been close, but after her Uncle Mac passed away two years ago, Verity had made a point of spending as much time as possible with Aunt Lucy, strengthening their bond even further.

Aunt Lucy and Uncle Mac lived in a beautiful stone mansion overlooking the Ottawa River. Having no children of their own, they treated Verity like their own daughter. She treasured fond memories of playing on their vast, well-manicured lawn that sloped down to a wooden dock where she spent hours playing while Aunt Lucy watched from her teak chaise longue. They maintained the dock year-round—even through harsh winters when the ice wreaked havoc on the wooden structure, requiring an annual rebuild.

As Verity grew older, Aunt Lucy became her confidante. It seemed she could tell her anything without fear of judgment. From boyfriends and girlfriends to careers and cosmetics, Verity valued Aunt Lucy's opinion above all others.

When Verity graduated from Toronto Teachers College, Aunt Lucy invited her to the mansion for a private celebration. She had set the table with her finest linens and served champagne in crystal flutes. As they admired a colourful array of petit fours on a tiered tray, Aunt Lucy fell silent for a moment. Verity sensed she was about to say something important.

"Verity, my darling Verity..." Her smile was so sweet, and Verity would never forget that moment—or the look in Aunt Lucy's water-colour-blue eyes.

"...I want you to know that this will all be yours someday," she said, raising both arms with upturned palms, gesturing to the surrounding home and grounds. "I've left everything to you."

Verity was stunned. She had never really thought about the possibility of inheriting anything from her aunt and uncle. She assumed her parents would leave behind whatever they could, but hadn't given it much more thought than that. Verity never expected anyone to carry her; her goal had always been to stand on her own two feet.

"Oh, Aunt Lucy," she managed, her voice catching slightly. "I don't know what to say." She looked down at her hands pressed against her thighs, as if seeking steady ground. "It's really so far beyond kind and generous." Then she met her aunt's eyes again and added, "I think the world of you, just as I did of Uncle Mac. And I truly wasn't expecting you to leave me anything; I wasn't."

Verity paused, letting the weight of the moment settle, and reflected on just how important her aunt had been in her life. "You know you've always been like a second mother to me." Rising from her chair, she planted a gentle kiss on her aunt's cheek.

Aunt Lucy smiled with delight, bowing her head slightly as she composed herself. She drank in Verity's words, her pride and pleasure shining through. "And I want you to know, too, my dear, that your inheritance comes with no conditions or expectations. It's a blessing to be able to give such a gift to the only remaining love of my life."

"Well, Aunt Lucy, despite this amazing news, I think you know I am excited about my teaching career, and that I plan to continue with that, no matter what."

"I do, Verity, I'm just so proud of you. You're capable and self-reliant, and it seems as though you are driven to contribute to society, which is admirable. You don't need an inheritance, and money does not buy happiness. But it can make things a lot easier if you have it when you need it."

"Yes, I appreciate that. And I often think about your famous line:

You can have all the money in the world, but if you don't have your health, what good is it?"

They chuckled at the line that had become her aunt's trademark at family gatherings over the years.

"And, Charlie, he's the love of my life; even though you have expressed some reservations about him." She smiled coyly before adding, "We all know that no marriage is perfect and that it takes time to develop a deep, true love like you and Uncle Mac had."

"No marriage is perfect, that's for sure."

"I am just so humbled and honoured by your gift, Aunt Lucy. I hope you know you will have a place in my heart forever and that I will treasure our time together since I was a little girl."

That special day would remain emblazoned in Verity's mind for her lifetime.

DAY THREE

Getting dressed for work the next morning, Verity shared her excitement with Charlie. "I have a beginning typist class today."

"Okay, why is that exciting?"

"Because they're a clean slate. Nothing's tainted them yet—not like the group I had yesterday. They'd been with Nicole for the past eight weeks."

"Oh, I see. You want to shape them from the ground up. Mould them into little Verity Child clones."

"Exactly." Their laughter filled the room.

"Verity, good morning." Janet, one of her lunch club companions from Monday, greeted her warmly in the staffroom, seeming to set the tone for a good day ahead. Verity scurried downstairs to Room 102.

She opened a window to clear the stale air. The room had the same configuration as Room 101: five rows of individual desks with shelves underneath for books and other student belongings.

Some students were already typing when Verity arrived. She smiled and greeted the class, recognizing a few faces she'd seen around campus.

"Stop typing, please!" The room fell silent as the clattering gradually came to a halt.

"I'm Verity," she said, writing her name in blue on the shiny whiteboard. She was glad the days of chalk and blackboards were mostly over; still, she carried her chalk holder—just in case—to avoid getting dust all over herself should she end up in a room that hadn't caught up.

Thirty faces studied her as she explained that she'd be their new instructor until the end of the term.

"I see some of you already type, even though this is a beginner's class—and that's perfectly fine," she said. "I'll start with an assessment to ensure you're using proper typing posture, correct fingering, keeping your eyes on the copy, and so on. Then I'll provide a review of acceptable procedures and techniques."

Verity paused to look around the room, pleased to see everyone listening.

"As you know, this is a self-paced program. You'll work at your own rate and progress at your own speed." Another pause. "Now, this is important." She swept the room with her eyes. "Please don't compare yourselves to others. Some will move faster, some slower— and that's perfectly okay."

She noticed a few surprised expressions. "This isn't a competition. Not at this stage, anyway," she added with a smile. "The only person you're competing with is yourself. Just aim to beat your own best score."

Verity expected she'd have to remind them of this principle from time to time, but for now, she sensed a collective sense of relief in the room.

When no one raised a hand, she continued. "Did you get a chance to read the yellow sheet explaining how your final mark will be determined?" Several students nodded. "Let me know if there's anything you don't understand."

Still no questions.

"In the beginner classes, we'll start by learning the letters of the QWERTY keyboard."

A hand shot up.

"Sorry, Mrs. Child, what did you call it?"

"Thanks for asking," Verity said, checking her seating plan. "Let's see... second row, fourth seat—you must be Linda?"

"Right."

"Before I answer, let me ask the class—does anyone know why it's called the QWERTY keyboard?"

Silence.

"Take a look at your keyboard. Do you see the letters Q-W-E-R-T-Y anywhere?"

Several heads nodded. A woman in the front row raised her hand.

"Yes... Morgan?"

"It's the first six alphabetic letters on the top left row."

"Exactly. And it's been that way since 1873."

VERITY DECIDED to stay in during the lunch break to reconfigure the rows of typing desks, aiming to make the room feel more like a business office than a traditional classroom. Since she wouldn't be sharing the space with any other teachers, she assumed she didn't need permission to make the change.

She began by clearing the only two surfaces sturdy enough to hold the weight of the machines. Unplugging each typewriter, she coiled the long cords into neat loops and set them carefully on top of the machines. Then, one by one, she rolled all thirty chairs to the north wall, forming a tidy line.

Wrapping her arms around a clunky Smith-Corona, she hefted it onto the supply table. It felt like lifting a hatbox filled with cement.

Bending her knees to protect her back, Verity began the noisy process of dragging the heavy wooden desks across the tiled floor, slowly working each one into its new position.

The new arrangement angled each desk slightly away from its neighbors, giving every workstation the feel of a private office. With large windows along the north and east walls, most desks would have a view.

Verity's blouse was soaked through at the armpits—something she hadn't anticipated. The task was more exhausting than she'd imagined. She sat down to catch her breath, already planning to slip on her cardigan before the students arrived, uncomfortable as it sounded.

When she started again, she paused after each desk move to reassess the layout, trying to mold it into the vision she had in her mind. But it soon became clear she wouldn't finish in time— students would be filing in within ten minutes.

There was just enough time for a quick bathroom break. Afterward, she stepped outside through the side door at the end of the hall and inhaled a breath of crisp afternoon air.

As she returned to the classroom alongside students trickling back from lunch, she could already hear the buzz of conversation and shifting energy—a sure sign of the fuss to come.

"Oh! What happened here?" one student exclaimed.

"Where's my desk?" cried another.

"Should I call a moving van, Verity?" someone joked.

Verity stepped in quickly. "Okay, let's put your things down and get to work. Help me replace the chairs and typewriters, and we'll sort out seating once everything's in place."

With Verity directing the setup and plenty of willing hands, the room came together in under fifteen minutes. "Great job, everyone. Now go ahead—choose a workstation and have a seat."

Students laughed and jostled playfully as they hurried to claim their spots.

"I call dibs on the window!"

"Not smart if there's an earthquake!"

The room filled with the sounds of rolling chairs, shifting desks, and playful chatter. Verity's first-come, first-served policy meant students would rotate through a variety of typewriters over time, adding a little surprise to each day.

She smiled at the buzz of energy. The rearrangement had worked.

"Well, what do you think?" she asked the class.

"This is cool!"

"Way better than rows!"

"Wait—do I get a Selectric *and* a window view?"

The room settled as students returned to their drills, the tapping of keys quickly filling the space again. Verity felt a quiet satisfaction—it had been worth the effort.

Verity marked the attendance using the seating plan her students had filled out, assuring the class she'd know everyone's name by the end of the week.

So began her third day at Everton Community College—what she hoped would be the start of a long and fulfilling chapter. By the time class ended, Verity felt a sense of ease settle over her. She allowed her thoughts to drift.

She found herself back in Toronto, recalling her first day of teaching at a community college. Standing before a classroom for the first time, her heart had pounded in her chest, her mouth gone dry. Every ounce of energy had gone into appearing composed.

But the truth was, she'd felt like an impostor. When the end-of-term evaluations came in—mostly positive—she still couldn't believe they were sincere. Praise hadn't quieted the doubt that whispered she didn't belong.

The memory faded as the sound of approaching footsteps snapped her back to the present. Nicole appeared in the doorway, her expression drawn and tired, a deep frown creasing her forehead. She looked into the room.

"What on earth is this?"

Oh lord, not Miss Cranky-Pants again.

"Good afternoon, Nicole. Do you have a problem with my new arrangement?" Verity stood with her arms folded, ready for the challenge.

Nicole smirked. "Honestly, I think it's more of a non-arrangement, Verity."

Verity paused, refusing to take the bait.

Nicole stepped inside and scanned the room. Then, she gestured toward the windows with a sharp flick of her arm. "This setup just invites students to stare out the window—watching cars, other students walking by, anything to avoid doing their work." Her voice was stern and clipped, making Verity feel like a scolded schoolgirl.

With a calm, 'sorry-not-sorry' tone, Verity replied, "Well, Nicole, I'm sorry you disapprove. I thought a more realistic office layout might motivate the students—and frankly, all of us."

Nicole paused, considering for a moment before launching a new jab. "Ha! Lucky for you, it's just you using this room—for now. But don't be surprised if you have to reconfigure it when that changes." She tossed her nose in the air with a sharp little scoff.

Verity bit back the urge to argue, managing a cool, one-word reply:

"Noted."

Without another word, she turned and walked out, leaving behind the only sour note of the day.

WHISPERS

Thursday's advanced typing class started with a question from a student sitting near Verity's desk.

"This might sound silly, but if offices are moving toward auto-correcting typewriters, why are we still spending time learning how to make the perfect erasure?"

Verity smiled warmly. "First of all, Penny, in my class, there are no stupid questions. Now, let me ask you this: What if your employer doesn't have a Selectric?"

"Right, ha! Maybe I should bring my own to work." Some students chuckled, and Penny, satisfied, sat down to begin her work.

If only Kendra and Jared could face the reality of the business world, they'd invest in the equipment offices use today.

Already, Verity liked the students. They seemed to have a purpose for being there, and it showed in their attitude and effort.

Janet, one of her lunch club companions, shared her thoughts during the morning break in the staffroom. "For many, just applying to this program was a big decision. Sometimes it took a lot of courage."

Verity found Janet's care and understanding comforting. She

could easily imagine her legal secretarial students feeling comfortable enough to confide in Janet.

"Returning to school as an adult isn't always easy, you know. Many have no work experience, limited education, and few of the resources others might've had on their journey through life." Janet spoke with a kindness that didn't feel patronizing. Instead, it felt like she was sharing hard-earned wisdom to help a less experienced teacher.

"Even though PeoplePower sponsors most students and pays for their courses in full, some still have serious issues to deal with while they're in school. Those problems don't just disappear."

Janet took a sip of her tea, and Verity mentioned that she thought she had smelled alcohol on the breath of one of her beginning typists the day before.

"Yes, some struggle with addictions, many live in poverty, some are in abusive relationships." Janet paused, studying her teacup. "And you might not have heard about this because it happened just before you started here." She leaned forward and whispered to Verity, "One student in the spring intake—a young woman whose dream was to work in the television newsroom—suddenly stopped coming to school. A few days later, we got a notice that she'd discontinued the program."

Verity listened closely.

"I wasn't the only instructor caught off guard by this. Her teachers all said she was unusually keen. You couldn't help but notice it. She arrived early, stayed late, asked lots of questions, and always handed in her assignments on time—and well done."

Verity frowned slightly. "What do you think happened?"

Janet smiled knowingly. "When I want to find out what's going on, I just ask my students. Here's what I learned." She took a slow sip of tea and leaned in closer.

"They said she'd been complaining about Jared coming on to her when she first met him to learn about programs in the Business Division. And there were more attempts when she stayed late at school and Jared was still around."

Verity's jaw dropped, her eyes widening. "Janet, I can't believe this. I think I'm going to be sick." She turned toward the window, needing to put distance between herself and the awful truth.

When Verity refocused on Janet, she continued quietly, "Jared tried to discredit her, saying she was already making up stories before she even got into the newsroom."

Janet sat up straighter, taking another sip of tea. She absently fiddled with a button on her sweater—Verity could tell the memory still weighed on her, even though it had happened nearly six months ago.

Incredulous, Verity pressed on, "Did she complain to the principal? The College Board? School counselors?"

Janet shook her head slowly. "I doubt it. Otherwise, we would have heard more. But the story seemed to fade away, as if it never happened. Her friends said Jared's behavior left her so disheartened that she couldn't face returning.

"That's just so sad." Verity tried to put herself in the student's shoes. "I guess these things are hard to prove. It'd be her word against his, and without concrete evidence, she probably didn't stand a chance."

"But at least if she'd complained to the higher-ups, they'd have had to investigate. It would've been satisfying to see him squirm," Janet said, pressing her lips together.

Verity shook her head. "I don't know how well I'd hold up if I had to face challenges like that."

"Neither would I."

Janet seemed ready to move on from the unpleasant topic of Jared. "But I'm proud of the students for taking steps to try to make things better. It's admirable, no question. Our job is to help them become their best selves, despite the challenges they face."

"Oh, Janet, that's beautifully put. And the self-paced programs probably accommodate individual differences much better than the old lock-step system, where everyone had to move forward at the same time."

"Exactly. That approach wouldn't work for some students. It'd be like setting them up for failure." Glancing at the clock, Janet gulped the last of her tea and headed off to her next class.

Though it was only Verity's fourth day at Hillside, she had already glimpsed some of the campus's deeper struggles. Her curiosity about what lay behind the scenes was growing.

DON'T LET THINGS BOIL OVER

As Verity walked down the outside cement steps from the main floor at lunchtime, she spotted Jared heading toward the parking lot.

"How's it going?" His clear, deep voice carried easily without him needing to raise it.

"Good, thanks. It's hard to believe it's already my fourth day here. It feels great to be part of things." Verity grasped the railing to steady herself on the steps.

"And how does your husband feel about the new job?"

Verity smiled. "He can see I'm happy, so he's happy."

Reaching the ground, Verity quickened her pace to catch up with Jared near the parking lot entrance.

He glanced back, smiling, then stopped so they could talk more comfortably. "Well, let me know if there are any problems at work. Don't let things boil over."

Verity's thoughts jumped to the issues she'd already faced during her first week on campus. She hesitated, unsure whether to bring up the uncertainties about her role or the conflicts with Nicole, particularly Nicole's unprofessional behavior toward students. Then the harsh reality hit her: what was the point of talking to Jared about unprofessionalism now that she'd heard the rumour about him coming on to that student?

Jared waited expectantly, and Verity had no choice but to respond. "Yes, I'm keeping my ear to the ground, like you asked, but I have to admit I'm a little unclear about what role I'm supposed to play."

She glanced up at him, feeling somewhat foolish, while he fidgeted with his keys. His silence grew awkward, so she tried to ease the tension. "Maybe we could meet sometime once I've settled in a bit more?"

"Sure, we can do that. Just let me know when you're ready." As they parted ways, Jared headed toward a bright red convertible Mustang with the top down.

Of course, he'd have a red convertible.

Verity headed toward Riley's for Friday's lunchtime meet-up with her colleagues. It seemed like Jared still wanted her to keep him informed about anything she might uncover, but she suspected he wasn't keen on making that role official. And with all the talk about 'problems,' she couldn't shake the feeling that Jared himself might be part of the problem.

VICE

*J*oining Christie, Angela, and Janet for lunch that day, Verity knew she couldn't mention her secret role—but she hoped she might learn more about Nicole. There had to be some explanation for her off-putting attitude.

Once everyone had settled at the table, Verity said, "As you probably know, I've had to rely on Nicole to help orient me to the typing program, and let me tell you, my patience is hanging by a thread."

She was rewarded with smiles and knowing nods from all three.

"Can anyone tell me exactly what Nicole's title is?"

Janet nearly choked on her coffee, Angela grinned, and Christie burst out laughing.

"She's an instructor, same as the rest of us," Janet managed, still recovering.

Angela looked directly at Verity. "Why do you ask?"

"Some of my students said that during orientation, Nicole introduced herself to the class as 'vice-principal.'"

No one looked surprised.

"Yes, I've heard that from my students, too," Angela said.

"I remember going over the college calendar, including the staff listings," Verity added. "I didn't see anything about a vice-principal."

"Oh, there's plenty of *vice* on this campus," Janet said with a smirk.

Verity raised an eyebrow. "Is Nicole married?"

Christie's eyes widened. "Legally, yes—but from the sounds of it, it's more of a business arrangement. They live in separate houses, let alone separate bedrooms. Nicole says she drives eighty miles to see him on weekends."

"What does he do?" Verity asked.

"He's a logger," Janet supplied. "Stays in the camps."

"She must be lonely," Verity murmured.

Janet raised her eyebrows and took a deliberate bite of her sandwich. The others offered vague nods, avoiding eye contact.

POWER

Back in Room 101, Verity watched as her class settled into their typing drills. With everyone working quietly and productively, she decided it might be a good time to catch Kendra in her office.

Through the open door, she saw Kendra's back as she rifled through a filing cabinet drawer.

"Excuse me, Kendra. Do you have a moment?"

Kendra jumped, then turned with a frown. "What is it, Verity?" she asked, her tone clipped as she hastily shoved a white business envelope into the drawer.

"I was hoping you could clarify something for me."

"Have a seat," Kendra said, moving behind her desk.

"It's about Nicole." Verity paused, watching Kendra's face for a reaction.

Kendra said nothing—just stared, waiting.

"I just wanted to let you know that, according to several of my students, Nicole introduced herself as the vice-principal during orientation. I wasn't aware she held that title, so I'm just seeking clarification." Verity offered a polite smile.

Kendra didn't hesitate. "No, Nicole's not the vice-principal. She's a teacher—same as you, same as everyone else. She has no more authority than that." Then she added, "Jared is aware of the problem."

Ah. So this was one of the 'problems' they'd both been skirting.

Verity felt a flicker of satisfaction. It was oddly validating to hear, officially, that Nicole had no special status.

"You have to be assertive with Nicole," Kendra went on. "It's the only way you'll get along."

That was more than Verity expected. And even though she was relieved to learn that Nicole might not be tucked in Kendra's back pocket after all, she couldn't help wondering what was being said behind *her* back.

"Yes, I've had to be assertive—even during my first week," Verity said.

"Okay," Kendra replied. Then, peering over the top of her glasses, she added, "But don't get the impression that *you* have any more authority than you do, either."

"I wouldn't dream of it." Verity kept her tone even, though the comment stung. "I'm well aware of my professional boundaries, Kendra." *Maybe more so than you are.*

"That's good," Kendra said smoothly. "Because those who aren't don't last long here." She smiled that syrupy smile Verity remembered from their first meeting.

At the end of the day, Verity settled at her desk in the staffroom to review the next day's activities. Across the room, she noticed Nicole at her own desk, twirling a gold pen between her fingers, lips parted as if caught in thought. Then, removing the pen, Nicole looked up, her expression oddly animated.

"Oh, Verity—you might be interested in this."

Verity glanced over, surprised by the unfamiliar tone. "Oh? What is it, Nicole? Something juicy, I hope."

"Do you remember Shirley? She used to work here. I'm not sure if you ever met her."

"Only briefly. Why?"

"She's trying to sue the college for wrongful dismissal." Nicole flashed a grin—showing teeth Verity hadn't seen before. "That woman's like a pit bull. But honestly, going up against Kendra and Jared? Total waste of time."

Verity raised an eyebrow. "I suppose you know Kendra and Jared well enough to make that call. I'm the newcomer, after all—I don't know anything about what happened before I got here."

Nicole's eyes glittered. "Let's just say Shirley's one of many do-gooders who didn't know when to keep her mouth shut."

"Do-gooders who didn't know when to keep their mouths shut."

"Keep their mouths shut about what?" Verity asked lightly.

Nicole's eyes gleamed. "Oh, now—you might want to practise your discretion, Verity. But only if you enjoy working here."

Verity didn't take the bait. She rolled back to her cubicle with a polite nod. "All interesting, Nicole. Very interesting."

Is she worried I'll stumble onto something I shouldn't know—and talk? Or is she comparing me to Shirley? Either way, I'm getting more than a little tired of the secrecy, the veiled threats, and the backstabbing around here.

ON FRIDAY MORNING in the staff room, before the first class of the day, Nicole tilted her head toward her desk, motioning Verity over.

Verity rolled her chair close enough to see the paper Nicole was holding.

"This is how I grade the advanced typing students," Nicole said. "Acceptable work gets a checkmark. If there's even one proofreading error, I draw a line through the whole page. They get one chance to redo it."

"I see," Verity replied evenly. "I like the emphasis on accuracy and proofreading."

Nicole went on. "Production work—letters, memos, invoices, reports—earns an A, B, C, or Fail."

"And is there a grading outline that explains what each letter grade means?" Verity asked.

"There isn't one," Nicole said matter-of-factly. "Most students are Cs."

Verity clenched her teeth but forced herself to stay quiet and listen.

Nicole smiled. "I can take one look at a student and tell right away if they're a C or a B."

Verity tilted her head, masking her reaction. "Oh? How can you tell that, Nicole?"

"When you've been here as long as I have, Verity, you just know."

"Uh-huh. That's an interesting theory, Nicole."

A wave of nausea rolled over Verity as she began to wonder if Nicole had the power to assess—and terminate—students on a whim. She pictured hopeful newcomers being cut down, victims of Nicole's cruel judgments.

"This is not a system I'm familiar with. Have Jared and Kendra approved it?"

"Oh, really, Verity?" Nicole rolled her eyes and snapped with a degrading tone. "I don't make all the decisions on my own, you know."

Then she stood up, hands on hips, clearly enjoying herself. "We three worked out all the details together."

Verity reminded herself to keep breathing, trying to make sense of Nicole's strange reaction to a straightforward question about approval. *Was she taunting me?*

It was time to head to class. Verity pushed her chair back to her cubicle, thinking, *What an asinine marking scheme.*

∼

AT MORNING BREAK, Verity stepped into the staffroom and noticed Nicole was nowhere to be seen. She approached Susan, the head of the typing program.

"Hi Susan, do you have a minute?"

Susan looked up and offered a faint smile. "Mm-hmm."

"I was wondering about the marking scheme for Office Procedures 180 and 181. Nicole went over the system for the advanced students, but I haven't seen anything for the beginners yet."

Susan shrugged. "Nicole's working on that—don't hold your breath."

Verity nodded. "If you need any help with it, I'd be happy to assist."

Susan smiled politely. "Thanks, Verity, but this is Nicole's baby. It's been hers since day one."

Verity thought to herself that Susan seemed little more than a figurehead. *Maybe on paper, it wouldn't look good for Nicole to be wearing too many hats. What other powers did Nicole have that weren't listed in the college calendar?*

As Verity entered her classroom, she overheard one student complaining to another. "Nicole's hardly ever here! I guess the vice-principal can come and go as she pleases, but that's not fair to us."

Verity walked to her desk, thinking about how many times she'd caught Nicole sitting in the staffroom while everyone else rushed off to their classes.

MUSK

Two weeks into the term, Verity felt settled enough in her routines at Hillside to revisit an issue that had been left unresolved.

When she spotted Jared in the parking lot after school on Wednesday, she seized the opportunity.

He was stepping into his Mustang, one hand already on the door to close it, when she approached. He paused, rolled down the window.

"Jared, hi." Verity offered a tentative smile, trying to read his mood. "I was wondering if we could talk—privately?"

Her voice had come out higher than she meant it to. *I need to sound more confident,* she thought.

"Sure," he said curtly.

Jared's tone wasn't exactly inviting, Verity thought.

"I was just heading back to the main campus. Can you meet me in my office in, say, twenty minutes?"

"Yes, that works," she said. She looked for some trace of warmth in his face, but his expression remained unreadable.

"See you then," she added, aiming for a lighter tone.

During the ten-minute drive to the main campus, Verity couldn't shake the worry that Jared might be expecting some dramatic exposé about the so-called troublemakers.

When she arrived at Everton, the receptionist's desk was already empty for the day. Jared's office door stood open. Peeking in, Verity saw him standing at the window, gazing out.

"Come in, Verity. Have a seat."

He turned and gestured toward a small seating area away from his imposing desk. As she passed him, she caught a faint whiff of musk. Jared followed and sat down opposite her, settling into one of the padded leather chairs arranged in a loose circle around a coffee table. The setup might have aimed for comfort, but to Verity, it felt like it had the polish of hospitality, but none of the warmth.

"What's up?" Jared asked abruptly, glancing at his watch.

"I was hoping to get a bit of clarification on my role at Hillside—if that's all right."

Jared leaned back and met her gaze. "Of course. What exactly feels unclear?"

Verity hesitated, suddenly unsure of herself. The way he looked at her made her feel as though she should already know the answer. She sank slightly into the chair. *But how could I, when no one's explained it?*

Verity made herself continue. She didn't intend to sound evasive, but the *spy* role still felt like dangerous ground.

"You'll remember," she began carefully, "that during my interview, you mentioned the possibility of my serving as an informant."

She paused, hoping for some sign of acknowledgment.

Jared shifted in his chair and tapped his knee a few times, offering no response.

The silence left Verity dangling. He still hadn't formalized anything about the role, and now she wasn't sure how far to go.

"I just wanted to let you know—I've been making notes. In case you still wanted me to keep an eye on things."

Jared's gaze sharpened. "What kind of notes?"

"Just... observations. Suppose something seemed strange or out of place. I've avoided gossip—stuck to things I witnessed."

Jared leaned forward slightly. "And who have you written about so far? Any incidents stand out?"

"I've taken notes on pretty much everyone, honestly—mostly for my reference," Verity said. "I'm used to journaling. I like to write."

She paused, watching for a reaction, but Jared remained silent.

"Not everything I've recorded would interest you," she went on, "but I want you to know that I've included both positive and negative observations."

Jared raised his chin and tilted his head slightly. "And who falls into the negative category?"

The gesture made Verity uneasy. *What if I say the wrong thing?*

She cleared her throat. "I mean, it's still early—I've only been at Hillside two weeks," she said, her tone apologetic. "But maybe that's significant in itself, that a few things have stood out already."

Jared's patience was thinning. "So, again—who do you see as the main troublemakers so far?"

Verity hesitated, then spoke carefully. "At the top of my list would be Nicole. But, if you don't mind my saying so... I've become quite curious about the dynamic between her and Kendra. And Teresa, for that matter."

Jared shifted again and began adjusting his tie. He looked straight at her. "How so?"

"Correct me if I'm wrong, but it seems to be no secret that Nicole receives special consideration compared to the rest of us."

"What do you mean? Give me some examples."

Verity paused. "Well, Kendra told me you were already aware of Nicole's abrasive behavior."

She waited for Jared to respond, but when he didn't, she began to wonder if Kendra had misled her.

Jared folded his arms and studied her for a moment before replying, "Tell me something I don't already know."

Verity felt diminished by his dismissive tone, as though her efforts meant nothing.

"Okay, well then," she said, glancing down at the coffee table between them, "let's just say there are certain standards not being upheld—things like consistent marking practices, appropriate teacher-student boundaries, and coordinator-staff relationships."

Jared raised his eyebrows. "Those are big accusations, Verity. You've only been here two weeks."

"Believe me, it doesn't take long to notice important things. And yes, they are big issues, Jared. That's exactly why I thought it was better for us to have this conversation now rather than later."

Jared stood up and walked over to the window. With his hands in his pockets, he stared out at the row of poplars lining the entrance to the campus. When he turned back to Verity, still seated, his face was unreadable.

"Those are all good observations, Verity, and I appreciate your thoughtfulness—and your effort in keeping notes. But there's no need for you to continue."

Verity blinked. *What?* She could hardly believe what she was hearing.

"I want your full focus to be on teaching your classes and everything that entails—for the duration of your contract."

For the duration of my contract? Verity felt the words lodge in her chest, cold and heavy. There was something final in his tone—something that made her feel small and dismissed.

Unworthy to spy, and nothing more than a substitute.

And yet, beneath the sting, fury flared. *After all this?*

She shot to her feet, fists clenched at her sides.

"What? I've done all this work for nothing? I let your urgency about so-called troublemakers hijack my thoughts since day one—and now you're just dropping the whole thing?"

She couldn't help herself.

Her voice was sharp, her face flushed. The fury spilled out, raw and unfiltered—so unlike her usual careful calm.

Why? Why had Jared changed his mind?

Maybe he's already found out who the troublemakers are.

Or maybe... I was never the right person for this, and he just realized it.

Trying to fit the pieces together, Verity struggled for answers, knowing there wouldn't be any.

"Does this have to do with Nicole? Has she been feeding you lies about me?" Verity felt foolish asking, but she was at a loss trying to understand why her job status had suddenly changed.

"I mean, she warned me to mind my own business or risk losing my job. Where does she get off threatening me like that?"

"No, this has nothing to do with Nicole." Jared's hands stayed in his pockets as he paced slowly away from her.

"You never even told me why you wanted an informant, Jared. You've kept me in the dark—no answers, no clues. Tell me, what were you looking for?"

"Fair enough, Verity. If it makes you feel any better, I'll say this: we suspect someone on staff is feeding information to the principal, maybe even the college board—we're not sure."

Verity pressed on. "What kind of information?"

"Information—lies, really—trying to make us look bad. That's all I'm going to say about it, so please forget it."

Not ready to let go, Verity added, "I want you to know I love teaching here, but there's been a lot of uncertainty and confusion ever since my interview with you."

Jared turned, still pacing. "Yes, I know, Verity, and I'm sorry." But the apology didn't sound genuine.

He smiled, moved toward the door, opened it, and stepped aside. "I have to go now. Dinner with my wife. Have a good evening."

With that, Jared closed the door behind him, leaving Verity to head back to her car. Spotting a pine cone on the walkway, she kicked it hard, almost losing her balance.

∽

BACK HOME AGAIN, Verity glanced through her notes. Although she now thought of them more as a personal journal to help process her strange experiences at Hillside, she wondered if someday they might hold far more value than Jared ever imagined.

August 20, 1973

Kendra seems dedicated to her job, though I'm still not entirely sure what her role entails. I see her car in the parking lot when I arrive early each morning, and it's often still there when I leave.

Her tailored suits, black patent shoes, and neat hairstyles certainly add to her professional image. She's like a 'walking-around boss,' always keeping her ear to the ground, watching what's going on.

She writes numerous memos, schedules frequent meetings, communicates regularly with Jared, and consults with Nicole often, sometimes including Teresa. Kendra is effective at managing things.

As much as I want to believe she's a good coordinator and role model, I'm already wary of her true motives. Her constant back-stabbing and gossip aren't exactly admirable, especially not from someone in her position.

People need role models to look up to, to help keep everyone on track. I can't say I look up to Kendra. Instead, I'm left with too many questions. She has a history of forcing out some of the most capable teachers. I can't help but wonder if she goes after those who ask too many questions—people like me.

MEETINGS

As late August turned into September, Verity had settled into the college's routine, as much as one could amid continual turmoil and tension. One constant was staff meetings.

Even though they'd just had one last Friday—only three days ago—Verity found a new memo on her desk in the staff room that Monday morning:

Please note: There will be a brief, follow-up staff meeting during today's lunch break, beginning at 12:30.

She caught Stella's eye. "There sure have been a lot of staff meetings lately. In my experience, colleges usually hold them once a month—unless something special comes up."

Stella was quick to grab the carrot, giving a knowing nod. "Oh yes. Whatever it takes to push through the current agenda."

"What I've noticed is I start to get edgy if three weeks go by without a staff meeting," Verity joked.

Stella leaned in. "It makes them feel important, you know." She winked at Verity and scooted out the staff room door.

As instructors slid their chairs into a rough circle in the open space of the staffroom, Verity noted the usual look of disinterest on her colleagues' faces.

"Too bad we don't get paid for staff meetings," Janet muttered under her breath.

"I know. This is cutting into our lunch break," Verity replied, glancing up at the wall clock.

At the sound of clop, clop, clop—Kendra's unmistakable heels clicking down the hallway—silence fell over the room. She entered briskly and took her usual seat near the doorway.

"Hello, everyone. Let's get started—we don't have a lot of time," she said, her tone clipped. She looked across the room toward Nicole's cubicle. "Nicole, would you mind taking the minutes?"

Verity had long given up expecting an agenda. Minutes were taken inconsistently, and the minutes from the previous meeting had never once been reviewed at any meeting she'd attended. Still, she ventured to raise her hand.

"If you don't mind, Kendra, I have a question regarding the minutes..."

Kendra glanced in Verity's direction as she shuffled the notes on her lap.

"It's customary," Verity began, "for the minutes of the previous meeting to be read at the start of the current one. I was wondering why that procedure isn't being followed."

She noticed the slight, approving smiles that flickered across several instructors' faces.

"The reason for this," Kendra said crisply, "is that we don't want to waste precious time repeating what's already been agreed upon."

Janet, her legal background impossible to suppress, chimed in. "You do realize, Kendra, that's a serious procedural violation."

Unfazed, Kendra replied, "We really can't get into this now. We have less than fifteen minutes to get through today's agenda."

Verity tried again. "May I suggest, then, that the minutes be distributed to all instructors as a handout the day after each meeting?"

"That's a possibility," Kendra conceded.

Teresa jumped in, sounding eager to please. "If you like, I can oversee that."

Kendra and Nicole lashed out at once.

"No, that's not your job," Nicole snapped, nearly on top of Kendra's curt, "Teresa, we must move on."

The overlap made their message messy but unmistakable. Teresa, red-faced with embarrassment, turned away and busied herself with her cup of tea.

Kendra pressed forward, moving to topics that mattered more to her.

"Now, there are a few important role changes to announce. "Effective immediately, I will be overseeing student quotas and conducting admissions interviews. That will no longer be Nicole's responsibility."

Nicole gave a brief nod as she supposedly recorded the change in the meeting minutes. Most of the instructors looked on, blank-faced.

Verity had begun to suspect that these hastily called meetings served one purpose: to slip in policy changes, often related to student evaluation, under the guise of routine updates. And now, added to the mix was Kendra's new authority to admit more students than before.

It wasn't hard to see the advantage. With Kendra now overseeing admissions, Nicole's tendency to clash with applicants would no longer be a factor.

"And finally, the next role switch involves expenditures—both operational and capital." At that, the staff seemed to perk up. Some sat up straighter, others leaned forward, all eyes now on Kendra.

"From now on, I'll have first approval for all spending requests. So if you have one, please submit it to me, not to Nicole."

Glancing at her watch, Kendra added, "Looks like we're out of time. Thank you for coming, and have a good afternoon." She flashed her syrupy grin before clomping out the door and down the hallway.

"Wow," Verity muttered to Angela and Janet, "with one wave of her wand, Kendra crowned herself Controller of Funds and Controller of Enrollment."

"Two biggies," Angela replied.

Janet was quick with her sarcasm. "Well, she's already Controller of Jared, so I can't wait to see what her next level of achievement will be."

"Why do you think she's increasing her power and cutting Nicole out?" Verity asked.

"More than likely," said Janet, "Nicole's landed in her bad books."

"That's a pretty abrupt shift, from what I can tell," Verity said.

"Yes, my dear," Janet replied. "Welcome to Hillside."

As teachers dispersed and Verity headed downstairs, she reflected on how staff meetings seemed like a ritualistic waste of time, benefiting no one but Kendra, Nicole, and Teresa. For some staff members, the meetings offered a welcome escape from teaching and a break from routine; for others, they provided comic relief and fresh material for gossip.

The impression that Nicole and Teresa were favoured—whether by design or default—was obvious to anyone paying attention. Still, Verity wasn't sure just how deep Teresa's involvement ran. She might need to get to know Teresa better, though that could prove challenging

Back home in her apartment that afternoon, Verity jotted down a few notes to add to her journal.

September 3, 1973

If Kendra makes it easier for students to succeed by revising the evaluation system, admits more students by approving nearly everyone, and raises the entrance quotas, it'll all look good on paper. The increased revenue could make her appear like an effective manager. But she's not looking at the big picture.

These meetings serve a purpose. They give Kendra the spotlight to assert her authority—and give Nicole and Teresa a stage to display their loyalty. It's a power dynamic. A performance.

Are the meetings the gears that turn the mysterious inner workings?

With Charlie still at work, Verity had plenty of time to reflect on her journey at Hillside so far. She made an effort to be friendly and upbeat with everyone. One day, she spent time with teachers who were pro-management; the next, with their counterparts. Through this, Verity gathered all kinds of information — some she wanted to know, some she wished she didn't.

Initially, spying on her colleagues felt offensive to Verity, but things had changed. Her genuine desire for the program and for herself to succeed kept her from distancing herself from the problems. Too much was at stake.

Getting to the root of these issues now seemed crucial to Verity's future success as a community college instructor at Hillside.

After all, this was the position she'd longed for, and she wasn't going to let any problems that developed before her arrival interfere with her ideals. She believed she had plenty to offer this campus, even if the foundation was a little shaky.

When the lunch club met the following Wednesday, the staff meeting was still on Verity's mind.

"It looks to me like our staff meetings are all about Kendra, Nicole, and Teresa," she said.

Janet nodded. "Yes, and apart from Kendra parading her power, Nicole and Teresa get to prove their loyalty to her."

"And why is that important?" Verity asked.

Angela spoke up, "To stay in Kendra's good graces with management."

Verity paused, considering, then asked, "Are you saying they suck up to Kendra to keep their jobs?"

Janet scoffed. "I don't think Nicole worries about job security. But Teresa? Maybe."

"Why's that?" Verity pressed.

Christie jumped in, "I don't know Teresa at all — she's kind of unknowable to me. Whenever I try to be friendly, she never returns it."

"I agree," Janet added. "And I don't get why she seems so insecure. She's a single mom — that might explain it. She probably needs the job to support her son."

Everyone nodded in agreement as they got up to leave Riley's and return to campus.

After the conversation, Verity felt even more determined to get to know Teresa better.

INSTINCTS

On Thursday morning's break in the main-floor hallway, Teresa passed Verity on her way to the staffroom. When Verity first started teaching at Hillside, Teresa had a habit of passing close by, smiling sweetly, and even saying hello. She didn't initiate conversation and seemed to guard her privacy, sharing little beyond occasional updates about her son's activities.

"Michael joined the soccer team," Teresa had mentioned once.

Verity's instincts told her Teresa wanted to make friends, though it was difficult for Verity to get a foothold. Without children of her own, Verity knew she couldn't fully relate, even as she hoped to have kids someday.

Teresa's staffroom cubicle was directly behind Verity's, but they rarely overlapped. When they were there at the same time, Teresa often seemed sullen and unapproachable. Verity suspected Teresa met with Kendra and Nicole more often than with her.

Verity also knew Teresa was likely privy to some of what went on behind Kendra's closed door, but she had no idea how much.

Later, as Verity gathered papers to mark after her Communications classes, Stella appeared in the doorway of room 103.

"Stella, how nice to see you. How are things?"

"Oh, ticking along as usual, Verity," Stella replied with a warm smile and sparkling Irish blue eyes. Then, glancing toward the open door, she leaned in and lowered her voice to a whisper. "I've been thinking that you might not be aware of a part of our system here we call 'the elite triangle.'"

"Huh?" Verity asked, intrigued.

Stella stepped back to close the door and grew serious. "Most of us refer to Kendra, Nicole, and Teresa as 'the elite triangle.'"

"Well, I get the Kendra and Nicole connection, but Teresa?" Verity said. She had noticed Teresa's support of Kendra in meetings — almost like a loyal 'yes-woman' — but didn't know much else.

Stella chuckled. "You'd have to be living under a rock not to notice that connection. Teresa always supports Kendra in staff meetings — always."

Verity nodded, having observed that from her very first meeting.

"But you might not have noticed that Teresa is almost always included in the meetings between Kendra and Nicole, especially before staff meetings."

"No, I didn't know that for sure. I've seen Teresa hanging around Kendra's office, though, and it looks like they take their morning breaks together."

"Oh, you bet. Three peas in a pod, those three."

"Teresa's so quiet; I find her hard to read. I haven't had much interaction with her."

"Oh yes, she keeps to herself — doesn't want to rock the boat."

"Well, I do plan to try and make friends with Teresa and get to know her better."

"Oh, good luck with that, my friend," Stella laughed, then turned to leave. As she reached the door, she called back, "Let me know if you find out anything."

"I will. Thanks for the visit, Stella. Have a good evening."

After that brief conversation, Verity felt even more motivated. If

Teresa was that close to Kendra and Nicole, she could indeed be a valuable source of information.

CRACKS IN THE FOUNDATION

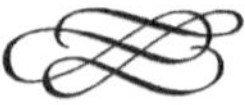

"What were you thinking when you put those two colours together?" Nicole seemed to fancy herself a fashion expert, and when she walked into the reception area on Thursday morning, her eyes immediately zeroed in on Ethel's outfit.

Verity stood by the open filing cabinet drawer, looking up in surprise. Navy blouse, black skirt.

Ethel looked embarrassed as Kendra peeked out from her office door to see what Nicole was fussing about.

"Black and navy together — what's wrong with that?" Kendra asked. "Come on in, Nicole. I suspect you haven't had your morning coffee yet."

Kendra appeared to tolerate Nicole's behaviour, and even some of the teachers seemed to put up with her rudeness and unprofessionalism. Was it apathy? Intimidation? Perhaps a sense of futility—maybe they'd learned from experience that complaints about Nicole fell on deaf ears. Whatever the reason, some chose to turn a blind eye, Nicole shamelessly continued to wield her authority with an abrasive manner, as though consequences were never a concern.

All the more surprising, then, was when Kendra confided in Verity on Thursday afternoon during a routine visit to her office.

"Nicole started to decline about six months ago. She suffers from fatigue, depression, and anxiety." Kendra's familiarity with these symptoms was clear.

"She gets hyper; she just keeps getting more and more hyper instead of calming down. I've told her, 'Look, you've got to stop being so abrasive; you're rubbing people the wrong way.'"

Verity could hardly believe her ears, never imagining she'd hear Kendra badmouth her own 'buddy.' The remark echoed the same tone Kendra had used with Verity about Shirley: a faux empathy that felt forced.

No one is safe here, and nothing is sacred.

"Nicole feels ostracized," Kendra told Verity.

"She is being ostracized," Verity agreed. "Why would it be any different, Kendra? Nicole continually drives people away with her rudeness, apathy, and irritability."

"Yes, and I know she hasn't been feeling well lately; she looks tired much of the time and has complained of nausea."

Kendra seemed to take on a motherly tone regarding Nicole, who, according to her, had a difficult relationship with her biological mother.

"I can't help feeling sorry for Nicole in some ways," Kendra explained. "She was locked out of the house as a teen for disrespecting her curfew, and she was a constant target of her mother's frustrations the entire time she lived at home. She left as soon as she turned sixteen."

"Anyway, Verity, I must get back to work. I have a lot to attend to since I'll be away next week. And, by the way, Shirley will be here for the final week of her contract. I suggest you disregard her chatter if she tries to engage."

"Oh, I see. What classes will she be teaching? You told me I was taking over her classes."

"Not to worry, Verity. I've arranged for her to tutor some of the students who are struggling, like the foreign language students. Nicole can find some work for her if she needs to. It's not an issue. Really."

VERITY LEFT Riley's earlier than Janet and Angela that afternoon, needing extra time to prepare for her communications class. As she made her way across the mall parking lot, she reflected on a comment Janet had made at lunch: "Oh, you can be sure that everything said to Nicole goes directly back to Kendra."

Angela had added, "And, of course, anything said to Kendra goes back to Nicole and maybe even Teresa."

Approaching the campus, Verity mused on the irony of having Kendra as coordinator—someone who was supposed to bring together programs, instructors, students, and sponsors into a relationship that fostered harmony and efficiency. Instead, Kendra appeared to blatantly coerce a chosen few as if they were somehow beyond reproach.

Before working there, Verity had never experienced a manager who freely spread gossip to serve her own purposes. Kendra seemed comfortable confiding in some teachers while excluding others. She could not be trusted to make unbiased decisions; few trusted her at all. Decisions were made according to Kendra's will and whatever followers she could inveigle, rather than for the good of the majority. Verity supposed that values like good leadership weren't in Kendra's vocabulary.

It became clear to Verity that Kendra coordinated events primarily to bolster her position, with little regard for the effect they had on other stakeholders. But just how far would Kendra go to secure and advance her standing?

Verity began to wonder whose side Kendra was on. She treated Nicole as her 'right-hand man'—the two were constantly conferring, often in whispers. Nicole filled in for Kendra when she was away and brought her butter tarts and other treats at lunchtime.

But Kendra and Jared seemed to be the real team, Verity surmised. She hadn't seen much interaction between Nicole and Jared or Teresa and Jared.

Verity figured the elite triangle managed Hillside's business behind the scenes, with Kendra consulting Jared on the major decisions.

VERITY IMAGINED THAT KENDRA, Nicole, and Teresa discussed issues beforehand, giving the three cohorts a clear advantage during staff meetings. They effectively took control of the agenda and direction. *I've got to get to know Teresa better,* Verity thought.

"That woman at work," she told Charlie that evening, "she's such a mystery to me."

"How so?" he asked.

"I don't know… she's usually so quiet and sullen. She tries hard at her job, and I'm not sure about her teaching, but I mean her other role—helping Kendra and Nicole at meetings."

"How does she help at meetings?"

"Honestly, she's like a puppet, nodding yes or no at the right moments, doing whatever it takes to advance Kendra and Nicole's agenda for that meeting."

"She sounds like someone worth getting to know."

Charlie's sarcastic comment spurred Verity on.

"Seriously! She could be the key to the mystery I've been trying to solve. Teresa might be a treasure trove of secrets that could explain why that crazy place keeps running without any real scrutiny from the higher-ups."

"How do you know it isn't being scrutinized?"

"I don't." Verity paused, considering Charlie's remark. "But, now that I think about it, maybe they *are* watching. Remember Jared telling me about *their* suspicion that someone on staff was feeding negative info to his superiors?"

Verity reflected on the latest staff meeting. "Maybe that's why there's this big push to increase enrolment. Kendra just gave herself a huge boost of control in a fifteen-minute staff meeting."

"Yeah? How'd she manage that?"

"Oh, the mechanics are ridiculous—she wants it, she takes it. No voting, no discussion. She's now in charge of funds and enrolment. See where this is heading?"

"I do. Kendra's quite the wheeler-dealer, isn't she? I hope it doesn't backfire on you, Verity. I know you're no puppet yourself, but I don't want to see you regretting sticking your nose where it doesn't belong."

"Yeah, yeah, yeah, Charlie — my ever-watchful protector. I've been studying this crew for three months now, and it's time to dig deeper."

"Okay, my love. I wish you the best." He kissed her lightly before heading out for his Thursday evening tennis match.

Verity's thoughts drifted to Jared. He was treated specially by Kendra, which she supposed wasn't unusual for an underling. But there seemed to be more to it—Kendra's obsession with looking perfect, her strong perfume, now her push to increase enrolment despite classes being near capacity. Fund management was probably another reason for frequent consultations between Kendra and Jared. Verity couldn't recall sensing any tension between them since she joined the staff over three months ago.

Her thoughts shifted back to Nicole and Kendra. Verity figured she was probably the last to learn about Nicole's supposed illness. Before Verity was hired, Angela had told her that one day, Kendra had called all the teachers together to announce Nicole wasn't well.

"You've probably noticed how her hands shake sometimes. Unfortunately, she has the beginnings of a neurological disease caused by anxiety," Kendra had said.

Verity felt some empathy when she heard the news, but working alongside Nicole—and seeing all the mystery and pretentiousness around her— made Verity doubt the full truth. Still, she wondered if that's why Nicole got away with so much bad behaviour.

Verity mused that if Kendra ever felt threatened by Nicole, the illness might become the perfect excuse for her next attack. Nicole didn't have the temperament, knowledge, experience, or skills to be an effective manager (not that Kendra did either, Verity suspected). But now Nicole's supposed illness was public knowledge.

Hmmm — maybe this was a pattern, like Shirley's highlighted affliction with Graves' disease.

Her thoughts turned to Shirley, and she decided she'd ask the lunch club for more about Shirley's relationship with Kendra.

Wednesday's lunch club meeting satisfied Verity's curiosity.

"Did you know Shirley and Kendra used to go to movies together on weekends?" Angela dropped the tidbit as Verity set down her coffee cup.

"With Kendra's husband away much of the time and Shirley being single, it seemed like a good arrangement."

Verity's interest piqued. "What happened?"

Angela went on, "Apparently, Shirley made lots of suggestions to Kendra about how to improve things at the college. That's when Kendra started to fear Shirley might be better suited for the job."

Janet added, "Kendra launched a campaign to discredit Shirley. She spread ridiculous lies, saying Shirley was connected to the mafia, that she was here to infiltrate the college system so the Russians could eventually receive kickbacks."

Janet paused, then looked around the group. "Why go to such lengths when Shirley's contract was only probationary? All Kendra had to do was tell Jared she was unhappy, and Shirley would be out."

"Except," Angela chimed in, "Shirley was loved by everyone— teachers and students alike. So Kendra had to get creative."

Verity began to piece together the answer to her question: Just how far would Kendra go to protect her position?

Janet nodded, confirming the suspicion. "There are few boundaries for Kendra. One minute, she acts like a close friend sharing secrets; the next, she's engineering your last day at work."

DAGGER

"You're so terrifically conscientious—you're appreciated, you know that?" a student said the next morning in Verity's Thursday Typing 180 class. "It's not what we're used to, believe me."

The woman's soft brown eyes held sincerity, and her warm words were deeply appreciated.

Dutifully, Verity said nothing about the implication that such conscientiousness wasn't the norm at Hillside.

Without stands to hold the drill books upright, the books lay flat on the desks, making the drills harder to read and forcing the students to keep their eyes fixed on the page.

jjdddkkksssllllaaa;;;
asdjklaskjklsd l;kl;sdf
aaa;;;ssslllldddkkk jj
asd kl;asd kl;asd kl;

Verity's beginning typists were puzzled at first—why memorize only the middle row of the QWERTY keyboard? They were always impressed when she recited it with ease—*a s d f g h j k l ;*— and proud when they, too, picked up this essential touch-typing foundation so quickly.

She demonstrated proper posture—sitting upright with her back against the chair, feet flat for balance, fingers curved and poised above the home row, wrists low and relaxed, not resting on the typewriter frame, forearms parallel to the keyboard.

With her eyes fixed on the copy, Verity's fingers flew across the keys at her usual speed—80 net words per minute.

"Strike the keys squarely, using quick, sharp keystrokes," she instructed.

She took quiet pride in learning every student's name by the end of the first week, despite the arrival of 30 new students each month.

That afternoon, on her way to the lunch club meeting, Verity spotted Christie's red hair from a distance and quickly caught up with her. Christie was unusually quiet, trudging along, shoulders slumped, eyes fixed on the ground.

"Christie, is something wrong?"

"Yes, but... if you don't mind, I'd rather tell everyone all at once."

Verity noticed the puffiness beneath Christie's eyes, the new thinness in her face.

Once everyone had their lunch on the table, Christie inhaled deeply.

"I just wanted you all to know I'll be away for a while. I'm having surgery on Monday. They found a lump in my breast, and it turned out to be malignant, so it needs to be removed."

Verity was the first to speak, concern etched across her face.

"Oh, Christie, I'm so sorry to hear this."

"That's such shocking news to hear just now. But I'm sure it'll all go very well," Janet said, her voice a mix of empathy and hope. "We'll all be thinking about you, so please let us know how it goes."

"The same thing happened to my sister," Angela offered. "They got all the cancerous cells, and she's been cancer-free for five years now."

"How are you holding up?" Verity asked gently.

"The truth is, I haven't slept in weeks."

Janet urged her to take all the time she needed to recuperate, and the others nodded in agreement.

"Yes, Kendra told me to stay away as long as I need," Christie said. "Nicole will take over my classes, just like she did last week."

Verity's heart sank. Nicole taking over Christie's classes could lead exactly where Verity feared. It wouldn't take many quiet comments or subtle criticisms to start unraveling things again.

The cloak-and-dagger method of getting rid of instructors is alive and well here.

The tone of the gathering shifted. Silences grew longer, and the conversation felt stilted—unusual for such a habitually upbeat group.

When they left Riley's and headed back to campus, the air was fresh and crisp, offsetting the heat and busyness of the cafeteria, where sad news seemed to linger with nowhere to escape.

Back in the staffroom, Verity headed down the hallway toward room 101. As she passed Kendra and Teresa, huddled together outside the washroom door, she caught snippets of Kendra's voice.

"When Nicole took over Christie's classes last week, she was appalled at how disorganized everything was. Honestly, I think Christie's just not mature enough to handle the job."

Kendra's voice trailed off as Verity reached the stairs and began her descent to the lower floor. *There she goes again,* Verity thought—badmouthing one teacher after another. First Shirley, then Nicole, now Christie.

Recalling that it was Nicole who had badmouthed Christie to Kendra, Verity's concern for Christie's job deepened. Things could easily spiral when you weren't there to defend yourself.

Several weeks later, as Verity emerged from the staffroom, she spotted Christie and Kendra walking down the hallway, moving away from her. Kendra had her arm draped around Christie's shoulders—a very telling image, as far as Verity was concerned.

That afternoon in room 102, Verity explained the differences among various letter styles

"Full block is the easiest to type and the easiest to remember."

Just as she reached to turn on the overhead projector, Nicole burst into the room.

"Verity, have you seen the keys to my filing cabinet?" she demanded, her tone sharp.

A ray of sunlight caught Nicole's emerald necklace, making it sparkle brightly—a striking contrast to her brusque entrance.

"Oh, excuse me, Nicole. We're right in the middle of something here," Verity said calmly, "but I haven't seen those keys since yesterday. I returned them to the middle drawer of this desk, and"—she opened the drawer—"they're not here."

Without another word, Nicole turned and stormed out.

Verity felt a flush of anger at Nicole's rude intrusion, but her professional commitment took precedence. She took a deep breath and carried on as planned.

~

AFTER THE LESSON, Verity left class before the dismissal bell and headed straight to Kendra's office. Finding the door open, she stepped inside.

"Kendra, I'm between classes, but this really can't wait. Do you have a moment?"

"Okay, Verity, what is it?" Kendra replaced the receiver on her desk phone, perhaps deciding to make her call later.

"Honestly, Kendra, I'm usually pretty resilient and understanding. But this was unprofessional—frankly, rude. I thought you should know."

Verity recounted Nicole's intrusion, then waited for Kendra's response. She hoped for validation or some accountability for Nicole's behaviour, but instead got what felt like a canned answer.

"Yes, I'd be upset too, Verity, and thanks for telling me. Nicole has a few quirks, as we're all aware. But she also has her strengths and contributes a lot to the program."

"I'll speak to her about it; don't worry."

It puzzled Verity that Kendra would defend Nicole, especially after stripping her of some power at the last meeting. Despite Nicole's erratic and unprofessional conduct, she kept getting away with it. Kendra's loyalty made it hard for Verity to express her concerns—and she suspected others felt the same.

While searching through files in the front office reception area before leaving for the day, Verity overheard Kendra and Nicole deep in conversation through the open door of Kendra's office.

"Maybe I'll ask Jared for some extra time away; what do you think, Nicole?"

"I agree. Two weeks isn't enough for our educational planning sessions. We just get settled in and have to leave again."

"And this time, I'm thinking Molokai—I'm getting tired of Maui."

Reflecting on that first interview with Jared, Verity wondered how he expected her to be a spy when those she was supposed to report to seemed to be in cahoots themselves.

As Director of the Business Division, Jared was responsible for Kendra and the division's instructional staff at Hillside, in addition to his duties at the main campus. Verity saw him on campus at least once a week, meeting with Kendra in person and probably more often by phone. He rarely attended staff meetings; when he did, it signaled that the meeting was important.

Angela and Janet had explained the protocol: if a staff member had a concern about Kendra, they should first discuss it with her directly. Only if no resolution was reached could the instructor make an appointment with Jared. And if the issue remained unresolved, the instructor could escalate it to the College Principal, Dr. Farmer, who would likely refer them to the Faculty Association.

Since Jared was ultimately responsible for everything that happened at Hillside, Verity held him at least partly accountable for mismanagement.

She recalled telling Jared the day Nicole threatened her with dismissal if she didn't keep quiet.

What kind of manager would ignore that?

BUBBLY

7 3-10-22

Dear Mrs. Child,

It is my pleasure to offer you a further "short-term" appointment as defined in the Handbook for Faculty. The term will be from Monday, November 2, 1973, to February 1, 1974. The salary will be $1,405.67 per month (subject to change, (subject to change as negotiations are presently taking place).

Dr. Farmer, the College Principal, signed the letter. Verity had ten days to accept by signing the letter and forwarding it to the Bursar. An addressed envelope was enclosed for her convenience.

The offer arrived on Friday, and Verity was able to share the news with the lunch club that same day.

"Whoa! There you go, Verity; maybe you're not such a threat after all," Angela laughed, causing Christie and Janet to chuckle as well.

"Or maybe, just maybe..." Christie smiled mischievously, a twinkle in her eye, "you paid a visit to that famous penthouse apartment of his."

This set them all laughing loudly, drawing the attention of other diners, some even smiling along at the scene.

When Verity recovered, she said, "I didn't think it would be renewed, not after the way Jared talked about my teaching up until my contract ended, ha!"

"Maybe you need to have more confidence in yourself," Janet advised. "Yeah, Charlie's always telling me that." Verity smiled as she visualized her handsome husband with his supportive arm wrapped around her shoulders. Lunch break flew by that day, and they all had to rush back to campus to avoid being late.

THAT EVENING, Verity waited for Charlie to get home. When he unlocked their apartment door at 8 p.m., some of her excitement about the contract news had already faded.

"Evenin', Mister." She met him at the door, wrapping her arms around his neck and tilting her head up to meet his warm, full lips. "I bet you're glad to be home."

"Oh, yeah, sure am, hon." He set down his briefcase, hung his keys on the hook, and said, "I'll catch up with you in about fifteen— just going to jump in the shower, okay?" He glanced up and noticed the vase of flowers on the coffee table. "Nice flowers. Who're they from?"

"They're from me," Verity laughed. "Okay, babe, let's meet on the sofa and celebrate the end of the week."

"Sounds good to me." Charlie headed into the bathroom.

Verity heard the shower running as she went into the kitchen to grab two champagne flutes. Opening the fridge, she took out the chilled bottle of Veuve Clicquot she'd splurged on that afternoon. She'd bought it on a whim after pulling into the liquor store lot on Pacific Boulevard. Maybe it was a bit over-the-top, she thought, but then she reminded herself that she and Charlie hadn't celebrated anything in a long time.

She picked up a bouquet of mixed flowers and some hors d'oeuvres from a nearby deli to complete the occasion. *Maybe this was a bit over the top,* she thought with a smile, *but if I do end up with a permanent contract someday... well, I guess we'll have to go to the Bahamas.*

When Charlie emerged from the shower, he headed into the bedroom to get dressed. Once ready, he joined Verity in the living room, where a platter of chicken skewers, cheese balls, pineapple spears, and deep-fried shrimp awaited him.

"Wow, Verity, that looks fantastic. And all this to celebrate the end of the week? There must be more to it than that—if not, I must say, I like your style."

She lifted the champagne bottle from the bucket of ice and filled their flutes, both watching the golden bubbles rise like sparkling springs.

"Cheers, darling." Verity clinked her glass gently against Charlie's, and they took their first sip of bubbly.

Settling onto the sofa, Charlie reached for a shrimp. "So, is there anything else you want to tell me?" he asked, sinking his teeth into the tempura.

Verity smiled. "Of course there is, Charlie."

He looked a bit nervous, she thought, bouncing his knee and squinting slightly, as if bracing himself for surprising news.

"No, I'm not pregnant, babe—sorry to disappoint." She placed a hand on his shoulder, still enjoying the moment.

"The news is that my contract was renewed. I have another short-term appointment, ending February 1st."

"Congratulations." Charlie looked relieved, then turned to her and kissed her on the lips.

"So, I gather you're pleased, despite all the grumbling I've heard since you started at Hillside."

Verity laughed knowingly. "Pleased? Not exactly. It's not like, 'Oh yay, my dreams have finally come true.' The director's a philandering ass, the coordinator's inept—I don't know how they keep their jobs, honestly."

"Maybe the higher-ups don't realize what's going on," Charlie offered.

"Or maybe Jared and Kendra just don't want the higher-ups to find out about their poor management," Verity said thoughtfully. "Although, now that I think about it, if some of their victims are like that poor student Jared came on to, maybe those victims just shrink away under pressure and don't make a fuss."

"That wouldn't be you, babe." Charlie laughed. "You might not always think you're worthy—however you measure that worth—but watch out, Hillside campus. Verity Child's got another shot." He reached for a pineapple spear and a chicken skewer.

Verity paused to gather her thoughts. "But here's the thing, Charlie—the real crux of it." She looked into his eyes to make sure he was listening.

"My strategy is to keep working there while pushing for positive change—for the students, the teachers, the whole Business Office Training program."

"Uh-huh. I get that, Verity. It's always been your goal with whatever you take on. But have you really thought about how that school seems to consume your life? I mean, it's all you ever talk about." He glanced at her, and Verity nodded as she reached for a chicken skewer.

"Not much different from you, Charlie. It's just that I don't see you at work. All those extra-long hours you put in at the office are going to catch up with you sooner or later."

Charlie chuckled. "I know, babe. Guess we're just a couple of workaholics."

"I'll drink to that." Verity took a final sip of champagne, and Charlie reached for the bottle to refill their flutes.

He set the bottle back in the ice bucket, then placed his hand on the back of her neck, sweeping her hair up as he drew her closer. "Just don't let that philandering ass anywhere near this beautiful bod," he murmured, pressing his lips to hers so she couldn't say another word.

GUTSY

On Monday morning, November 5, in the front office area, Verity caught sight of Kendra dressed in a crisp white skirt and matching blazer. She worked hard to maintain her figure and always looked her best. Kendra was eating an apple and carrying a cup of yogurt.

Verity checked her mailbox and, just as she was about to head to class, Jared appeared. "Good morning, Jared."

Verity's smile came easily now that she knew her contract had been renewed.

Jared returned a brief smile and continued toward Kendra's office, his expression brightening when he saw her.

Verity slowed her pace, pretending to leaf through papers on her clipboard so she could watch discreetly. She saw Kendra, looking equally pleased, touch Jared's arm and guide him inside her office, even though he hardly needed the help.

"Good morning, Jared. Just in time for coffee and muffins," Kendra said, her voice bright.

As she walked away from the reception area, Verity remembered Angela mentioning that Kendra and her husband talked on the phone every day. Verity herself had seen them holding hands in the parking lot during lunch breaks. One sunny Sunday afternoon in October, she'd even spotted them strolling hand-in-hand through the botanical gardens at Queen Elizabeth Park.

Verity mulled over the new information. She figured either she'd misjudged how close Kendra and Jared were, or Kendra was playing a damn good game of cover-up.

∾

Curious about Kendra's marriage, Verity brought it up at Wednesday's lunch club meeting.

Angela spoke first. "They raised three kids together. Kendra worked as a seamstress to help pay college tuition. I think her husband, Norm, was in the navy, so she was on her own a lot."

Janet chuckled. "Once the kids were grown, they built a smaller house so the kids couldn't stay over, or so they said."

Then her eyes sparkled with amusement, as if she had a juicy tidbit to share. "But yeah, Kendra worked as a seamstress. I remember the time I confronted her about breaking staff confidences."

Janet peered over her glasses. "You know me — I don't pull punches when I'm sure of myself. And this was a big one."

All eyes were fixed on Janet.

"She told me one day, in her office, that Mary, one of the teachers, had been treated for a gambling addiction. That's not something you want leaked when you're starting a new job, is it?"

Angela shook her head, smirking. Verity watched Janet's animated retelling closely.

Raising her eyebrows and glancing sternly over her glasses, Janet said, "I told Kendra her behavior was deplorable—that she had no business breaking confidence and risking Mary's reputation."

I left her sitting there, stunned. She said nothing, and I wasn't sticking around for her excuses."

"Next thing I know, Jared calls me into Kendra's office. He was alone. No need to hold back. He said he was disappointed in my disrespect toward Kendra; I told him I was disappointed in her disrespect toward a fellow instructor."

"And on it went, round and round in circles."

Janet made a shooting motion with her thumb and forefinger. "Kapow."

"If you had any idea how to run this place, you wouldn't have hired Kendra—a student with no experience beyond sewing garments—in the first place."

"Now, look," Jared said, rising from his chair. But I refused to be silenced — now that I'd come this far, I stood up, too, and let him have it."

Verity and Angela fixed their gaze on Janet, grinning widely, eager for the next part of the story.

"And you might think you're fooling people with your so-called secret rendezvous at your swanky uptown penthouse," Janet shook her head, "but you're not fooling anyone, Jared." Then she shook her head again, this time 'no.'

"And before he could accuse me of slander, I bit my tongue about naming any students. Instead, I said, 'Adios, I have better things to do than waste my time sitting here with the likes of you,' and I got up and left his office, slamming the door behind me."

Janet laughed carefree, like someone ready to retire. She had the union's strength behind her now — she wasn't going anywhere. She said it was no longer necessary to show respect at every turn when she felt otherwise.

The others looked intrigued.

"That was pretty gutsy of you, Janet, to say the least," Angela said, and Verity nodded.

"And he had it coming, sounds like," Verity added.

"I'm still trying to figure out the alliances," Verity said. "But my impression is that if you cross Nicole, you cross Kendra. And if you cross Kendra, you cross Jared."

"Yup," Angela agreed. "Sounds about right."

"But still," Verity said, "it's annoying that I have to worry about this at all."

Janet and Angela nodded in agreement.

Verity continued, "I want to focus fully on teaching. But I'll tell you one thing—my ideal of open and honest communication between colleagues and management just seems to get buried deeper and deeper as the weeks fly by."

"It just keeps getting more and more ridiculous," she complained to Janet and Angela as she sank her teeth into her toasted ham and cheese.

"You'd wonder, wouldn't you," Janet said, "how such a corrupt system manages to hold together? With Kendra's new quota system, she'll be buying new furniture and equipment to handle an influx of students, when we're already close to capacity... unless they hire new teachers, ha! And with evaluation techniques designed to push more students through, even if their skills are questionable, our reputation's at risk."

Angela chimed in, "That's the worst part—the damage to our reputation. It won't show up right away, but eventually, People-Power will catch on, and there goes their sponsorship."

"As far as I can see," Verity added, "we need an influx of good teachers—ones who are excited to be here, qualified to teach, and well-versed in their subject areas."

Angela and Janet nodded in agreement.

"I guess we sound like a broken record," Verity said as they pushed back their chairs, preparing to head back to campus. "But let me ask you two—especially you, Janet, since you've been here the longest—do you honestly see things changing for the better anytime soon?"

Janet paused, and the others leaned in, waiting. "It'd take a miracle —I don't see things improving anytime soon. Unless our esteemed director gets the boot—along with his sidekick Kendra—I don't see much hope on the horizon."

Verity frowned, curious. "I know very little about business, but I do know that if the numbers look good, the managers look good. So I'm thinking the numbers will probably look even better now that Kendra's hell-bent on bringing in more students."

Angela nodded. "Exactly. And the Jared-and-Kendra team will be the stars of the show."

WALKING BACK FROM RILEY'S, Verity wanted her closest colleagues to know how much she appreciated them.

"You know," she said, glancing at both Angela and Janet to make sure they were listening, "meeting with you two at Riley's is like walking from a deep, dark cave filled with venomous spiders and scorpions into an open garden filled with sunshine, flowers, and fresh food at the ready."

All three grinned at the joke, with Janet tilting her head back and bellowing with laughter.

SERGEANT

*V*erity made occasional attempts to be friendly with Nicole, hoping she might let something slip—some important piece of information that could bring Verity closer to unraveling the mysteries of the school's inner workings.

One day, Verity caught up to Nicole as they were both walking outside. "So, I hear your husband's a logger."

"Uh-huh."

"I'm guessing you don't go for forest walks together in your leisure time?"

Nicole was unamused. "We're not together; I only see him on weekends."

"Oh, that must be difficult, Nicole."

"No, it's okay. He has colitis, so he's not the best person to be around 24/7. He goes through one roll of toilet paper after another."

"Oh, I'm sorry to hear that. Poor guy. Sounds like it's not exactly a mild case."

"You have no idea."

"I can sort of identify with you—I usually arrive home to an empty apartment, even though I'm married."

"Believe me, you couldn't come anywhere near identifying with me, Verity."

Verity felt a wall being put up between them once again. She was growing weary of making fruitless efforts to connect with Nicole.

"And maybe that's for the better, Nicole. I was trying to be friendly, but it seems making friends isn't exactly high on your priority list."

Nicole scoffed. "Don't do me any favours, Verity; I've got all the favours I need."

Verity took the shortcut back to campus.

WHEN KENDRA BOOKED a week off from November 12 to 16, Nicole stepped in as coordinator. She answered phone calls on Kendra's behalf, carried a ring of keys as large as a circus hoop, and always seemed to know when a fire drill was coming.

Her abrasive demeanour toward staff and students ramped up noticeably. She came and went as she pleased and was often spotted at her desk in the staffroom, even during her scheduled teaching hours.

At Riley's on Wednesday morning, Janet seemed amused. "Looks like we're in for a week of Sergeant Nicole stomping around with her circus-sized keyring, bossing everyone, and acting like she's the Director of Everything Negative."

"Where's Kendra off to this time?" Verity asked. "Let me guess... Maui."

"Jared's away this week, too," Angela added.

"Hmm," Janet said. "How do you know that, Angela?"

"I tried to schedule an appointment with Jared for this week."

"I overheard Nicole and Kendra talking about packing," Verity said. "Sounds like Kendra's got a whole new wardrobe of linen shorts, Hawaiian shirts, and Maui Jim shades."

"Maybe she got a raise for taking on extra duties," Janet raised her eyebrows.

"Eww," Angela said, "the thought of those two having sex." The three of them laughed.

As they headed back to campus, Verity spotted Stella walking toward her car. Breaking away from her lunch club friends, she called out, "Stella."

She hoped to catch a moment with her—maybe Stella knew more about Nicole's real condition. Kendra's explanation about Nicole having a neurological disease caused by anxiety didn't sit right with Verity.

"Lunch on the fly, I see," Verity said as she watched Stella take a bite of her sandwich. "Where are you headed?"

Stella replied as she got into her car, "Off to see Murph at the park for a few minutes." The distinct scent of peanut butter gave away what was in her sandwich.

"Murph?" Verity asked.

"Murph Kennelly. Know him?" Stella said as she turned the ignition and settled into the driver's seat.

"No, I don't," Verity said, deciding now wasn't the time to probe further about what Stella might know about Nicole.

"I'll introduce you sometime. He's on the College Board—real nice guy." As she shut the car door, Stella called back, "Gotta run."

IN THE STAFFROOM before the next class, Nicole informed Verity, "A shipment of Business Communications textbooks just arrived. These are for the April intake, and we're giving them out for free. That'll keep the students happy. Usually, if you give students something for free, they tend to keep quiet."

Yes, I suppose you do want the students to keep quiet, Verity thought. *I wonder what other bribes they're handing out around here?*

Nicole added, "Oh, and Verity, I see Eileen Baxter is on your new intake list. She's a real troublemaker, you know."

Verity remained skeptical of Nicole's judgment. "Nicole, Eileen's doing exceptionally well so far. She not only excels in class but also has a delightful personality. She's quite popular among the students, too, and adds some fun to the classroom."

STATUS QUO

*B*y now, the term "elite triangle" was so ingrained in instructors' minds that most thought of the three as a single unit. They were also known as 'the cloak-and-dagger team.'

"They're masterpieces of misinformation," Stella quipped.

By Friday, December 7, Verity found herself more focused on the status quo at Hillside than on the new December intake.

At the lunch club meeting, Verity asked about the Selection Committee. She'd heard whispers about it since she first started.

"Oh, we call that the Firing Squad," Janet said, prompting Angela and Christie to smirk.

Verity listened as Janet explained, "In the past, instructors have unanimously refused to sit on the Selection Committee because the terms of reference were never clearly defined. To be blunt, we refused to be the firing committee for the current short-term staff."

Tick, tick, tick. Verity's understanding of the management's workings was becoming clearer.

Janet continued, "When a teaching position opens up, Kendra hand-picks the Selection Committee—choosing people she thinks will support her preferred candidate."

"So, what you're saying, Janet, is that the whole idea of a Selection Committee is nothing but a farce," Verity concluded.

"Pretty much," Janet said. "This approach has successfully eliminated seven competent teachers in Kendra's three years here—teachers who either didn't support her methods or disagreed with her in other ways."

Angela chimed in, "The pretense that the so-called 'Selection Committee' helps choose the best candidate is well known among the old-timers. The protocol was put in place to make it look like standard hiring procedures were being followed."

Verity considered this and then replied, "I see. So, in reality, the committee members are like a choir without voices, you might say."

"Exactly," Janet smiled, clearly enjoying the comparison. "Eventually, teachers refused to sit on the Committee. 'Oh, sorry, Kendra, we're having a test at that time.' 'No, sorry, I can't help—I'm revising my course modules and need the extra time.'"

"Sorry, not sorry," Angela laughed, joining in.

Verity poked at her lasagna, bitterness simmering beneath her words. "You know," she said, "when I started here just five months ago, I was naïve." She put down her fork.

"Maybe I was too idealistic, but I believed a college teaching career meant being part of a community of clever minds with shared goals and purpose. I thought the leaders would be people we could look up to—people who'd motivate and inspire."

"Yes," Janet agreed. "I get it. When those who claim to lead with professionalism—and whose jobs rely on public approval and funding—fail to meet even basic standards, it throws everything out of balance."

Angela was quiet, eyes distant.

Verity pressed on, grateful to unload her thoughts among trusted friends.

"It seems laughable now, I know. But I feel like I stepped into a house of cards—one that could collapse from the slightest tremor. Hiring the cheapest labor, buying the cheapest materials, not even considering the skills needed to do the job right—get it up and running, and worry about the mess later, if at all."

"I can't disagree with that analogy, Verity," Janet said gently, "but don't let it get you down."

"Well, Janet, to tell you the truth, I feel like I did as a kid when my uncle crossed boundaries he had no business crossing. He'd built such trust with me that I regarded him as a second father—and then my world turned upside down."

Angela lowered her eyes and squeezed them shut as if trying to absorb the shock of what Verity had just shared. "Oh, Verity, I'm so sorry to hear that."

"Yes, I didn't mean to shock you," Verity said softly, "but I wanted you to understand the strength of what I'm feeling right now. When the very foundation of what you thought was solid starts to crack and crumble, with no change in sight, what else is left but to take it down and rebuild?"

The others nodded silently.

Verity added, "But I no longer feel I have the energy or the will to help with that process."

As they headed back to campus, all three silently agreed—they were glad it was Friday.

SUBJECTIVITY

Friday, December 14, signalled the end of term, and Verity was sitting in her cubicle in the staffroom, preparing student assessments two days ahead of time. Only moments ago, Nicole had been sitting in her own cubicle just ahead of Verity's, and Verity was surprised she hadn't seen Nicole leave.

Returning to her work, Verity looked up when Nicole pushed open the staffroom door, looking pale and tired.

"Nicole, are you all right?" Verity asked as Nicole headed back to her desk.

"If you call having to race to the bathroom to throw up being all right, then yeah, everything's just rosy."

"Oh, I'm sorry to hear that. I know some of the students have the flu right now—I guess with the high-stress Christmas season upon us. Do you think that's what it is?"

"Doubt it. Is there something you wanted to see me about?"

"Yes, if you don't mind. It's about Eric McGregor, who transferred from your Typing 181 class to mine with the December intake. Since he's been with me for only two weeks, I thought you'd be better able to assess his progress."

"He's a C," was the inevitable reply.

Nicole's subjective marking is not only sheer laziness on her part, not to mention just plain wrong, but it's also inconsistent with what the rest of us are doing—duty-bound to record every mark and keep fastidious records. Nicole is a disgrace to the profession. But who do I complain to?

"And I'll just let you know," Nicole continued, "that certain teachers' marks are too high. You'd be better off keeping your marks on the low side."

Nicole looked directly into Verity's eyes. "You already know we have two objective marks to guide us," she said, "one for production work and one for typing speed. The final mark, however, is to be determined subjectively." She added, "No percentage is designated to the subjective mark."

In Verity's experience, the subjective mark usually made up around 10% of the final grade. At Hillside, the weight of the subjective mark was left entirely to the teacher's discretion. That opened the door for any teacher harbouring a grudge against a student, or simply disliking them, to use the marking scheme as a lever against those not in their favour.

Verity pictured Nicole wielding the subjective mark to push her student of choice into failure or forced repetition. Such misuse directly contradicted Kendra's new plan to boost enrolment.

HAVING EXCHANGED holiday wishes with her colleagues, Verity welcomed the peace and comfort of her and Charlie's love nest. Even though it was dinner for one on Friday night, she poured herself a glass of sparkling wine and settled into the soft cushions of their sofa, bobbing her head to Elton John's "Crocodile Rock."

She resolved to do her best to clear her mind of Hillside's problems over the next three weeks.

BLAB

January 7 heralded the start of a new school year, and two days later, the lunch club reunited at Riley's on Wednesday, as usual.

Christmas bulbs and evergreen garlands still adorned the windows at Riley's as Verity, Angela, Christie, and Janet joined the bustling crowd inside.

The welcoming scent of cinnamon and sugar greeted them—Riley's was still featuring their Christmas special, cinnamon buns. Verity placed her order, then went to secure a table, leaving Angela to bring their lunches when ready.

Once everyone had gathered at the table, Verity, Janet, and Angela shared highlights from their time off.

Noticing Christie's quietness, Verity asked her directly, "How was your holiday, Christie?"

The morning's gathering took on a sharply contrasting tone. Christie swallowed hard and bowed her head.

"I withdrew my application for a continuing contract yesterday."

Angela and Janet fell silent, struggling to absorb the news. Verity wasn't surprised. She told the others that Nicole had blabbed about the withdrawal two days before Christie herself even knew.

"I had a brief conversation with Nicole in the parking lot at the end of the day. I wished her a good evening and was about to leave, but Nicole had more to say."

"Yes, it'll be quite a good evening, knowing Christie won't be teaching here anymore," Nicole sneered, clearly wanting me to know she had the privilege of hearing the news first—and shamelessly breaking confidence."

Verity glanced at Christie, who shook her head.

"That news left me cold, Christie. I drove away without saying anything—didn't want to give Nicole the satisfaction of seeing my disappointment."

"Isn't that typical of the ongoing indiscretions here at Hillside?" Janet asked.

Christie remained quiet for a moment, seeming resigned. Then she said softly, "I never really felt comfortable at Hillside anyway." The sadness in her voice was clear to those who knew her well.

Verity was deep in thought. Christie wants to stay here; they all knew that.

"When did you withdraw your application, Christie?" Verity asked.

"On Tuesday, after meeting with Jared and Kendra."

"Well, that's strange," Verity said. "Because I met with Kendra in her office after classes on Monday, and she told me you had already withdrawn." Janet bristled at the news.

"How would Kendra know about your withdrawal before you'd even made the decision?"

Christie looked puzzled. The others put two and two together and could only surmise that Christie's meeting with Jared and Kendra had been purely procedural. Kendra and Jared had already made up their minds about her withdrawal. What they said to persuade the insecure Christie to follow through remained a mystery.

Verity wondered why Kendra had told her that Christie had withdrawn. Then she remembered—Kendra knew she and Christie were friends.

Was she testing my loyalty? Did she think I might cause trouble over this? Or was her main purpose to remind me that I'm disposable too?

The conversation turned to the idea that being let go from that campus had become a kind of twisted badge of honour. Reflecting on those who'd shared Christie's fate, the more seasoned members of the group—Angela and Janet—could easily name the good teachers who had come and gone. It was even suggested that the lunch club compile a list of respected colleagues who had vanished since Kendra and Jared took over leadership.

"I wonder if they already have another target in mind," Angela said.

Verity pictured Kendra seated in her office, rubbing her hands together as she plotted her next move. No wonder she never had time to complete her seventeen coordinator duties—she was too busy pulling strings for her own advantage. Kendra thrived on control, but she couldn't see beyond the short term.

Sombrely, the club headed back to the college. No one had a bounce in their step this time.

WANING

Kendra returned from her Hawaiian vacation looking bronzed and refreshed. She wore a bigger smile than usual that Monday morning, offering cheerful greetings to everyone during a brief appearance in the staffroom.

By Wednesday, Verity noticed a sudden shift in Kendra's demeanour. She'd also overheard a rumour that Kendra had called Janet a liar.

Verity decided to ask Janet directly when they met for lunch at Riley's that day.

With her hands wrapped around a hot coffee cup to ward off the January chill, Janet set the record straight for Angela and Verity. "No —it was I who called Kendra a liar."

Both Verity and Angela fixed their gaze on Janet as she continued.

"It was around 2:30 yesterday afternoon. Ethel will tell you I stormed in and out of Kendra's office in five seconds flat."

She gave a wry smile, clearly amused by Ethel's retelling.

It was hard for Verity to picture the usually composed Janet exploding like that, but as Janet went on, her outburst seemed not only understandable but necessary.

"I'd had enough of Kendra's lies and backhanded comments. I marched down the hallway, saw the office door was ajar, and swung it open without even checking with Ethel.

Lucky for me, the DO NOT DISTURB sign was flipped to the blank side," Janet said. "Not that it would have stopped me."

She paused, then added with satisfaction, "I just shouted, 'You're a liar!'—plain and simple."

"Then I turned and walked out. But not before catching the look on her tanned face. Eyebrows up, eyes wide—she looked shocked. Maybe even a little scared."

"Honestly? Worth it."

Angela and Verity leaned in across the café table, eager for more.

"What happened?" Angela asked. "What pushed you to that point?"

Janet's expression hardened. "Kendra told some of my students that I'd been fired as a legal secretary in Edmonton. And that the old phrase 'those who can't do, teach' applied to me."

Verity felt her stomach drop. Janet's cheeks were flushed now, her usual poise replaced with anger.

"Kendra must've run straight to Jared, like she always does when she's out of her depth. Ethel came into my class and said Jared wanted to see me in my office right away."

"Did you go?" Verity asked.

"Of course not," Janet snapped. "I was teaching contract law. By the time I wrapped up, Jared had already left."

Janet's riveting story left Angela and Verity so absorbed that they arrived late to the afternoon staff meeting. As Verity pushed open the door, she immediately sensed the tension in the room.

She slipped into the seat beside Teresa as quietly as possible and turned her attention to Kendra, who was already speaking.

"Jared has asked me to form a committee to oversee student job placements," Kendra said, crossing one leg over the other as she surveyed the group, clearly expecting compliance.

"Who would like to volunteer for this important initiative?" she asked, scanning the room.

One hand went up quickly. Then a pause. Several seconds later, another followed.

"I need one more volunteer, please," Kendra said, her gaze circling the room again.

Finally, a third hand rose—hesitant, elbow still bent, palm lifted cautiously.

"Thank you," Kendra said. Then, turning to Teresa, she added, "Please record all three names in the minutes."

Looking pleased with the progress, Kendra took a sip of her coffee and moved on.

"Now, I need someone to lead the committee." She had barely finished the sentence before Nicole chimed in, "I'll do it."

Teresa, without waiting for Kendra's confirmation, began writing again, already noting Nicole's name, as if it had been decided in advance.

Janet and Angela exchanged knowing glances. Verity didn't miss it. It confirmed what she already suspected: Nicole's appointment had been prearranged.

Given what Verity had observed of Nicole so far, she could already picture her assigning the most thankless tasks to those she didn't like.

"Good. Done. Thank you, everyone. We now have our committee," Kendra said, clearly satisfied.

❧

Later, back in Room 101, Verity refocused on her students. One in particular weighed on her mind: Yusuf, her sole foreign student. His struggle to communicate and understand English was a constant challenge for both of them.

"You need to learn more English, Yusuf, and then you can be successful here," she said gently. "If you like, we can ask your sponsor if they'd be willing to pay for you to study English first, instead of continuing in this course right now."

She tried to offer encouragement, to break the work into manageable steps. But deep down, she knew the support Yusuf needed wasn't readily available at Hillside.

Verity's plan to help him never got off the ground. At Hillside, school policies seemed to shift almost daily, and Kendra often contradicted herself.

The marking scheme for typing was revised to the point where it was nearly impossible for a student to fail.

Though Kendra argued that students should be allowed to complete the course and fail on their own merits, rather than be dismissed early, she later claimed that the international student should never have advanced beyond introductory typing.

Yet it was Kendra herself who had the final say on student progression. Despite Verity's recommendations to the contrary, Kendra approved the student's advancement.

Eventually, Verity understood the real reason: the more students who finished the course, the better it looked for the college, and the more likely it was to receive continued funding from PeoplePower.

MEMO

73-09-01

To: Verity

From: Jared

. . .

*The enclosed represents a normal appeal on a mark awarded to a college
student. From the student card, it would appear you were the instructor
involved in the awarding of the C in T180.*

*Could you please provide a brief statement so that I may understand the
situation fully when I discuss the matter with the student in question?*

As Verity read the memo, it struck her that college correspondence
was not always grammatically correct, and there were often punctuation errors and inconsistencies in form. She was amused at the
thought that perhaps they hired their own graduates.

The "student in question," Lexi Moore, wrote this in her letter of
appeal:

"I received a C, which I felt was unjust because I never missed
classes, was late only once, and completed the production work with
all the marks over 90%.

I discussed this with the teacher involved, and she said I received
a C because she felt my behaviour was not suitable in an office situation. She was referring to a disagreement we had in the classroom on
November 19. I feel I was treated unfairly, and I appreciate this
opportunity to appeal my mark."

Reading this letter, Verity was reminded of Nicole, the Queen of
Subjectivity. And then the uncomfortable question: *Had I fallen into
that rabbit hole myself?*

Verity reviewed her mark book and reflected on Lexi's work as a
student in her class. Then she replied to Jared:

"She received a B for Production and an A for Speed. Her final
mark is reflective of her general disposition and her failure to apply
herself to the best of her ability.

Lexi takes up more of my time than any of her classmates (while she is probably more capable than most of them), and she has never shown any degree of appreciation for my help up until the time of our 'disagreement'. Lately, she has been asking questions that she could easily answer herself. Repeatedly, she submits work that she has failed to proofread.

Concerning the disagreement we had on November 19, I found Lexi to be disruptive, immature, and lacking in common courtesy. As I was conducting the morning drill, I became aware of her loud voice, coming from the third row. I frowned at her several times while doing the drills, and she admitted that she had received my message.

She continued to talk to the student beside her, and also to the two behind her, loudly enough to disrupt the class proceedings. I stopped the drills and said, "Lexi, I will not compete with your voice."

She continued ranting to the point where I finally said that if she couldn't stop disrupting the class, she would need to step outside. Even then, Lexi persisted in talking back.

Incredulous, I asked if she intended to continue. I thought I heard her say no.

Eager to get the class back on track without further disruption, I resumed the drills.

After class, I approached Lexi and asked if she understood why I was upset. I did not get the impression that she fully understood, nor that she even cared.

I find her to be discourteous, inconsiderate, and undeserving of the special attention she demands. Since she is unlikely to succeed in an office situation with such a disposition, I gave her a final mark of C. I also explained to Lexi that if she improves her disposition, her mark will likely improve, as she undoubtedly has the ability."

MEMO

73-01-10

To: Jared
From: Kendra
Cc: Verity Child
Re: Lexi Moore

I SPOKE with Lexi at length today, and we've agreed that the C she received in T180 will stand. However, I am allowing her to take T181 with a different instructor.

VERITY FELT satisfied with the resolution. Still, she couldn't help but think of Nicole—and the growing suspicion that management had likely received many student appeals regarding grades Nicole had assigned. But did those appeals go through the same channels? Or did they somehow get brushed aside?

She recalled how often Nicole's students ended up reassigned to her classes.

When Verity consulted the school calendar, she noted that students progressed at their own pace and received a certificate as long as they completed within the six-to-eight-week maximum. That every student got a certificate, Verity figured, probably counted as "success" in Kendra's mind. In her mind, however, that certificate could mean little—just another piece of paper, depending on the student's actual performance.

Stella had openly challenged the policy, pointing out that students felt pressured by the timeline. One of her students had put it bluntly: "I came for an opportunity, not a challenge."

"What happens after eight weeks?" Stella asked. "What becomes of the student who passes production but hasn't yet achieved a valid timing?"

"That's just one of those fine details that don't seem to get accounted for," Verity replied.

Then there was the strange rule prohibiting students from working at home. Instructors all knew that students *did* work at home, just as they knew some snuck into vacant typing rooms to use the typewriters and catch up or get ahead. It was yet another example of the system's contradictions. Verity and her colleagues agreed: sometimes the only sane response to a foolish rule was to bend it.

Though Verity tried to stay positive and do what she could within the constraints imposed by those in charge, she felt her resolve to push for real improvement slowly slipping away.

DUTIES

MEMO

74-01-15

To: Kendra
From: Verity

It would be beneficial for students in Typing 180/81 to acquire metric rulers since all measurements in the textbooks are metric. Presently, most students employ the inefficient method of converting millimeters to inches in order to determine margins and spaces. Please make this item a required purchase.

DISAGREED. Kendra maintained that students would still use inch rulers, regardless.

ON THE OTHER HAND, *it is to the Typing 180 student's disadvantage, financially, to purchase the manual Stationery and Business Forms since they will use only five sheets from that book to complete the course. Production exercises for 180 may be typed on plain bond; the students may type their own letterhead.*

Agreed.

You may already be aware that we have a typewriter in room 101 with a French keyboard. Since none of the symbols on the keyboard match those on the element, everyone avoids using this machine. In effect, we have only 29 typewriters in room 101, not 30.

Kendra said she'd look into this.

Is it at all possible to acquire at least one machine with unmarked keys? Perhaps we could trade the French typewriter.

No reply.

∽

MEMO
74-01-16

To: Kendra
From: Verity

Students in Typing 181 first encounter footnotes as a production job and do not, therefore, have a trial run before being marked. Since many students have difficulty with this aspect of typing reports, I suggest adding VI.22, p.

212 to the problem section of the outline.

Verity's request was relayed to Nicole. No reply.

MEMO
74-01-17

To: Kendra
From: Verity

I WOULD LIKE to suggest a new marking scheme for Typing 180, designed to tighten parameters and help prevent personal judgements from interfering with professionalism: 45% speed, 45% production, 10% office manner.

The marking system would be explained clearly to students in both written and spoken form so that everyone knows what to expect.

AGREED. Carried out January 17, 1973

AT THE JANUARY meeting of the lunch club, Verity voiced her confusion about Kendra's role as coordinator.

"I know what a coordinator is supposed to do, and I think we all agree Kendra is failing miserably at promoting harmony and efficiency, right?" She looked from Janet to Angela.

Angela gave a self-satisfied smile. "More like disharmony and inefficiency—with a heavy dose of narcissism."

"Exactly," Verity said. "But seriously—what does she do besides chair staff meetings, meet with Jared behind closed doors, and conspire with Nicole and their sidekick Teresa? I honestly don't know. Her duties have never been made clear to me."

"I can tell you exactly what her duties are," Janet said. "The staff asked Jared the same question not long after Kendra came on board."

She promised to bring the list to the next lunch club meeting, scheduled for the following Wednesday.

On Wednesday, January 24, Verity was eager to see the list Janet had promised. True to her word, Janet handed over a copy of a memo outlining the coordinator's duties.

"We were shocked," Janet said, raising her head and then lowering it deliberately, pausing as she repeated the word with dramatic effect—"simply shocked"—before looking up at Verity.

"Turns out, of the seventeen job duties listed, all but three were supposed to be performed by the department chair, not the coordinator."

Verity let that sink in before turning her attention to the memo. The three duties assigned solely to the coordinator were:

• Timetabling and allocation of faculty for all departmental programs, including University Transfer and specially funded courses.

• Work with the director in the evaluation of existing faculty.

There it is, Verity thought. *Both Kendra and Jared evaluate faculty.*

• Assign offices and classrooms to faculty.

"After we saw the memo," Angela said, "we asked Jared if a chairperson had been assigned. Want to guess what he said?"

"Hmmm... sounds like a yes," Verity replied.

"Right. Now, guess who the chairperson is," Angela said, leaning forward, a glint in her eye. Janet studied Verity's face, waiting for the reaction.

"Oh, Gawd," Verity exclaimed. "So Nicole pushing her weight around and acting like she owns the place makes perfect sense."

She read aloud Chairperson Duty #17: "Assist the director in special assignments."

They all laughed, imagining what those *special* assignments might be.

Verity suspected Jared had assigned only three duties to Kendra because she likely couldn't handle more, and because he wanted her to appear successful. Maybe there were personal reasons, too.

"Of course, we now know that Kendra appointed herself in charge of funds and enrollments," Verity added. "Which is a major shift from what's actually in the list."

"Huge," said Janet.

Angela nodded in agreement.

The closeness between Kendra and Nicole suddenly seemed more understandable. They relied on each other, and Nicole's 'importance' was now, in Verity's view, a necessary evil for the program's survival... a practical alliance, reinforced by the camaraderie of vacationing together.

Verity began to suspect that whenever she made suggestions to update or improve course modules, Nicole viewed them as threats to her authority. Nicole may not have aspired to be a coordinator, but with Kendra shielding her, she had all the safety she needed to wield power on her own terms. In turn, Kendra leaned on Nicole to carry out nearly all the duties assigned to the chairperson, not the coordinator.

Like any symbiotic relationship, their partnership had a certain logic to it. Together, they performed like a polished livewire act at the circus. And a circus it was. Verity imagined Kendra as the ringmaster, Teresa the trained monkey, and Nicole the bejeweled pony, prancing about and overestimating her power.

Verity grew quiet, trying to absorb what she'd learned. "Tell me—how did Kendra get that job in the first place? Does anyone know?"

"Oh, yeah," Janet replied. "That's a well-known story."

She leaned in and launched into it. "Kendra was a student in the program herself. After graduating, she became secretary to the male coordinator at the time. Then one day, she marched into Jared's office and told him she could do a better job than her boss."

Verity's ears burned with interest.

"Jared was a seasoned manager by then—nearly twenty years in the role. And Kendra? She had only a Grade 10 education, no leadership training, and no teaching experience. Yet somehow, she managed to get the job."

"Wow." Verity's mouth formed an O as she absorbed the impact. She began assembling more pieces of the puzzle. "So when Kendra saw how easy it was to oust the last coordinator, maybe when Shirley came along with her enthusiasm and ideas for improving the school, Kendra felt threatened. Maybe that's why she pushed Shirley out."

"You got that right," Janet said, stirring sugar into her tea. "And every smart cookie who came after, with bright ideas and good intentions, became a threat. So you'd better watch your back, Verity."

"If it's that easy to steal someone's job," Verity joked, "maybe I'll weasel my way into Jared's chair."

They laughed, but as the three headed back to campus, Verity's optimism faltered.

If trying to improve things only led to retaliation, then what was the point?

BUMP

*I*f there was such a thing as an ordinary day at Hillside, Tuesday wasn't it.

Kendra burst from her office and made a beeline for poor Ethel, who was preparing for morning announcements.

"Ethel, do not put through any more calls from Revenue Canada. When they call, I'm in a meeting—period."

She pivoted sharply and stomped off toward the staffroom.

Verity, watching from a safe distance, was relieved not to be in Kendra's path. She reconsidered her plan to dig through the front office filing cabinet—better to wait until the coast was clear.

Just then, Nicole appeared, dressed from head to toe in sleek black. Most striking of all was her necklace: three emerald stones, brilliant against the dark fabric.

"Nicole, good morning," Verity said, catching her just as she reached Kendra's door.

"Yes, Verity. What can I do for you?"

"Nothing at all," Verity said quickly, "but I have to ask about that necklace. It's stunning. Was it a gift?"

A small smile softened Nicole's usually guarded face. "Yes. A gift from a very special man," she said, her tone playful.

When Verity said nothing, just waited, Nicole added, "My father was a jeweller."

Right then, all three women looked at each other in alarm as they heard a loud sound—like a train barrelling through—although they all knew there were no train tracks anywhere near Hillside.

They froze, caught in suspended animation for a few seconds, until the building began to shake.

Ethel crouched beneath her desk.

Nicole moved quickly to the doorway of Kendra's office, bracing herself with her feet against the open door so it wouldn't slam shut.

Verity steadied herself against the filing cabinet, eyes scanning frantically for a safe spot. Within seconds, and despite the trembling, she lowered herself to the floor, wedging her back against the cabinet and jamming her feet against the opposite wall, vulnerable but better shielded from flying objects.

Then, just as suddenly as it had started, the shaking stopped.

They waited a minute, bracing for the aftershock. When it didn't happen, all three women began to piece themselves back together.

As Nicole manoeuvred to her feet and Verity made her way toward Ethel's desk to check on her, she noticed a small white slip of paper on the floor. Nicole must have dropped it. Bending to pick it up, Verity couldn't help but see the word *OBGYN* written in black letters, followed by a phone number.

"Oh, Nicole, you dropped something."

Verity stepped just inside the doorway to hand it over. Nicole extended her hand, but Verity didn't miss the tinge of pink colouring her cheeks.

"Ah," Verity teased, "so those weekend visits to see your husband have paid off, I see."

She'd thought she'd noticed a slight bump the other morning when Nicole turned sideways in the staffroom. But Nicole hadn't said anything, and Verity knew better than to assume—after all, to suggest a pregnancy when there wasn't one could be the ultimate insult.

Nicole stumbled slightly. "Oh, no—my sister is pregnant. This phone number is for her."

Verity couldn't wait to chat with the lunch club that afternoon. Naturally, everyone wanted to know where the others had been when the quake struck, what they'd done, and whether anyone had been hurt.

Once they'd exhausted that topic, Verity leaned forward with a twinkle in her eye. "Have any of you noticed Nicole's emerald necklace?"

"Hard to miss it," said Janet. "Isn't it gorgeous?"

"Yes—and I found out it was a gift from her father. Nicole told me he's a jeweller."

Angela scoffed. "What? Nicole told us she was an only child. She said her dad had died in some horrible accident involving his wheel-chair and a train. Right, Janet?"

Janet nodded, laughing. "Oh yes, I remember that."

"Oh," said Verity, chuckling, "I guess I swallowed that one too fast. Should've checked in with the Truth Squad first."

Angela smirked. "What do you think she's covering up this time?"

Verity shrugged. "You know, sometimes it's not even worth wasting your brainpower trying to figure out what makes these people tick."

Janet and Angela shook their heads in agreement, but their curiosity was piqued. Sensing the moment, Verity leaned in and shared the story of the piece of paper—*OBGYN* scribbled on it, the blush on Nicole's face, the awkward explanation about a so-called pregnant sister.

Angela and Janet listened closely, then exchanged a glance.

Angela tilted her head. "Well, there it is again. If Nicole were an only child, then I don't believe she has a sister who's pregnant."

"Oh, I give up trying to figure that woman out," said Verity, exasperated. "I think I'm happier the less I engage with Nicole."

She pushed back her chair, preparing to return to campus, and both Angela and Janet followed suit.

"Well," said Angela, placing a hand gently on Verity's shoulder, "if she is pregnant, at least that'll mean some time away for her."

"Can you imagine Nicole as a mother?" said Janet.

All three women shook their heads, walking toward Hillside in silence, their unspoken thoughts loud enough.

SIREN

After seeing Nicole carried away on a stretcher one week later, Verity could barely get through her morning classes. She was thankful it was a lunch club afternoon—she needed to talk it through with her friends.

All three made their lunch selections and were seated in no time; they all knew what the topic of conversation would be. Angela was the first to bring it up. "Does anyone know what happened to Nicole?"

Janet was quick to respond. "I asked Ethel the first chance I got, and she said it was probably Nicole's nut allergy."

"What do you mean?" asked Verity.

"Don't you know Nicole is allergic to nuts?" Angela said.

"Yes, I think we all do," Verity replied, "but what happened, exactly?" She turned back to Janet.

Janet explained, "Ethel said Nicole had joined Kendra, as usual, in her office during morning break. Since they often have muffins with their coffee, Ethel figures one of the muffins must've contained nuts."

"What did Kendra say about it? Does anyone know?" Verity asked.

"Ethel couldn't get a word out of her and finally gave up. She said Kendra looked like she was suffering and didn't want to add to her grief."

Verity recalled the day when Kendra told Teresa not to buy banana nut muffins because of Nicole's nut allergy.

"I've heard Kendra request muffins without nuts, out of consideration for Nicole's allergy," Verity offered. Then she added, "But have you seen those products that warn there may be traces of nuts in them?"

"Yes," said Janet. "I suppose it's possible neither Kendra nor Nicole realized their break-time food might have been exposed to traces."

"Or maybe the product wasn't properly labelled," Verity said.

"Anything's possible," Angela agreed.

"Any word on how Nicole's doing?" Janet asked.

No one had heard anything.

SLAP

*I*n the package of marking information left for instructors that afternoon, Verity noted item #7 under the improperly punctuated heading, "Marking, General Points to Consider for Final Letter Grade."

"*Attitude of the student: Eager? Flippant? Willing? Is there a temper tantrum when things do not go right for the student?*"

On another page entitled "Marking Information for Typing":

The instructor will determine the final mark for each component. Students must realise, however, that all work is considered subjectively for the final mark."

There it was. Another slap in the face for Verity. It looked like Nicole had overridden Kendra's decision to reduce the weight of the subjective mark to 10%.

Verity left the school along with the students that day, skipping her usual routine of staying late to do marking. Like a punctured balloon, she felt deflated—no longer of use, all her energy gone.

At home, she opened her journal and reread the most recent notes she'd written. It felt strange, almost surreal, to see her thoughts about Nicole on the page after witnessing her being carried out on a stretcher that very morning.

JANUARY 17, 1974

I have accused Nicole of displaying a negative attitude toward students and of behaving unprofessionally. I support my accusations as follows:

Approximately three weeks ago, in the staffroom after 3:20 p.m., Teresa asked Nicole, "Who's Maggie Compton?" Nicole replied, "She's a nondescript person—not one of our better students."

About another student I was enquiring about, Nicole remarked, "Don't worry, she's coming up for assessment," in a tone that suggested she held unilateral power over the student's status. When I asked if she truly had that authority, she replied, without expression, "Yes."

In a separate conversation regarding Marion Birk's suitability for office work, Nicole described her as "fat" and criticized her clothing.

I overheard Nicole refer to a student as "stupid."

On May 3, several staff members heard her declare, regarding the April intake, "They're all a bunch of dummies." A student was present in the staffroom at the time.

I am left with the strong impression that Nicole's subjective mark— and she emphasized to me that it "counts very heavily" toward the final grade—is largely influenced by her personal opinion of the student, rather than objective assessment.

WHEN CHARLIE SETTLED in at home after work that evening, he immediately noticed something was off. "Is something wrong, hon? You seem a little down."

"Yeah. Things have been getting to me lately," Verity admitted.

"It's like that old saying—hitting yourself on the head with a hammer only feels good when you stop. Or… however it goes."

She told him about Nicole being taken away by ambulance and the strange uncertainty surrounding it all.

Charlie listened patiently, then offered gently, "Maybe it's time to stop, babe."

"I don't know, Charlie. Maybe it is. My contract's up February 1, so I've only got two more weeks—if I can hold it together that long." She paused, then added, "I don't want to lose my ideals. But Hillside doesn't feel like a place where they can survive. At least, not mine."

Charlie pulled her close. "Wow. That's a big shift. You've always had so much heart for this work. It's hard seeing you so beaten down." He rested his chin lightly on her head. "But maybe it's time to listen to your heart, you know? A job isn't worth it if it breaks the parts of you you most want to keep."

"Maybe," Verity said softly. "Though for some people… maybe a job is worth more than we can even imagine."

TRUST

After thinking it through, Verity decided the best way to connect with Teresa might be to ask about her son. And since everyone had to eat, maybe she'd invite her to lunch. Even though Verity's sleuthing energy had faded, she'd been around long enough to know: just when you're about to give up, the truth often finds a way through.

Late Tuesday afternoon, Teresa stepped into the staff room to gather her things. Verity had waited at her desk, hoping she'd come —she'd noticed Teresa had left her purse behind.

It was rare to find anyone lingering in the staffroom after 2:30. Most teachers bolted the moment classes ended. Maybe Teresa had been meeting with Kendra; she was, after all, the only remaining member of what used to be the 'elite triangle.' Now, it was more like a bird with a broken wing.

As soon as Teresa swung open the staffroom door, Verity jumped at the chance. "Teresa, I'm just heading out too. Mind if we walk together?"

Teresa looked up briefly, then returned to gathering her things. "Yep, I'm heading out."

It would take some work to thaw the ice.

As Verity opened the outside door for Teresa and they walked down the steps together, neither of them spoke. Heading toward the parking lot, Verity decided to get right to the point.

"You know, even though our cubicles have been side by side for months, we hardly ever talk."

"Yeah, I guess that's true," Teresa said, pulling her keys from her purse.

"Honestly, I'd like to get to know you better, Teresa. So, if you're open to it, I'd love to take you out for lunch."

"Oh, that's not necessary, Verity," Teresa replied with a brief smile, turning to give her full attention.

"Sometimes meeting outside of school puts things in a whole new light," Verity said. "There's a new bistro I've been wanting to try —it's only a five-minute drive. We could take my car. Tomorrow at lunch works for me. How about you?"

Verity didn't want to leave room for a childcare excuse, so she figured a lunch outing might be manageable. She held her breath as Teresa considered.

"All right. I'll meet you here in the parking lot at noon. That work?"

"You bet it does," Verity said. "I'm looking forward to getting out of Dodge for a bit. See you tomorrow at noon."

THE BISTRO WAS BUSTLING, so Verity was glad she'd thought to reserve a table by the window. She hoped the setting would help Teresa feel at ease—if that was even possible.

With less than an hour to make a good impression, Verity opened with a question about Teresa's son, Michael.

The conversation unfolded lightly, with a few laughs along the way and no mention of school. Verity steered clear of anything that might hint at her true reason for the invitation, and Teresa didn't bring up any issues either.

BACK ON CAMPUS, Verity made a point of chatting with Teresa more often and even invited her to a lunch club meeting. Getting the others to agree, however, hadn't been easy.

"Look," she'd argued, "Teresa could be a valuable source of information. Anyone who spends that much time behind closed doors with Kendra is bound to have access to something."

What Teresa shared with Janet and Angela was longevity—each had spent years at Hillside. So when the conversation at Wednesday's lunch turned to stories from the early days, an easy camaraderie began to form between the three. Verity, meanwhile, listened closely for anything useful.

TERESA'S DELIGHT at being included in the Wednesday lunch club was unmistakable. Back at Hillside, she walked a little taller, smiled more easily, and even cracked the occasional joke.

She so enjoyed the newfound camaraderie that she rarely missed a meeting.. Verity was encouraged by the change—gaining Teresa's trust had seemed unlikely just weeks before.

As the group grew more comfortable with one another, they began to share personal stories. In her gentle, caring way, Janet asked Teresa what it was like raising a child on her own.

Teresa didn't hesitate. She spoke openly about surviving an abusive relationship that lasted ten years. The final wake-up call came when she was seven months pregnant and took a punch to the stomach. Until then, she had managed to deny just how serious the danger was. Even after that moment, it took her two more years to find the courage to leave. When she finally did, she gathered Michael in her arms and never looked back.

She shared how he had actively isolated her, discouraging her friendships and family ties, so that when she finally needed support, she felt utterly alone. It wasn't until a routine prenatal checkup that the floodgates opened. The doctor's simple question that day—"Is your husband excited about the baby?"—unleashed years of hidden pain.

With the support and encouragement from the lunch club, Teresa began to see them as a kind of new family. The mood was light and jovial at Friday's meeting when Teresa surprised everyone with an invitation.

"You know what," she said to Verity, Angela, and Janet, "My son Michael will be at a sleepover next Saturday. How about you all come over to my place for drinks and hors d'oeuvres?"

Seeing their pleased reactions, Teresa added, "And any—or all of you—can stay over if you like, since Michael won't be home."

Verity's face lit up at the invitation—getting to know Teresa in her own space felt like a perfect next step.

"Can we make it a Hawaiian night?" Teresa asked, eyes sparkling. "With flower leis, skirts slit up to there, and anything you can bring that screams palm trees, cocktails with colourful umbrellas, tropical fruit garnishes, and fun times." She smiled broadly, clearly delighted with the idea.

Joining in the fun, Verity said, "The drink of the evening has to be Harvey Wallbangers. I'll bring the Galliano." She pictured her favorite golden liqueur in that tall glass bottle.

"Okay," Angela added, "I'll bring the vodka. Janet, can you bring the orange juice and garnishes?"

"You bet," Janet replied with a smile.

Caught up in the planning, they almost forgot the time until Janet glanced at her watch. "We'd better get going," she said.

As they pushed back their chairs and stood, Teresa reminded

them, "I'll have plenty of ice on hand. And please, everyone, bring food that fits the theme."

On the way back to campus, they chatted about ideas for dishes, and Verity thought staying overnight might be a perfect plan after all.

PARTY

Angela and Verity were the first to arrive and exchanged cheerful "Aloha" greetings before turning their attention to Verity's coconut shell bra—a playful nod to the theme. Janet soon arrived, wearing a Hawaiian-style sleeveless shift dress with a black background adorned with red hibiscus, bird of paradise, plumeria, and lush green leaves. A real hibiscus flower was pinned elegantly in her upswept hair.

Angela sported a Hawaiian shirt that looked like it might have come from her husband's closet. Teresa was ready to party in a red tropical-print mini skirt with a halter-back top; the skirt featured a daring slit along her right thigh.

Verity took on the role of bartender, mixing cocktails as the strains of "Blue Hawaii" filled the air. As the evening progressed, the music shifted to Bob Seger's "Old Time Rock and Roll," Three Dog Night's "Joy to the World," and other classic rock hits that wouldn't offend Janet, at least not during the early part of the night.

The Harvey Wallbangers went down far too easily, and the bartender might have been a bit too generous when mixing Teresa's drinks. Everyone was having an absolute blast, their laughter growing louder and more infectious with every passing minute—even when the jokes weren't all that funny. Together, they belted out the lyrics to "The Loco-Motion" by Gerry Goffin and Carole King.

If nothing else, they all nailed the hip-swinging moves. Teresa started a conga line, with everyone placing their hands on the hips of the person in front. They bounced around the room, vaguely following Teresa's shouted directions to kick left, kick right—until Angela lost her grip on the hips ahead, causing the whole line to derail when the *engine* was no longer in control.

As darkness fell, Janet thanked everyone and, waltzing out the door, declared she hadn't had this much fun in years.

Verity offered to make Angela one last drink before she left—her husband was picking her up, so she kept an eye on the time.

"Teresa," Verity coaxed, "if you have another Wallbanger, that'll make three of us."

Standing by the stereo, Teresa shouted over the music, "Maybe we could make our own threesome, like Jared, Kendra, and Nicole." She doubled over in laughter at her bold joke.

As she straightened and settled back onto the low sofa, the slit of her mini skirt opened fully, revealing bright red lace panties.

Verity's eyes widened, as if trying to soak in every detail of Teresa's surprising revelation. The playful flash of Teresa's red lace panties was nothing compared to the news of the threesome. Angela was left speechless, her brow furrowed in confusion.

Verity considered shutting off the music but hesitated—she didn't want to discourage Teresa from sharing more intriguing details.

Angela finally broke the silence. "What do you mean by a *threesome*? Like, a sexual threesome?"

"Oh, ha! I gez I'm not s'possed to talk 'bout that..." Teresa's speech was slurred, and she had slumped back onto the sofa, on the verge of drifting off.

"It's okay, Teresa; you're among friends here. Can you tell us anything more about this threesome?" Verity tried to keep her tone steady and matter-of-fact.

"Waz there tuh tell?" Teresa mumbled, pausing for a long moment. Verity gently shook her shoulder, trying to rouse her.

"How did you find out about the threesome?" Angela enunciated carefully, her voice louder than usual.

Teresa laughed, her head falling back against a cushion. "Oh, I was a bad, bad girl." Her eyes fluttered closed, heavy with sleep.

Angela quickly shut off the music, and Verity grabbed an ice cube from Teresa's drink, rubbing it gently against her cheek. Teresa startled awake.

"What do you mean, 'bad girl,' Teresa? Please, tell us."

"I opened the wrong door at the wrong time, and there it was—staring me in the face like some cheap porn movie."

"Do you mean Kendra's office?" Verity kept her voice steady.

"Uh-huh. Who'd 'spect to see THAT in the middle of the day?"

"See what, exactly?" Angela pressed. "Please, tell us what you saw."

Verity and Angela exchanged looks, listening intently, hardly able to believe what they were hearing.

Teresa began giggling again. With a sudden burst of energy, she sat upright on the sofa. "Let me show you exactly—well, not *quite* exactly. That'd be impossible."

She dissolved into another fit of laughter she couldn't contain. The more she laughed, the harder it became to stop, until she was guffawing in loud bursts that seemed far too big for her small frame.

At last, she sagged back, breathless, giving Verity an opening.

Not wanting her to drift off again, Verity pressed, "Okay, Teresa —show us what you saw."

Teresa slipped into instructor mode. "Okay. Pretend I'm Jared. He was in his favourite chair, legs wide open like this." She spread her knees. "Angela, you sit on this one, just like Nicole did." She patted her right knee. "But face me."

Angela's curiosity outweighed her discomfort, and she followed the instructions.

"Verity, you're Kendra. Sit on this knee, but face away from me."

Teresa's eyes fluttered shut, and she began to sway. Verity gently shook her awake, then turned around and carefully perched on Teresa's left leg, waiting for her to continue.

Angela tried to picture the scene. "Did you happen to notice a *Do Not Disturb* sign on the door, Teresa?"

"Nope. It was turned around, so I figured it was okay to go in."

Teresa wrapped her left arm around Verity, placing her hand between Verity's thighs, one finger pointed. "Now, I'm Jared, remember? My fly's unzipped and I'm standing at attention—or should I say, waiting for attention." She laughed at her joke, clearly entertained.

Then, with theatrical flair, she slipped her right arm around Angela's back and placed her hand squarely on Angela's backside.

"Okay, we get the idea, Teresa," Verity said quickly. "You've described the scene very well."

Both she and Angela scrambled off Teresa's lap and settled onto the floor, trying to process what had just happened. Meanwhile, Teresa flopped back onto the sofa, eyes closed.

Eventually, Verity and Angela set about cleaning up after the party, turning the music back on, hoping it might ease the shock of the evening.

Verity no longer wanted to stay the night but couldn't, in good conscience, leave Teresa alone in her condition. She wasn't looking forward to the inevitable vomiting or the morning hangover, but the information they'd uncovered felt like a fair trade.

What she and Angela would do with this gem of a revelation, they had no idea.

THE NEXT MORNING, over coffee and a slow-moving conversation, Teresa revealed her actual role at the office.

"Yeah, I'm just window dressing," she admitted. "I show up at meetings to support Kendra. It helps make it look like it's not just her and Nicole calling the shots."

"I see," Verity said thoughtfully. "The more I get to know you, Teresa, the more I realise the person at work seems quite different from the one at play. And I mean that in the nicest way."

Teresa blinked slowly and repositioned the ice pack on the back of her neck.

"But tell me," Verity asked gently, "what happened after you discovered the threesome?"

"I was sworn to secrecy, of course, with the promise of job security in return for my loyalty." A faint smirk tugged at Teresa's pale face.

～

As VERITY LEFT Teresa's place that morning, a wave of sadness came over her. Teresa's history of abuse was already enough to endure—now this twisted workplace arrangement likely dragged her self-esteem even lower.

With Nicole gone and Teresa's role more transparent, Verity found herself wondering: would Jared and Kendra be looking to fill Nicole's spot in their infamous threesome?

Nicole had been useful—until she wasn't. If her illness meant she could no longer keep up her dual role, Verity suspected they had already decided it was time to move on.

Nicole's gossiping and backstabbing would no longer be tolerated—because it no longer had to be. The trade-off had run its course. With her gone, she could no longer scare off students or undermine Kendra's mission to boost enrollment."

Once Teresa recovered from her hangover, Verity planned to probe further.

LATER THAT SUNDAY EVENING, Verity spoke briefly with Angela on the phone.

"Now that the threesome's been exposed," Verity asked, "do you think we could use that information to our advantage?"

"Well, it certainly explains a lot of the bizarre behaviour we've endured since Kendra came on board," Angela replied. "In that sense, it's satisfying."

"I agree," said Verity. "And such deplorable, indefensible behaviour doesn't deserve to be kept secret, that's for sure."

"True," said Angela. "But still... I feel uneasy about the whole thing. Don't you?"

"Definitely. No one would believe us, for one. And we have no proof—not without betraying Teresa, who made us promise not to tell anyone. Her livelihood depends on that secrecy. I wouldn't want to jeopardize it."

In the end, they agreed not to expose the sordid secret shaping life at Hillside. Yes, they could threaten to tell the spouses—but to what end? Aside from tearing families apart and unleashing who-knows-how-much grief, rage, and heartbreak, what good would it do?

Their dirty little secret was safe. For now.

IN THE REAL WORLD

It was Monday morning in the staffroom. With Nicole gone, Susan had quietly resumed her rightful role as head of the typing program. She handed Verity a four-page document titled *Marking Information for Typing*.

There had been much discussion about a new method for grading timed writings. Verity had asked for clarification more than once—the proposal, as floated through departmental meetings, had always felt murky. Despite reservations from many instructors, Kendra had pushed it through at the last meeting before the holiday break.

Now, on this Monday morning, Verity stared at a memo on her desk. The directive was clear: the new grading system would take effect today.

She thought back to the day she'd questioned Kendra at that first meeting. "Who came up with this idea?"

"It was a collaboration between Susan and me," Kendra had replied.

Verity remembered how Susan had turned away to stare out the window, saying nothing. That told Verity all she needed to know. If the method flopped, Kendra could blame Susan. If it worked, she'd no doubt claim full credit.

Back in the staffroom, Verity held the paper in her reluctant hands and examined the new system. To determine the so-called "composite score," instructors were to multiply the gross typing speed by two, add the net speed, and divide by three.

No rationale was given for the math. None of it made much sense.

Verity did know one thing: the scheme was bound to inflate students' typing speeds on paper. And that, she surmised, played neatly into Kendra's ongoing mission—make the numbers look good, regardless of the reality behind them.

Students were uneasy. Some voiced concerns that their actual typing ability wasn't being fairly reflected. Those who had been at the school for months and were already applying for jobs said employers didn't recognize the scoring method. They felt awkward explaining it in interviews, only to be met with blank stares.

Kendra remained firm. She argued that employers cared about speed above all—how fast someone could type, not how accurately. Accuracy, she insisted, was secondary.

To Verity, it was clear: the entire system had been designed to benefit students who consistently struggled to pass timed writings under the current six-error limit.

Kendra's solution? Issue cards to graduates stating a clean, unqualified speed, something like *50 words per minute*. No mention of accuracy. No explanation. Just a number that, in the real world, would be assumed to represent net speed, because that's what matters.

The achievement shown on the card was the composite score. Some of Verity's students didn't hesitate to voice their concerns. "I feel like we're cheating with this new system," one complained. "Just another deception cooked up by our campus leader," said another.

Kendra was overheard in the hallway downstairs, urging students to increase their speed. "Let your fingers fly," she encouraged. "Don't even think about the keyboard."

One particularly accurate typist, Kitty Hampshire, was so upset by the introduction of the composite score that she missed a day of school, breaking her previously perfect attendance record.

The new scheme provided plenty of fodder for the January 16 lunch club meeting. Verity hadn't even started on her mac 'n cheese and salad, while the others were nearly finished.

"I can't tell you how upset I am about this stupid idea of calculating a composite score for timed writings." She took a quick sip of water and accidentally spilled some on her blouse.

Dabbing absently at the stain with her napkin, Verity continued, "And then issuing cards to each student so they can 'prove' their so-called achievement to unsuspecting employers."

The others listened quietly as they ate. Angela didn't teach typing, so the issue didn't resonate with her as much.

Janet was quick to jump in. "Of course, I wasn't having any of it. Kendra should have known better than to even bring that up with me."

She popped a spoonful of yogurt into her mouth and swallowed. "So Kendra decided the composite scoring wouldn't be used to assess typing progress for the legal program, because legal documents have to be accurate."

"But accuracy? Not so important in the rest of the business world, in her 'brilliant' opinion," Janet said with a roll of her eyes—an expression the whole table soon shared.

"It's disgraceful!" Verity stabbed her fork into the casserole. "Did she not take her ill-conceived plan far enough to consider how this would affect students on the job?"

Taking a bite, mouth still full, she pressed on, "What about the reputation she's 'building' for Hillside College? What effect might this have on sponsors like PeoplePower?"

Angela waited until Verity finished chewing, took a sip of her coffee, and said, "Kendra's chief concern is what looks good on paper. If she looks good and the paperwork looks good, then she'll keep impressing Jared and the higher-ups."

~

EVEN THOUGH IT was already 8 p.m. when Charlie got home, Verity couldn't help but vent. He'd settled into his leather lounger, pouring his favourite Carling Black Label into a tall, frosty glass.

As he lifted the glass to his lips, he caught the faraway look in Verity's eyes as she relived the story of the composite score.

"Trying to dissuade Kendra from that ridiculous scheme won't be easy," she said. "But I can't support it, Charlie. And honestly, I don't want it to tarnish my reputation as an instructor. I mean, I can hardly claim innocence if I'm using the system myself."

It seemed Charlie wanted to humour her. "No, that'd be like aiding and abetting a crime — and you wouldn't want that on your record." He took several gulps of his beer, his eyes twinkling with amusement.

Thursday's departmental meeting was convened specifically to revisit the composite scoring system after its implementation. Kendra, Verity, Susan, and Teresa gathered in Kendra's drab little office.

Kendra's skin looked sallow—Verity suspected it was from losing her tan. "This meeting shouldn't take long," Kendra began, flashing her syrupy grin. "Is everyone comfortable with the new scoring system by now?"

Verity spoke up, "No, not at all, Kendra, for reasons I've already outlined. But today, I thought I'd share some real examples of the system's effects so far."

Kendra's demeanour darkened, and Teresa sighed impatiently.

"With the new emphasis on speed, students are now averaging 10 to 15 errors per five-minute timed writing." Verity paused for emphasis. "This is simply unacceptable."

Susan shook her head in despair. "I wish I'd never heard of the composite score!"

Verity pressed on. "Some of my students have chosen to ignore the new system altogether, focusing instead on improving their accuracy and measuring success by the traditional method."

She wasn't holding back. "Others grin with delight as their fingers fly across the keyboard, knowing how easy it is to achieve an acceptable score with this new scheme."

After a brief pause, Kendra responded, "Thank you, Verity; that's certainly interesting. But we're still in the early stages of this system, so let's continue for now and perhaps re-evaluate in the spring."

Though the system was already in place, Verity felt compelled to voice her deep concerns. She sent a letter to Jared, copying Kendra.

MEMO
74-01-24

To: Jared
From: Verity

Unless accuracy is emphasized over speed for beginning typists, students will fail to develop a proper respect for accuracy—a skill that, I believe, will affect their performance in other routine office tasks. While occasional speed tests based solely on gross words per minute can be useful to encourage faster typing, they are impractical as a measure of true achievement in the real business world.

Speaking for myself and the majority of my students, the current composite scoring method encourages typing as fast as possible with little attention to accuracy, at least until the tenth error is made.

I propose that a combination of gross speed and error percentage would provide a more accurate reflection of a student's true ability. Additionally, I recommend the use of timed writing charts so students can visually track their progress over time.

~

MEMO

74-01-25

To: Verity

From: Jared

THE "RECORD OF TIMED WRITINGS" sheet appears an excellent idea and a supply has been ordered.

Thank you for the suggestion.

VERITY FOUND Jared's reply waiting on her staffroom desk Monday morning. It felt like a slap in the face—she clenched her teeth. It seemed only courteous to acknowledge her comments and suggestions about the evaluation system, regardless of whether he agreed.

She fought the urge to crumple Jared's memo and toss it in the wastebasket. Instead, she decided to step outside for some fresh air.

As Jared ascended the front steps, a chance encounter was inevitable.

"Oh, good morning, Verity. Did you get my memo about the record of timed writings?"

"Yes, I just read it about five minutes ago."

"I do appreciate your efforts, you know; they don't go unnoticed."

"Oh, really? Because I can't say the same about your latest memo."

"What do you mean?" Jared asked, pausing to think. "Oh, right—the new evaluation system." He nodded slowly, studying Verity as she stood just outside the door.

"Look, maybe we should discuss this further. I can see it's important to you."

"It sure is."

"Let's talk over dinner tonight, if that works for you. Say, seven o'clock at the Seabreeze? I'm tied up until then, so I can't do earlier."

Verity hesitated, unsure how to respond. On the one hand, she was glad he was open to discussing the issue, especially since Kendra seemed to be stalling, hoping everyone would accept the new system. But why not just meet at the main campus tomorrow?

Still, another part of her jumped at the chance to speak with Jared in private. And she couldn't resist the temptation to see how he acted outside of work.

"Yeah, that sounds fine," she nodded. "Seven at the Seabreeze. I'll make a reservation—though it probably won't be busy on a Monday night."

She smiled at Jared as she continued down the steps, deciding to take a longer walk out in the field.

EVEN THOUGH IT was too cold to sit outside, and the oceanside windows were shrouded in darkness, the iconic restaurant still held an enticing ambiance.

Green glass fishing buoys encased in rope were artfully arranged among displays of starfish, cone shells, conchs, clams, mussels, and other sea treasures unfamiliar to Verity. The nautical theme was a refreshing change from the stuffy rooms of the Hillside campus.

Verity was escorted to a corner table by the window, as she'd requested. A candle, protected by a glass chimney, flickered softly in the center of the table, which was draped with a crisp white linen cloth. She appreciated the fine details of the upholstered chairs— their fabric patterned with little reddish fish swimming among corals on a sea-green background.

Only one other table was occupied. As Verity gauged the privacy they'd have until another guest arrived, she noticed Jared speaking briefly with the receptionist. He handed her his coat, and she led him to their table.

He looked refreshed, as if he'd gone home, showered, and changed clothes. "Verity, I hope you haven't been waiting long."

"Oh, no, I just got here," she replied.

As the server lit the candle and announced the evening specials, Verity found herself only half listening. *I feel like we're on a date.*

"Will you have something to drink, Verity?"

"Yes," she said, looking at the server. "I'll have a greyhound, please."

Jared ordered a scotch on the rocks, and they both began scanning their menus.

"I'm pretty hungry. What about you?"

It took Verity a moment to settle into the novelty of the situation. When their drinks arrived, they were ready to order.

"I'll have the sablefish, please."

"I'll take the New York strip, medium rare."

Light jazz played softly in the background as Jared lifted his glass toward her. She met the gesture, and they smiled, saying in unison, "Cheers," their eyes locking briefly.

The first taste of vodka washed over her palate, and Verity reminded herself to take it slow. Jared smiled with his eyes as he sipped his drink.

"Jared, if you don't mind, I'd like to start our discussion by saying I was a bit insulted that you didn't address the concerns I raised in my letter."

"I understand, Verity. Let me explain the logic behind the new evaluation system."

"Logic? Oh yes, I'm eager to hear that." Verity made a point to stay polite, telling herself to remain calm no matter what.

"As you may know, we're always looking for ways to improve our programs, to be innovative where possible, and to nurture our relationships with our sponsors and the community."

Oh man, Verity thought, *Jared sounds like he's addressing a Board meeting.* She made a conscious effort to keep her face neutral.

"And when we looked at the numbers, it became clear that there were too many dropouts and too many failures."

"I see. Was any research done to find out why those students dropped out or failed?"

Their conversation was interrupted as the server placed their meals before them. Verity's attention was immediately drawn to her entrée.

"Oh, this looks delicious! Such a beautiful presentation!" she said, smiling as she thanked the server.

The server smiled back. "I hope you enjoy it," she said, then turned and walked away.

Jared cut into his steak as Verity savoured the exquisitely tender first bite of her sablefish.

"This sablefish just melts in your mouth. Want to try some, Jared?"

"No, thanks. But this might be one of the best steaks I've had in a while."

They ate in comfortable silence for a moment, not wanting the whole evening to feel like an extension of the workday.

"Have you been here before, Jared?"

"Many times. It's one of Linda's and my favourite spots. What about you?"

"This is my first time, but I'm sure I'll be back."

When the server cleared their plates, they ordered coffee, and Jared resumed their conversation.

"Well, to make a long story short, we needed a way to keep students enrolled and help them experience success."

"Yes, I understand that the composite scoring system supports that goal. When students achieve success, they feel confident, and their sponsors see them as strong candidates for further support. Higher enrolment looks good for the school and boosts revenue. On the surface, it seems like a win-win."

Jared regarded her with quiet admiration as she spoke with confidence.

Just then, their coffees arrived. As Verity stirred in a spoonful of sugar, Jared said softly, "I know, Verity, I truly understand your concerns." He smiled warmly, his teal eyes softening.

Though he was likely more than twenty years her senior, Verity allowed herself a brief, fleeting thought of him in a romantic light. His light grey shirt complemented the salt-and-pepper hair, neatly styled with precision. She recalled his red convertible Mustang and wondered if it was waiting outside. Verity had always been drawn to a clean-shaven look, and Jared's lean build and tall stature held an undeniable appeal.

"But I hope you can come to accept our new system in time. I'm asking you to give it a chance."

She smiled up at Jared's handsome face. "Are you asking me to go against my principles... again?"

Jared caught the joke immediately. "I suppose you could see it that way—or as an opportunity." He drained the last sip of his coffee and set the cup gently on its saucer.

"I'm not usually one to miss an opportunity." Verity hadn't planned to look alluring tonight, but judging by the way Jared's eyes lingered, she wondered if she'd gone a little too far.

"That's good to hear, Verity." He winked at her. "By the way, I've extended your contract for another two months, through to March 29. You'll get the paperwork tomorrow."

The server appeared with the check, and Jared reached for his wallet. "This one's on me, Verity. My pleasure."

Sensing the danger of lingering any longer, Verity decided to thank him and make a quick exit as soon as she could.

They both stood, gathered their coats, and stepped out of the restaurant.

The night was clear and cold, a vast canopy of stars glittering overhead.

"I'll walk you to your car."

"Oh, no need—it's right here." As she slid her key into the lock, Jared stepped a little too close for comfort, Verity thought.

"I enjoyed your company, Verity. I hope we can do this again sometime. Have a good night."

Verity slipped into her old Cadillac, her mind swirling with questions about the evening. As Jared drove off, he waved goodbye, a satisfied smile on his face.

THE WORLD OUTSIDE OF WORK

The stress from work began to spill over into Verity's home life and her relationships outside the college. Things got so bad that she felt embarrassed to say she worked at Hillside.

"Why do you stay?" her new friend Mimi asked one afternoon.

"It sounds crazy, but teaching at the college level was always my goal, like for many other teachers. And honestly, there aren't any openings at other colleges around here."

The events at the college weighed heavily on her mind. "You'll know what I mean when I say the elite triangle…"

Her running group exchanged knowing looks and murmurs such as "Duh" and "I guess!"

"I know you're not teachers, but we've all been students at some point, so maybe you'll appreciate this." She launched into the tedious details of the composite scoring system.

Spread out on the park lawn, her running friends gradually turned away, staring out at the sea or packing up early.

"Well, thanks for the riveting stories, Verity, but I've got to hit the road now."

Still, Verity persisted. "You know," she said to her landlord, "the school is so poorly managed, you'd wonder how they continue to get away with it."

"Sounds like a bloody soap opera to me."

Verity eventually saw that people grew weary of hearing her complaints. She recognized that the bizarre events she continued to experience and necessarily participate in didn't even sound real. She sometimes wondered if people thought she was making the whole thing up, attempting to throw a good light on herself; paint herself as superior, somehow.

Verity harped on about the low standards while realizing that she was not being a good representative of Hillside College and, implicitly, the main campus, Everton. The composite scoring system, the elite triangle, inconsistencies in the grading system, low staff morale, angry students, and incompetence... were all regular themes.

People were incredulous when Verity told them that the director was aware of most of these problems, yet didn't try to help improve the situation.

But Verity had gained a new understanding of what Jared had wanted when asking her to find out who the "troublemakers" were. He wanted to know who was plotting to upset the status quo, meaning the status of Jared's world. In his mind, there was nothing wrong with the way things were run at Hillside.

THE STRAIN STARTED to take a toll on Verity's marriage. Charlie would come home tired, having missed dinner and needing to unwind. Verity, meanwhile, needed to vent—her way of releasing the day's built-up frustrations. ("Don't let things boil," Jared had warned her.)

"I'M COMPLETELY DISENCHANTED with the way the college is run," Verity announced one evening. By now, she had become a proverbial broken record to Charlie. He took another sip of whiskey, leaned back in his chair, and said with a trace of sarcasm, "Oh, I can't wait to hear this."

Not exactly a welcoming vibe.

Could she blame him? No. But the work felt impossible to leave behind. The intensity followed her like a shadow, clinging tightly during the short drive from school to home. She'd replay the day's scenarios over and over, thoughts lingering long after she'd tucked herself into bed.

Work wrapped around Verity like a suffocating cocoon—and she had no idea what her eventual transformation might be.

There were few distractions from work. No kids, no regular social activities. Verity knew from experience that standing around an elegant food table in a sexy cocktail dress and high heels, chatting with lawyer acquaintances, was a treat, now and then. But it wasn't sustainable, nor did it nourish her soul.

She needed something she could call her own. And if that meant being a perfectionist about how she went about things, so be it. That was who she was.

Once, after Charlie had had a few drinks, she tried to explain herself. "I love the routine of going to work, of playing a role in society that helps people find jobs so they can earn a decent living. And I want to pull my weight when it comes to managing the living expenses."

Verity carefully removed the whiskey glass from Charlie's hand as he slipped into slumber, snoring softly on the sofa.

Charlie worked most weekends, although he tried to keep Sundays sacred as his day of rest. Saturdays had become Verity's day to clean the house, prepare meals for the week ahead, and, if she had any energy left after that marathon, she might go to a movie with friends or enjoy a shared dinner out or at someone's home. Charlie had recently joined a chess club that met every Saturday night. Sundays were the one day they spent together.

Those Sundays were a welcome break from routine, a chance to erase the college from Verity's mind. They usually went hiking, even when it rained.

But when Verity slipped her hand into his that Sunday, she felt a subtle reluctance from Charlie. She wasn't usually a hand-holder, but seeing Kendra and her husband holding hands in the parking lot that day had touched her. It was a quiet signal of connection for anyone nearby to see. She wanted that connection, too. But if affection between her and Charlie had become more duty than desire, she'd rather not engage at all.

Verity often considered herself single, because that's what it felt like much of the time. In that way, she had a small glimpse of what Nicole might have felt when she and her husband decided to live separately, ostensibly for convenience.

Verity filled the voids in their marriage with work. That was okay, she reasoned—at least she had something to fill it with.

She continued making notes in her journal.

NOTES UPDATE

1 Kendra persists in making defamatory remarks about teachers, at times verging on slander.. She even wondered aloud if Stella was a lesbian. Why a teacher's sexual orientation should be anyone's concern—or relevant to her employment—is completely beyond my comprehension.

2 Staff morale is surely at an all-time low. There's an undercurrent of tension, and confusion runs persistently through the team. Those on permanent contracts stick it out mainly for the pay cheque and the promise of a good pension.

3 The self-study program is suitable only for students who are self-motivated and well-organized. Many of our students haven't been in school for years, have little or no work experience, and are unlikely to thrive in a self-study environment. They need the inspiration and guidance of a good teacher, as well as the social satisfaction of belonging to a traditional class.

*V*erity rarely saw Stella in the staffroom. When she did, Verity always made a point of acknowledging her. Each time she approached, Stella subtly stepped back, as if afraid of catching germs. She always seemed to have something urgent to attend to—a convenient escape route, Verity supposed.

Curiously, Stella wanted to stay informed about college happenings, but only on her terms. She'd toss out a quick question while heading to her next class, then dash off as soon as she got an answer.

"Hey, do you know if Jared's going to be at the staff meeting today?"

"Yes, I believe so."

"Well, prepare for fireworks then." And just like that, she was gone.

Of course, the opinionated and judgmental need to know what's going on. Verity guessed Stella enjoyed stirring the pot a little, injecting some troublemaking to enliven the monotony of her days. It was as if Stella directed her own play from the sidelines, remaining in the background while the scenes unfolded without her.

At every staff meeting, Stella brought stacks of test papers to mark—or at least, that's how it appeared. This way, she could attend in body but not in spirit, sending a clear message that she was too busy for trivialities and pettiness.

THE COMPOSITE SCORING system remained a persistent thorn in Verity's side. Although credentials seemed to carry little weight at Hillside, in her mounting frustration, Verity reached out to her mentor at her alma mater. Seeking professional support she could trust, she wrote to Jayne Hart, Assistant Professor of Business Office Management at the University of Mapleton, Ontario, explaining the composite scoring system proposal and asking for her expert opinion. It felt somewhat embarrassing, but Verity saw it as a way to reinforce the concerns she had already voiced. She copied her letter to Jared and Kendra.

The staff overseeing the program at UMO embodied the highest standards of professionalism. Their department operated like a well-oiled machine, and the camaraderie resembled that of a convent of sisters united by a common purpose, which Verity imagined included worthy goals such as teaching, careful planning, foresight, staying current, and fostering innovation, all pursued to the best of their abilities. In other words, it was a world apart from the disarray she experienced at Hillside.

AFTER WORK ON FRIDAY, February 8, Verity unlocked her apartment mailbox and felt a thrill when she spotted a letter from Mrs. Hart. She hurried upstairs, set her books down, and settled into a chair at the kitchen table. Carefully tearing open the envelope, she read the contents—exactly what she had anticipated all along.

74-02-04
Dear Verity,

It was such a pleasant surprise to hear from you. I am happy to hear that you are teaching at a community college, and I remember that you also taught at Toronto Community College.

I have enclosed a brochure that shows, with examples, the point system we use here, as well as sample charts the students use to help determine their final scores. I hope that this helps you gain a clear understanding of the point system. We have used it for three years now, and find it to be both fair to the student and realistic to prospective employers.

We have established a rule to prevent a student from typing as fast as she could with no regard for accuracy.

Regarding the composite scoring system, I have not heard of it, and would have to have more information in order to comment intelligently.

Please do not hesitate to contact me again if you would like to know more about the system we use here.

Sincerely,
Jayne Hart, Assistant Professor
Business Office Management
The University of Mapleton Ontario

VERITY'S RESOLVE WAS CLEAR. The evaluation system devised by their management team seemed unique—if not entirely misguided. And although Jared had personally explained his reasons for it, she just wasn't convinced.

She made an appointment to see Kendra first thing Monday morning, before classes.

"Kendra, I think you'll find this interesting." Kendra looked up, eyes wide with curiosity.

Verity handed over a brochure. "This explains the point system used at the University of Mapleton Ontario. It includes plenty of examples showing how it works."

Kendra skimmed the brochure briefly before returning her attention to Verity.

Verity continued, "Not only does this system more accurately reflect students' actual achievements, which benefits students, employers, and the college, but it's also fair and well-proven."

"Oh, Verity, we all know how you feel about the composite system. But I've asked you—and everyone else—to give it a fair try until spring. I was hoping that would put an end to this," Kendra said, raising her left eyebrow.

"Yes, I know, Kendra. But in all good conscience, it's difficult for me to work with a flawed system—especially when I know there's a better alternative."

"Again, Verity, that's just your opinion."

"Yes, it *is* my opinion. And it's an educated one."

Kendra's voice rose. "Oh, so now you're implying I'm uneducated?"

"Look, I'm not implying that at all. I just thought that, as coordinator of the program, you'd want to do some research and comparisons—to help you and Jared find the best option for all of us."

"And now you're suggesting we didn't research it enough?"

Growing weary of Kendra's defensive attitude, Verity lowered her voice, trying to keep things calm. "You know, I can easily demonstrate how we could adapt it to fit the needs of college-level students."

Kendra shot back, "If we hadn't already decided on this evaluation method, I might be more open. Now, I need your support. I'm done with these discussions—we need to move on."

REPUTATION

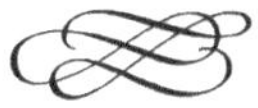

MEMO

74-02-12

To: Verity

From: Kendra

RE: O'MALLEY, Jennifer

Please provide me with a brief report on this student's class attendance and progress since joining your Typing 181 class with the January intake.

MEMO

74-02-12

To: Kendra

From: Verity

ATTENDANCE IS GOOD, and she has improved her typing score since becoming more relaxed in a new classroom. Composite score 37; Net 28.

Jenn requires a lot of encouragement and is most appreciative whenever assistance is provided. (She does not take up so much of my time as to deprive other students.)

Although she sometimes struggles to complete assignments, I believe she understands the concepts. It is my observation that these difficulties may be linked to her drinking problems. Jenn is easily confused at times; in fact, her mind goes blank sometimes, and she is unable to find the page number we are working on.

She experiences frequent episodes of shaking but generally manages to regain control. Although she is having difficulty with problem/production work right now, I think it's still too early to determine how she will do eventually.

Verity Child

VERITY TYPED her reply on the Selectric during the 12:15 lunch break. She disliked having to make such judgments, but it was part of her job. Sure, she could encourage and accommodate until Jenn could move forward, but in her heart, she knew she wasn't doing anyone any favours — including Jenn herself.

Verity removed the memo from the machine and delivered it to Kendra's secretary. She had only 15 minutes left to eat her lunch.

ON THE WEEKEND of February 15 and 16, Verity travelled to Victoria to attend a teachers' conference held at the Empress Hotel. Meg, the newest instructor at Hillside, was the only other representative from the college that weekend, although Verity had heard that many instructors from the main campus would be in attendance.

At morning break, Verity wandered into the hallway, where tables draped in linen tablecloths were laid out with cups and saucers, cream, sugar, and teaspoons for coffee and tea.

Having glanced through the main campus staff directory and program offerings, Verity recognised a colleague from the Business Division pouring herself a cup of coffee.

"Pat! Pardon me, but I think I recognise you from the college calendar—you're a computer programming instructor, aren't you?"

The woman turned toward Verity with a smile, holding her cup and saucer. "Yes, I'm Pat McCullough. And you are?"

"Verity Child. I teach in the BOT Division at Hillside. It's nice to get away to Victoria for the weekend."

"Oh, you're from Hillside." Pat's lower lip turned down slightly, and Verity noticed a change in her tone.

Verity nodded slowly, studying Pat's eyes.

"Then perhaps I should offer my condolences." Verity was at a loss for words.

Pat continued, "We've heard all the rumours about what's been going on at Hillside, but if it's any comfort, I want you to know that Hillside is not representative of the community college as a whole. Now, if you'll excuse me, I need to catch up with my friend Myrna. Enjoy the conference." With that, she disappeared into the crowd.

While Verity understood the sentiment, it still stung to hear her workplace referred to as the outcast of the college family. The conversation cast a shadow over her weekend, and she returned home earlier than she had planned.

SNOOP

Verity stayed late on Friday afternoon to prepare for the February intake of students. She headed to the reception area just outside Kendra's office to check some student files. Unlocking the file drawer with her key, as all files were kept locked at the end of the day, she noticed the janitor working inside Kendra's office.

None of the office doors were locked, allowing easy access for the cleaning staff. Verity assumed any confidential papers were secured in Kendra's lockable filing cabinet.

It was well known at Hillside that Kendra suffered from severe migraine headaches. She had been very clear about her need for privacy and routinely reminded teachers to respect her *Do Not Disturb* sign. Of course, for Verity and Angela, that sign held an even deeper significance.

Verity watched as the janitor left Kendra's office, closing the door firmly behind him. The *Do Not Disturb* sign hung prominently. She pictured herself opening the door and glancing inside—the very presence of the sign made the room all the more tempting.

Glancing around to ensure no one was nearby, Verity quietly

turned the doorknob and slipped into Kendra's office, gently closing the door behind her so the *Do Not Disturb* sign stayed clearly visible.

Her heart pounded so hard it felt like it might burst through her chest. She reminded herself to breathe. Tiptoeing to Kendra's chair, she eased into it and reached for the large centre drawer of the desk. If someone walked in, she'd claim she was using the phone.

To her surprise, the drawer slid open easily—no key, no resistance. She had imagined needing to search the office for a way in. Her eyes were immediately drawn to a familiar blue-and-white pack of Player's cigarettes.

Why would Jared leave cigarettes in Kendra's desk, especially when Kendra detested the smell of smoke?

Quickly riffling through the papers in the largest section of the drawer, Verity came across a white business envelope that had already been torn open. The return address read *Robson Street Employment Agency.*

At first, it didn't strike her as unusual—after all, every training program at Hillside included a work experience component. She was about to set it aside when a figure written in red ink caught her eye: **$1,325**.

She removed the letter and unfolded it. It contained an itemized list showing student names, typing speeds, and corresponding dollar amounts linked to each speed.

Verity paused, taking in the information. But conscious of the risk, she didn't linger. She closed the drawer, careful to leave everything exactly as she'd found it.

She tried all three doors of the filing cabinet—locked. Glancing around the room for anything else out of place, she repositioned the chair with care and slipped out as quietly as she'd entered.

I can't believe I just did that.

Verity hadn't given the letter much thought as she focused on preparing for the new intake. But later that night, alone in her apartment, she caught sight of herself in the bathroom mirror and spoke aloud to her reflection.

You just committed a crime.

She turned the bathtub taps on full blast, stripped off her clothes, and tossed a handful of bath salts into the swirling water. As steam filled the room, she stepped into the tub, letting the warmth and lavender scent calm her nerves.

She lay back, fully submerging for a moment, as if she could wash away the entire day. When she sat up again, water streaming down her face, her thoughts drifted to the letter from the employment agency.

Student names. Typing speeds. Dollar amounts.

Why would anyone assign money to students based on how fast they typed?

And then it hit her.

All the energy she'd poured into questioning the composite scoring method—arguing its flaws, pushing for transparency—it had all been for nothing. Kendra hadn't just ignored her concerns, she had a plan—a plan to profit from inflated student scores. And she wasn't about to let anything or anyone get in the way.

SUNGLASSES

Thursday, February 21, had been astonishing. Every instructor who entered the staffroom that morning found a notice waiting on their desk. It had been weeks since they'd submitted their collective letter to Jared, formally requesting a meeting, and they'd made it clear that Kendra was not to attend.

Now, suddenly, the meeting was scheduled for tomorrow, Friday, immediately after classes.

"Yes, we asked for it," Verity muttered, glancing around the room, "but we didn't expect it to happen the very next day."

She crossed the room and stopped at Angela's cubicle. "Angela, what do you make of this?"

"I think our two requests—holding a meeting outside the regular schedule and excluding Kendra—pushed Jared to try and gain the upper hand before anything even begins," Angela said.

"My thoughts exactly," Verity replied. "He knows springing it on us with almost no time to prepare only works in his favour."

"Yeah," Angela added, "and with such short notice, some instructors might not even be able to attend."

Verity and Angela were still mulling it over when Janet walked up and joined the conversation.

Verity seized the opportunity. "Angela, do you think you, Janet, and I could meet after classes to do some prep?"

"Definitely. How about three o'clock at my place?"

By 3:15, all three had gathered around Angela's kitchen table to strategize and discuss. Verity was eager to begin and launched right into her notes.

"A wound has been opened, and we are now in a position to let problems that have been festering for months—maybe even years—come to light and be seen as they are."

"Wow, that's rather dramatic," Janet chuckled.

"I agree," Verity said with a nod. "It is dramatic. And as you both know, it's hard to keep emotion out of it. But fair point—I hope we can all keep our cool."

She went on. "Unintentionally, our plight has reached the ears of the college principal, Dr. Farmer, and we'll likely be expected to justify our complaints."

Verity paused, looking sombre at the thought of how Dr. Farmer might respond to the situation plaguing Hillside.

"But you can be sure he already has a good idea of the goings-on," Angela said.

Verity tilted her head. "Seriously, Angela? What do you think he knows?"

"Oh, I wouldn't be surprised if he has a pretty good idea about the whole thing."

"Angela, we know you have connections at the main campus through your interest in business and public administration, but please don't tell me that even the principal knows about Hillside's problems and still chooses not to act." Verity sounded incredulous, but she was also aware of the time and thought it best to move on.

Janet, who had sat through more staff meetings than she cared to count, many of which were attended by Jared, leaned in to offer her take on what to expect.

"The basic problem we've exposed—the elite triangle—is naturally a sore spot for Kendra. We can be sure that steps will be taken to minimize blame and shift the focus elsewhere. That seems to be the custom at Hillside."

She continued, "This will turn into a fight between staff and management. And you can bet management will be ready. They'll lead the proceedings. Jared already knows what questions he'll ask and who he'll direct them to. If he can, he'll twist the situation so it looks like management isn't at fault at all."

Verity took a moment to think before responding. "If we allow that to happen, the problems in the BOT Division will just keep piling up. We need to organize ourselves. Without a united front—and support from the permanent staff—we won't be taken seriously."

"That's right," Janet agreed. "If we start turning on each other now, after everything, then we haven't got a hope."

"Exactly. So let's be clear about our motives and intentions." Verity reached for her notes. "Mind if I read what I put together during lunch today?"

Angela and Janet nodded, leaning in with their arms folded on the table.

"I'd like to know if we can all agree to this," Verity said, unfolding the page. "First point: There exists what the teachers refer to as an 'elite triangle'—three individuals who make decisions among themselves before staff meetings, especially when it comes to what ends up on the agenda."

"No one would deny that, except Nicole and Teresa," said Angela. "And Nicole won't be there."

"Has anyone heard anything else about Nicole's condition—or why she was taken away in an ambulance?" Verity asked.

"Not much," said Janet. "Though I did hear that Stella's being questioned by investigators."

"What?" Verity and Angela said at the same time, voices raised in surprise.

"I don't know the details," Janet said, lowering her voice slightly, "but one of my students mentioned something about peanut butter on Stella's breath. And if Nicole was anywhere near peanut butter... well, we all know about her allergy."

"Right," said Verity, absorbing the information. "That's... something to think about. But we'd better stay focused. Let's finish prepping for tomorrow." She looked down at her list and continued reading.

"Kendra is chiefly concerned with what looks good on paper—not what works best for staff or students, not what's good for the Division, and definitely not what's good for the College as a whole," Verity said.

"Exactly," Janet agreed. "And we've got more than enough examples to back that up—like the evaluation system, or the shift from monthly to weekly intake. Honestly, I can't imagine we'll get through everything in just two hours."

"There's also the 'cloak-and-dagger' routine they use to replace teachers—anyone they've decided to get rid of for whatever reason suits them at the time."

"Leave that one to me," Janet said, her tone firm. Angela and Verity exchanged a glance, knowing Janet was thinking of Christie.

"There's a pattern," Verity went on, "a history of pushing out competent professionals who dare to disagree with the coordinator."

"I know you two have been here longer than I have," Verity added, "so maybe that's a point better delivered by you both."

Angela hesitated. "Maybe. But it's a long list, and the hard part will be proving it."

Janet nodded in agreement. "Yeah, it's tricky—most of what's happened isn't exactly documented."

Verity looked down at her notes. "Okay. What do you think of this? It's more of a summary, really..."

"We've lost faith in Kendra's ability to carry out the responsibilities of her position ethically and competently," Verity read from her notes. "Her actions continue to damage staff relations. They silence teachers, promote unprofessional behavior by example, and strip us of the pride and safety we should feel in our work."

"It's all true, of course," Angela said quietly. "Are you planning to read that out loud tomorrow?"

Verity shook her head. "No, I don't think so. It's more to help me organize my thoughts—so I can express myself clearly when the time comes."

"Still, it's powerful," Janet said. Then she turned to Angela. "Let's make our own notes too, just in case. That way we won't forget anything important."

When Friday morning came, Verity felt optimistic, even though the rest of the staff hadn't been included in the lunch club's discussions. She reasoned that the three of them were the most likely to speak up anyway.

At 2:15, Verity hurried upstairs to the staffroom. Most of the teachers were already there, along with Jared, seated in a circular arrangement. He wore a light grey suit and sunglasses that hid his eyes.

It always bothered Verity when people wore sunglasses during a conversation, especially when she wasn't wearing any herself. It was worse still when they wore the blackout kind that completely concealed their eyes. She likened it to playing cards with someone who could see your entire hand reflected in a mirror, while you couldn't see theirs at all.

Every hair of Janet's perm seemed glued in place, her chiffon scarf perfectly matched to her outfit; her shoes, handbag, earrings, and necklace all carefully chosen for the occasion. Verity, who could relate to perfectionist tendencies, figured that Janet's years in the legal field had likely shaped her need for order and precision.

A teacher quietly told Angela that Nicole was still in the hospital. When Angela asked Verity and Janet whether they should send a card, Janet replied, "Why be insincere?"

Verity shifted her focus back to the meeting. She was pleased that, for once, the teachers could present a united front, without the usual manipulation or control from Kendra. It felt like they might accomplish something, even if only partially.

Jared's mood was sombre as he looked out at the circle of expectant instructors. When the final two stragglers found their seats, he opened the meeting by reprimanding the staff for requesting it without Kendra. He appealed to their imagined sympathies, saying she felt "hurt" by the exclusion.

Janet stated the obvious. "We wouldn't say what we have to say if she were present."

Jared shot back, "What do you have to say that's so important she can't hear?"

He was clearly not in a receptive mood. His tone made it obvious he didn't appreciate the staff's attempts to make him understand the realities at Hillside.

Janet hesitated briefly, then spoke clearly and with purpose. "We feel Nicole has a very negative attitude toward her students; she's been rude to some staff members, and she seems to wield more authority than the rest of us."

Jared's face remained unreadable as he asked flatly, "Does anyone else have anything to add?"

Verity wasn't about to let Jared dismiss Janet's statement. She spoke up, "I can give you a couple of examples of Nicole's negativism toward students." She recounted the times Nicole had labelled various students as "fat," "nondescript," "having a chip on her shoulder," "a bunch of dummies," and "trouble-makers." Verity hadn't bothered to write these down as she usually would—each insult had stung her deeply, and she remembered every one.

Janet cut in, noting that a student was present in the staffroom and had overheard the "bunch of dummies" remark.

Verity felt a surge of satisfaction that these accusations were finally out in the open, for everyone to hear. A few teachers looked shocked. Jared's eyebrows shot up above his shades, feigning surprise as best he could behind those black lenses.

"The students think Nicole is the vice-principal," ventured Christie, who had returned specifically for the meeting.

"Where did they get that idea?" Jared asked.

"From Nicole herself," Christie replied. "She introduces herself that way. She also likes to brag about her possessions—things like her emerald ring and diamond pin that she plans to add to her collection."

Christie continued, "Nicole tells her students how to dress and has warned them they can't make a good impression on the job if they wear synthetics. And this is to a class of mostly women who are subsidized students and can't afford the tuition themselves."

Verity felt a surge of happiness witnessing Christie's newfound confidence—such assertiveness was the complete opposite of the Christie her colleagues had known.

Meanwhile, Stella sat behind and to the left of Jared, well out of his peripheral view, quietly nodding her head to encourage Christie, egging her on. So far, Stella hadn't contributed a word to the meeting; she sat with the usual stack of papers on her knee, ostensibly grading as the discussion unfolded.

Angela now joined in, her voice trembling slightly. "It looks to us as if Nicole is in league with Kendra. People don't speak out at meetings anymore because they believe all the decisions are made in advance—by Kendra and Nicole."

Jared raised an eyebrow. "Why do you think that?" he asked Angela, his tone provoking Janet's ire.

The normally composed Janet snapped. "The question of Nicole's position was raised by permanent staff at our recent meeting with you. You should have realized then that there were serious problems with staff relations."

Janet's face flushed—perhaps a mix of anger and embarrassment. It was one of the rare occasions Verity had seen her show such outrage.

Jared curled his upper lip, dismissing Janet's retort. "I haven't heard anything here that Kendra doesn't already know."

He then went on to condemn an unnamed staff member for going over his head to Dr. Farmer, sternly warning anyone else who might consider doing the same in the future.

What right did he have to try to intimidate us this way?

Jared's response to the staff's sincere attempts to expose real problems at Hillside—and to bring about meaningful change—felt deeply off-putting. Verity's anger simmered, and she began crafting a response in her mind.

Verity thought it was common knowledge that when an employee loses trust in the management skills of those who hired her, the next logical step is to escalate the issues to the next level. *No one should be publicly—or privately—condemned for taking such action, unless, of course, they work under a dictator.* But she knew better than to say that aloud.

"I've heard many complaints from a few instructors here about the lack of communication between staff and management," Jared said sternly. "So I'm going to answer those complaints with one simple question." He paused, slowly turning his head to survey most of the attendees. "How many of you made an effort to communicate with us?"

Verity's frustration and disappointment deepened. Here they were, handing him the problems on a silver platter, clearly and united—and yet, he refused to take them seriously.

More teachers spoke up, voicing complaints about the collusion between Kendra and Nicole, but Teresa shook her head. Jared, of course, zeroed in on Teresa's dissent.

"Kendra's not here to speak for herself, and it's not fair to accuse her behind her back," Teresa said quietly, her voice low and pleading.

The room fell silent. Teresa's eyes brimmed with tears as some instructors shifted uncomfortably, while a few rolled their eyes—Verity guessed they saw Teresa's defense of Kendra as a selfish, weak attempt.

Verity wanted her say and spoke clearly, calmly: "Teresa, nothing said here hasn't already been said to Kendra herself."

Teresa lowered her still-shaking head, gripping the sides of her chair with both hands.

Jared rushed to her defense. "That's enough!" he barked at Verity. She imagined the glare burning behind his dark glasses. Verity fought to remain neutral despite the sting of being yelled at in front of everyone.

How gallant, Verity thought—protecting the poor single working mother who kisses ass to keep her job, just like you protect Kendra, who kisses your ass to hold onto her power and so-called respect.

In futile attempts, several instructors took turns trying to explain that the core problem was the elite Kendra had created, whether intentionally or not. Stella continued to nod encouragement from the background, staying otherwise silent. Teresa seemed to summon all her strength just to keep from breaking down into tears. She looked at Jared with pain as he excused her from the room.

"Teresa, you don't have to participate in this. You know we appreciate your support in this and everything else you do for the College."

As Teresa made her way out, some teachers described how Nicole projected an air of authority through her abrupt, indifferent, and untouchable attitude toward both students and staff.

"And she's always the one asked to fill in when Kendra's away," someone added.

Jared seized the opportunity. "Did any of you volunteer to help out instead?"

Verity waited a moment, knowing that there would not be an

answer, and picked up a former thread by saying, "A good example of decisions being made beforehand is the time Kendra introduced the composite method of scoring timed writings."

Several teachers nodded, sat up straighter in their chairs, and seemed to welcome this remark. "The majority of us at the departmental meeting voted against composite scoring," Verity asserted. "It was implemented anyway."

Jared shifted uncomfortably, impatience barely concealed behind his dark glasses as he glanced at his watch.

"Anything else?" he asked.

"There's a cloak-and-dagger method of firing staff," announced Shirley, who, like Christie, had shown up to attend this meeting. Who had invited them, Verity did not know.

Jared seemed ready for this. "You were in the hospital, and on a short-term contract which had expired. We needed someone else."

"What about Christie?" Janet asked.

"She handed in her resignation," said Jared.

"Only because I felt I was forced to," Christie countered. "Kendra told me that I was never meant to be a teacher." Christie was brave; after all, she had nothing left to lose.

All eyes were on Christie as she painted her picture of defeat. "Jared, you encouraged me to take the position, knowing I wasn't experienced in office procedures and had no teaching background." Her voice trembled, but she drew strength from Stella's now vigorous nodding—Stella was even mouthing silent words of encouragement.

Janet stepped in, backing her up. "New teachers receive no initiation," she said.

Jared listened, appearing sympathetic. He tilted his head downward in what looked like acknowledgment.

He apologized to Christie for a "misunderstanding," although he didn't explain what the misunderstanding was. Verity couldn't help but notice that he seemed to have a weakness for women in tears.

The room felt grey and airless. Verity's focus drifted. Any hope she'd held for a productive meeting dissolved, eclipsed by the sinking realization that nothing would change.

She hadn't agreed to spy for Jared, but if she had, her reports would have mirrored what he heard now. Yet, none of it seemed to register—the truth wasn't what he wanted to hear.

Staff offered thoughtful, specific feedback—concrete examples, firsthand accounts, and observations that could guide real improvements. It was far more valuable than anything she could have gathered on her own.

In her heart, Verity knew the real issue was Jared himself. His misuse of authority lay at the center of the problems at Hillside. The irony was sharp: he'd asked her to uncover the source of the dysfunction, and now it was obvious. He was the source.

Comments eventually dwindled to a halt, and now it was Jared's turn to show his hand. "This entire meeting has been frustrating," he said, his tone edged with weariness. "And it's shown me that it's almost impossible for me to remain impartial."

He paused, letting the words settle over the room. "So here's what I suggest. I can provide the services of an impartial mediator to help address some of the concerns raised. Would you agree to that?" He looked directly at Verity.

She shrugged and lifted her brows. "Sure, why not?" It wasn't enthusiasm—just resignation. They had nothing to lose, and Jared was not the one to sort any of this out. Several teachers nodded in agreement.

"You're under no obligation to talk to the mediator," he added. "I want you to know I'm not at all happy with how this meeting went. Nonetheless, I'm willing to continue the discussion in fifteen minutes, for anyone interested."

His eyes lingered on Verity, Janet, and Angela as he pushed back his chair.

"I'll be back here at four sharp," he said before walking out.

Feeling the futility of further talk, Verity gathered her things, ready to return to her classroom. But Shirley and Angela weren't finished. "You know how long we waited for this damn meeting," Angela said, and Janet chimed in, "We might as well talk while we've got his ear, don't you think?"

What else could Verity do but join them? She'd invested too much trying to address the problems directly rather than letting them simmer beneath the surface.

Everyone looked spent. The air in the room felt thick with tension, the meeting having drained them emotionally. Verity no longer had a clear sense of purpose or direction. She certainly hadn't expected Jared to offer to continue the discussion.

Still, she followed Angela, Christie, Janet, and Shirley as they regrouped in the far corner of the staffroom. They began to giggle—fatigued and unguarded, their laughter spilling out as a release valve for the day's emotional toll.

Then Jared returned, his expression unreadable behind those ever-present dark sunglasses. He looked grave, or at least that was the impression Verity gathered from the set of his shoulders and the silence that followed his entrance.

He wanted to talk about Kendra. "Is she a good coordinator?"

Janet began cautiously, "We know things have changed since she had only three duties while Nicole had fourteen." She seemed determined to make that point. "But Kendra does have much more responsibility these days." She skirted around the question, clearly reluctant to answer directly.

Shirley spoke next, offering general remarks about leadership qualities, professional role models, and qualifications. Then Jared turned expectantly to Verity. When she remained silent, he removed his sunglasses, fixed his gaze on her, and asked directly, "Do you think Kendra is a good coordinator?"

Verity met his stare calmly. "I don't think breaking confidences between teachers is professional. And if Kendra were truly professional, she wouldn't have allowed this elite triangle to form. A manager must remain neutral and not let personal relationships influence decisions. In that regard, I think she's incompetent."

Jared's eyes flashed with fury behind his dark glasses as he shouted, "That's enough!"

This was the pattern Verity had seen from the very beginning. In Jared's eyes, both Kendra and Nicole were untouchable. It made no sense. He knew there were problems—he'd even asked Verity to help. So what exactly was he after?

Deep down, Verity knew she'd already lost with Jared. She was drained, emotionally spent, and filled with regret.

What she hadn't realized at the time, when those words slipped out, was that some of them could just as easily have described Jared Sinclair himself.

"Kendra is one of the pillars that hold this place together. What do you want me to do—fire her?" Jared threw the question to the others. They balked, and a chorus of "No" followed.

That's exactly what he wanted to hear, Verity thought bitterly. For her, this had been the perfect opportunity to underscore the gravity of the accusations. Instead, she felt abandoned by the others. She regretted staying for this final stretch of the meeting.

Jared had won. The group's alternative suggestions faded into meaningless noise for her.

POSTINGS

As Verity swung open the staffroom door on Friday, February 28, she spotted Joyce and Joe, the bookkeeping instructor, in close conversation. They glanced up as she entered.

"Morning, Joyce. Morning, Joe. What are you two whispering about?"

Joe replied with a grin, "Oh, heh, heh—just looking at the notice of teaching vacancies on the bulletin board."

"Oh? What areas are they looking to fill?"

Joyce smiled sweetly and took a sip of her tea. "Looks like the Business Office Training Division."

Joe elaborated, "That includes Legal, Accounting, Bookkeeping, Business, Secretarial, Shorthand, English, and Communications."

"Just to narrow it down, eh?" Verity said, unloading an armful of books and her lunch.

It was standard practice to offer these vacancies to short-term contract teachers, assuming their performance had met expectations.

MEMO
74-03-01

To: Verity Child; Gina Jack
From: Jared Sinclair

The R.A.C. under which you both hold short-term contracts with Everton College expires on March 29, 1974. Consequently, this opens up two vacancies.

Advertising has been placed to publicly note the instructional vacancies. Applications will be received until March 15, 1974, whereupon screening procedures and interviews will be held. I have entered applications from both of you in this competition.

Successful candidates will be offered two-year probationary appointments. Should either or both of you be the selected candidate, your time spent as a result of the short-term contract(s) will be credited against the probationary term.

Verity knew that Gina Jacks, who had replaced Christie, was now eligible to apply for a continuing contract—and that her own position had also been posted.

By Monday, March 3, Verity had something new to worry about.

"Verity!" Angela was drying her hands in the ladies' washroom when Verity pushed open the door. She lowered her voice. "I wanted to tell you what Kendra said when I met with her in her office this morning."

Verity quickly checked the stalls to make sure they were alone.

"Kendra cut me off before I could even explain the scheduling issue I was there about. She went straight into talking about the accusations against Nicole and said, 'The only one who claimed students criticized Nicole was Verity."

"That's a lie," Verity said sharply. "Kendra herself told me that students were rebelling against Nicole."

"Exactly. But it gets worse. She said, 'Verity never even had an interview, you know.'" Angela pronounced each word with deliberate care.

"I had two interviews," Verity snapped. "They just weren't in front of a formal Selection Committee."

Both women fell silent, the implication hanging in the air. They knew Kendra's game—and this latest twist marked the beginning of a new, calculated attempt to discredit Verity.

"Of course she knew you'd tell me," Verity said bitterly. "That's the point. She's sending a message."

Angela looked down, the weight of it all settling between them.

Kendra had built a reputation for sidelining anyone who challenged her authority. If a teacher made her uneasy, she found a way to push them out. She surrounded herself with those who echoed her views without question. Verity had never been willing to play that part.

INTRUSIONS

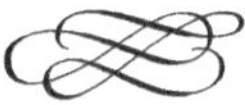

During Verity's Typing 181 class that afternoon, the door swung open and Kendra marched in unannounced—something about a transfer slip, transfer procedure, and the August intake.

"The timed writings have to be in by Tuesday, not Thursday," she declared in front of the class.

Verity knew full well that the deadline had just been changed—Kendra was making that up on the spot. But she wasn't about to give her the satisfaction of an argument during class.

"Yes, that's right," she said calmly, pretending she'd known it all along. Without missing a beat, she turned back to the board and continued writing, absorbing the disruption with grace.

It didn't escape Verity that Kendra was trying to provoke her. It was the same tactic Nicole had used during Verity's early days—barrelling into her classroom without warning. Verity had reprimanded Nicole after class and then reported the incident directly to Kendra... which meant Kendra *knew* how disrespectful this kind of interruption felt to her.

But Verity wasn't about to give her the reaction she was fishing for. Outwardly composed, inwardly seething, she refused to show the slightest hint of anger. Still, she couldn't shake the sense that Kendra was playing a petty game—trying to rattle her, to gather ammunition for some future complaint. And the sheer childishness of it ignited a quiet fury in her.

If Kendra's behavior that afternoon wasn't enough to unsettle Verity, what happened that evening gave her an entirely new reason to worry.

The unease began the moment she stepped into her apartment. Charlie wouldn't be home this early—she knew that—but an uncharacteristically intense feeling gripped her as she crossed the threshold. She wasn't the nervous type, but right now, she wished he were there.

Her heart quickened as she moved slowly down the hall, uncertain what she might find. She didn't bother removing her shoes, as she usually did. Instead, she tread lightly, almost as if sneaking up on someone. Glancing left and right, she continued to the study and set down her things. A vague but growing sense of dread pressed in on her.

Forcing herself onward, she checked the kitchen, the living room, and—more cautiously—the small bathroom. Everything looked exactly as she'd left it. She started to feel a little silly.

Then she saw it: a plain white business envelope sitting on the dresser in the bedroom.

She froze.

She was almost certain it hadn't been there that morning. And she'd left after Charlie, so it couldn't have been him.

Her heart raced again as she picked up the envelope, turned it over, and broke the seal. Inside was a single sheet of white paper, which she unfolded quickly.

A sudden, soul-chilling cold washed over her.

The page was dominated by a single eye—staring back at her, unnervingly inhuman. Verity couldn't fathom how the artist had captured such pure malice on paper, a gaze that seemed to pierce right through her. The message behind that eye felt dark and powerful, a silent threat aimed directly at her.

Her hands trembled uncontrollably.

She dashed to the kitchen to call Charlie. After what felt like a dozen rings with no answer, a sharp gasp escaped her lips. Snatching her keys, she fled the apartment, still shaking. Relief surged through her as she slid into her car, thankful she'd parked it on the street instead of the shadowed underground garage.

Angela's apartment was only a short drive away, up Mountainview Avenue. Taking three steadying breaths, Verity started the engine and prayed Angela would be home.

"Verity! What's up?" Angela was in her sweats, a mug of tea in hand.

They settled into the living room, and Verity recounted the unsettling experience—the break-in and the disturbing drawing of the eye. As the two absorbed the details, one thing became clear: this wasn't random. It had to be connected to the college. What kind of intruder steals nothing and leaves behind a single, eerie image?

"I feel so violated, Angela," Verity said, her voice low. "Not only did someone get into my apartment, but what they left behind… it was meant to scare me."

"It's such an invasion of privacy," Angela agreed. "And it feels targeted. Malicious, even."

"I need to call the police." She reached for Angela's phone and made the report.

They went over the event again and again, dissecting each detail until their energy wore thin.

"Thanks for being here," Verity said finally. "I know I interrupted your studies, but I figured you'd want to know."

"Of course. I'm glad you came."

Verity gave a weary smile. "Charlie's in for a surprise when he finally gets home tonight."

Later, back at her apartment, she checked the door lock more than once and double-checked the balcony windows. Then, still in her clothes, she collapsed onto the bed and fell asleep on top of the comforter—so deeply that she didn't even hear Charlie ease the door open and step inside.

ATTITUDE

*A*fter the disastrous staff meeting and the mounting incidents meant to unsettle her, Verity decided it was time to book a meeting with Jared. She'd never been one to sit back and let things happen without standing up for herself.

Monday morning, March 17, brought another unwelcome surprise. When Verity entered the staff room, she found her cubicle had been moved—repositioned near the door, directly in front of Joyce's.

She immediately drew the connection: Joyce was due to retire soon. Was this a pointed message? A petty slight disguised as logistics?

A memo sat on her desk, addressed to all faculty in the Division. It read:

"The following is a revision of assigned responsibility for Course Module Development to reflect work currently being accomplished by various members of the faculty."

Below was a list of seven instructors and their respective subject areas. Verity's name was nowhere to be found.

It was Thursday morning, March 20. Verity's contract would expire in just nine days. After her 8:00 a.m. class, she headed for the staffroom.

The moment she crossed the threshold, she saw it. A white business envelope—its stark shape unmistakable against the dark wood of her desk—was placed dead center, as if to ensure it couldn't be overlooked.

Typed across the front in bold capital letters: VERITY CHILD.

She hadn't expected it to be delivered so impersonally. Still, she knew what it was. This envelope held her future.

Aware of the others in the room, Verity set her books down and opened it with practiced calm, though her heart thudded in her chest.

Looking back, Verity would question why she had chosen to do it that way. She could have, after all, tucked the envelope into her notebook and looked at it in private.

But in that moment, she needed to appear unshaken—needed to pretend this wasn't everything—even as the ground beneath her seemed to tremble.

"It is with regret that I must inform you..."

The rest of the words blurred together, refusing to register. Verity kept her expression neutral, unwilling to give anyone the satisfaction of seeing her react. She knew eyes were on her.

She sat down, opened a file folder, and began to make notes that meant nothing. The motions were mechanical, a shield against the weight of what she'd just read.

She felt hollowed out. Even though part of her had expected it, the cold finality of it was hard to absorb. The anonymity of the delivery only added insult to injury.

Still, her inner voice was merciless.

Did you honestly believe they'd renew your contract after you called Kendra incompetent? Cross Kendra, and you cross Jared. You knew that.

In the next few seconds, Verity turned over the word *fired* in her mind. It felt heavy with shame, steeped in failure and disgrace. That word belonged to other people—people who cut corners or showed up late or didn't care. Not to her. Not to the farm girl who'd worked hard her whole life, who had a spotless record and prided herself on doing things the right way.

Fired.

It carried a stain that wouldn't wash out.

She remembered asking her mother, as a child, what the word meant. Her mother had said, "It means someone did something wrong and lost their job." In her young imagination, Verity had pictured someone being tossed into flames—burned up and discarded because they no longer had value.

And now, here she was.

Seven more days at Hillside. Seven more days of showing up like nothing had happened, while everyone knew exactly what had.

Still reeling, Verity stood, left the staffroom, and made her way downstairs to room 102. She closed the door behind her and picked up the phone, dialing Angela's number with shaking fingers.

Please be home, she thought. *Please pick up.*

"Hello."

The word echoed in Verity's ear like a lifeline tossed to someone going under.

"Angela, I didn't get the job." Verity blurted it out, her voice low, barely above a whisper. She didn't want anyone overhearing, didn't want to give her pain a wider audience. Before Angela could respond, Verity rushed on, needing to spill everything at once, like tearing off a bandage before the sting could grow.

"It was awful. When I saw that white envelope sitting on my desk, I just knew." She paused, the words hanging between them.

But somehow, just saying it out loud gave her a sliver of relief. The weight began to shift, if only slightly.

"Verity, what are we going to do without you?"

Angela's voice cracked the wall Verity had hastily thrown up around herself. That single line—that gentle, heartfelt truth—was exactly what she needed. It cut through the noise of failure and self-doubt and reminded her, if only for a moment, of her worth. *I mattered to someone.*

Time seemed to pause.

Angela, ever the practical one, didn't let them linger too long in the emotion. "You need to take this higher," she said. "File a grievance. This reeks of wrongful dismissal. Who knows? Maybe they'll reinstate you."

Verity clung to that fragile glimmer of hope, desperate to believe that sound educational practices would prevail—and that she'd be part of a new, synergistic movement to lift Hillside out of the mud. But the reality hit hard, leaving her weakened to the core.

"The possibility of being reinstated hadn't even crossed my mind. My contract expires on the 29th, and by now, they've probably hired my replacement. Just this morning, Joyce was heading into the staffroom as I was heading out, and I asked her if she knew who'd been hired to replace me." Verity's voice caught, and she choked back tears.

"And?"

"Gina."

Angela paused, taking in the news. "That doesn't change the fact that you were unfairly treated. And remember, we still have a heavy piece of ammunition in our back pocket, if we need it."

"Yes, I guess so. I need to back away for a bit, but I'll be in touch." Verity took a shaky breath. "Angie, thanks for being here for me."

"Always, Verity. Now, I guess you'll be headed to class soon? Try to clear your mind of all this, and we'll talk strategy later, okay?"

～

"Okay, I have over an hour before my next class; I might visit Kendra —if I can find her in her office."

Feeling a hint of pride returning, Verity headed to the front office, only to find Kendra's door firmly shut. Her secretary told her Gina was inside. Verity bristled at the thought of Kendra briefing Gina about her, painting her as 'not well.'

Determined not to lose momentum—or give Kendra the chance to disappear if she spotted her—Verity busied herself, pretending to sort through student files. If another teacher approached, she planned to say, "Go ahead; I have a lot to look up."

She hoped she wouldn't be kept waiting long enough to lose her nerve.

At last, the door opened and Gina stepped out, carefully avoiding Verity's eyes. Before Gina could close the door, Verity twisted around the half-closed door and slipped into Kendra's office.

Businesslike and composed, Verity asked Kendra if she could see her for a moment. Without waiting for a response, she took a seat in the visitor's chair.

Kendra stood with her back to the door. Caught off guard, Verity caught a fleeting look of pain as Kendra turned around, removing the hand that had been pressed to her forehead.

"Yes, Verity," Kendra said, more a statement than a question, her usual condescending tone unmistakable.

Caught off guard by the sudden visit, Kendra's discomfort was obvious.

You'd think I'd walked in on her and Jared in some secret tryst in this ugly office, Verity thought

Secretly satisfied that she had unsettled Kendra, Verity remained unshaken, bolstered by her conviction and the support of her best friend. Crossing her legs, she settled into the chair, pen and paper in hand, and got straight to the point.

"Why did you hire Gina instead of me?" Verity met Kendra's gaze directly, daring her to look away. She waited, expecting Kendra to slip up.

Then Kendra laughed—a sharp, descending series of laughs, throwing her head back against the high vinyl chair. With her guard down, her true nature surfaced.

Verity pictured Kendra as a female Dracula, relishing the moment she sank her fangs into her victim's neck and drew blood. Being laughed at to your face after asking a sincere question carried a cruelty all its own.

That moment seemed to condense every dark incident from the past. All the times Verity had despised, resented, and been disgusted by Kendra—all of it coalesced into one loathed, despicable presence sitting right there.

Verity could probably understand and forgive most of Kendra's actions with time, but she would never forgive this malicious reaction, one that seemed to satisfy Kendra's distorted sense of importance.

She wanted to scream, *"Forget your petty pretensions to power— you've turned this place into a circus!"* But she knew it would fall on deaf ears. What did it even matter anymore?

Her cheeks flushed crimson, pulse pounding, but Verity pressed on. "You specifically told me—right here in this office," she said, jerking her arm downward with her index finger pointed firmly at the floor, "that I was ahead of Gina if a new position ever came up."

In that moment, she felt like a child yelling at a parent over some petty injustice.

"I've been here almost eight months now. You know I'm well qualified—maybe even overqualified for this job..." She stopped herself, realizing it might sound like a threat to Kendra. But what did it matter now?

"Kendra replied, "Gina was chosen by the Selection Committee, not me," which only fueled Verity's frustration.

"Don't insult me by pretending the Selection Committee is anything other than a farce." Saying it gave Verity a brief satisfaction before she pressed on.

"Two months ago, you told me I'd be considered first, before Gina. How have things changed since then?"

"I don't know. I can't answer that."

"What do you mean, you don't know?"

Kendra's tone shifted. Turning her chair fully toward Verity, she folded her arms on the desk and leaned in. "Well, if you really want to know, it's your attitude."

Verity felt the sting, made sharper by the way Kendra seemed to enjoy saying it.

"My attitude?" Verity's voice rose, her eyes locked on Kendra's. "Would you care to explain that?" She was incredulous now. "Tell me about my attitude, Kendra."

Her voice climbed to a near shout as she carefully enunciated each word. "I have a right to know why you're saying I lost my job because of my attitude." She paused, her breath steadying. "Give me some examples."

As if suddenly seized by paranoia, Kendra stood abruptly. "I don't know. Ask Jared. Phone him. I have nothing more to say," she snapped, waving her hand as if brushing Verity away like a speck of dust.

Verity didn't budge. She deserved the full explanation she'd come for—and she wasn't leaving without it. Her determination was clear, and she took satisfaction in Kendra's evident struggle to end the confrontation.

"Are you seriously telling me the deciding factor at the Selection Committee was *attitude*? Was that even a listed qualification? Because if that's true, how on earth did Nicole ever qualify to teach here? Or did your personal relationship with her just override all that?"

Verity's voice sharpened. "And what about the staff morale? Do they all have bad attitudes, too?"

Kendra stayed silent, so Verity pressed on, dripping with sarcasm. "Oh, I see how this works—Nicole gets her subjective pass.

If you don't like someone, you tip the vote so you get to decide who stays and who goes."

"Please, just go," Kendra pleaded, opening the door. "This is my office," she ground out through clenched teeth. "Stop being such a troublemaker."

As far as Verity knew, she'd never been called a "troublemaker" before. People liked to slap labels on others, she knew that, but deep down, she knew who she was.

Verity savoured Kendra's discomfort. Facing the full force of Verity's convictions, Kendra exited her own office, the sharp clicks of her heels echoing down the hall.

Verity allowed herself a brief moment of triumph. This is how it should be—me here, her out there.

Satisfied with this small victory, Verity rose and left, unwilling to give Kendra the chance to rally allies—a typical Kendra move.

Verity followed Kendra's wake into the staffroom where, indeed, she appeared to be enlisting the support of Teresa, her one remaining 'friend'.

Verity started packing her things for her 10:00 class, quietly whispering to Joe, "I made her leave her office," unaware of how far she had slipped with this uncharacteristic gloating.

THURSDAY

s Verity slid into her car, her jammed thoughts slowly untangled, revealing a bitter truth: Kendra had succeeded in engineering the termination of what was likely the best job she would ever have. All the dedication, all the hard work—none of it had mattered in the end. Not to management. And in the end, that's all that mattered.

Deep in thought as she pulled onto the main road, Verity was jolted back to reality by the angry blast of a horn from an oncoming Ford pickup. Her heart slammed against her chest as the driver swerved past, glaring and flipping her the bird. Face flushed with embarrassment, she pulled over to the side of the road.

Inhale. Hold. Count to six. Release.

It took six full breaths before her nerves began to settle. She glanced around, hoping no one from the college had witnessed her stupidity. Then, after triple-checking her mirrors, she eased back onto the road, silently vowing to focus—really focus—on the drive home.

Verity arrived home to an empty apartment. Charlie often worked late—sometimes well into the evening—so she wasn't surprised. When he finally opened the door at 7 p.m., he found her slumped on the sofa, still in tears.

Normally, he'd head upstairs for a shower the moment he got home. But tonight, bypassing her would seem heartless.

"What happened, hon?"

"I didn't get the job," she said, voice trembling as she wiped her tears with the sleeve of her hoodie.

"Oh... I'm so sorry, sweetheart." He joined her on the sofa, wrapping an arm around her shoulders. As he pulled her in, she caught a faint whiff of perfume.

She stiffened. "Where were you just now?" she asked, lifting her head to meet his gaze.

"I came straight home from work, hon. Why?"

"Who else was there?"

"Just me, as usual, and the cleaner. There's a tight timeline on a challenging case, so I've had to put in the extra hours—no way around it."

Verity's gaze dropped to his collar. A tiny smudge of pink lipstick.

Her heart seized. Then, she exploded.

"You liar!" she shouted, shooting to her feet. "How much of an idiot do you think I am?" Her fists clenched, teeth jammed together, every muscle in her body stiff as she glared at him—daggers in her eyes.

"Verity, I—"

"Spare me the lies. Just take your crap and get the hell out of here!"

She stormed into the kitchen, grabbed her keys, then spun back toward him.

"You have all of your stuff—and especially yourself—out of here by the time I get back. Eight o'clock. On. The. Nose."

As Verity turned to walk out of the kitchen, Charlie was headed toward her. "Get out of my way," she growled at him. And, as she opened the front door, "If you're not gone by eight, I'll call the police."

With that, she slammed the front door shut, leaving Charlie to begin an uncertain chapter in his own life.

VERITY SAT in her car in the dark, underground garage, wondering where to go. She let out a heavy sigh, then turned the key in the ignition in case Charlie might run after her.

Up the hill at the exit from the garage, she turned right, heading toward oblivion.

Thursday evening traffic in the city forced Verity to focus on the drive. She decided to head toward Stanley Park, where she found a quiet spot to pull over. She sat there trying to assimilate the dramatic events of the day.

That's a Thursday I never wanted to happen.

It was already dark outside by 7:30, except for street lights, and the occasional blaring headlights from passing cars.

Verity replayed the brief encounter with Charlie as if watching a film in slow motion. The more she ran the scene through her mind, the more her anger dissolved into a deep, aching sadness.

Tears burst forth in a torrent, her upper body shaking uncontrollably. She pulled up the hood of her sweatshirt and turned away from the street, desperate to disappear inside her grief, anonymous in her misery.

PULLING into her parking space back at the apartment, Verity saw that Charlie's car was gone. *Probably overnighting with his girlfriend.*

Inside, it was clear he'd removed his clothing, shoes, and most of his belongings. She'd deal later with the jade grizzly bear—his parents' wedding gift. *Guess I'll need a sledgehammer to smash it.*

Catching sight of her tear-streaked reflection in the bathroom mirror, Verity decided on a warm bath to wash away the day. She poured herself a glass of white wine and sank into the bubble-filled tub, eyes closed, letting Bob Marley's "No Woman No Cry" blare louder than she should have.

After a long soak, she dried off, crawled into bed, and pulled the covers high under her chin. She didn't bother with a nightie. Spent to the bone, she drifted into a deep sleep.

FRIDAY

The last day of the week couldn't come soon enough. Verity drifted through Friday in a daze, grateful to return to her quiet apartment—her new haven. At least, it felt that way once she'd barricaded the hallway door. She wedged the back of a chair under the doorknob, feeling slightly more secure from intruders, including anyone bold enough to leave behind that drawing of an evil eye.

Surely his girlfriend didn't break in and leave that for me?

No. Get a grip, Verity.

She jotted down the local police emergency number and placed copies on her bedside table and by the phone in the kitchen.

There was nothing in the mailbox. Nothing was shoved under the door by Charlie. As six o'clock came and went, Verity had no appetite for dinner, no interest in TV. She didn't want to talk to anyone.

Not wanting to think about Charlie, Verity reached for the letter again. Her eyes landed on the middle paragraph, and nausea crept in.

"I can assure you that you were given careful consideration. In the final analysis, however, we felt the successful candidate had an edge in terms of teaching experience and business background."

Bitter resentment welled up. Many of the permanent faculty had box seats—close enough to watch, far enough to avoid discomfort. They coasted, keeping quiet while real players like Angie, Janet, and she said what needed to be said, did what needed to be done.

Her thoughts turned philosophical. *There are too many agendas at Hillside that don't align with my values.* Maybe being let go wasn't a failure, but a validation of her principles.

Sure, I managed to land three contracts. Maybe the outcome would've been different if I'd played the game. But would I want to stay at a place that couldn't be trusted, that ran on hidden agendas, that rewarded compliance over competence?

The hardest part was that the answer was yes. She had wanted the job—longed for it; dreamed about it. She had built her identity around it. And now, the cold, hard fact remained: she didn't get it.

Catching her tear-streaked reflection in the bathroom mirror as she rinsed her face, Verity asked herself a cold, hard question.

What did you think would happen?

SHADOW

Verity had one more week of work until her contract expired on March 29. She tried to hide her devastation by focusing on her classes, spending more time in her classroom than usual, and doing her best to hide her sadness in front of her students. She buried herself in paperwork, clinging to routine as a lifeline.

Susan Kidd, one of Verity's top students, approached her desk. Susan had been quietly observing the school's politics since she first enrolled at Hillside. Now and then, she would offer wry commentary, like, "I'm glad I'm such an organized person—if I had to rely on guidance from Kendra or Nicole, I might've thrown my hands up in despair... like I've seen other students do."

Today, she stepped forward and held out a piece of paper. "Verity, I wonder if you'd mind reading this letter I drafted for Jared Sinclair."

Even though Verity was going through the motions, feeling like a faint echo of the confident professional she once was, she accepted the paper with a grateful nod and began to read.

. . .

Dear Mr. Sinclair,

Before I leave Hillside College, I feel compelled to share my thoughts regarding my experience in the BOT Division over the past year.

Continual confusion aptly describes the state of affairs in the program. Policies seemed to change so frequently that students couldn't find their footing. If it weren't for the conscientious and consistent support of Verity Child, I believe many of us would have walked away from the program long before completing it.

One particularly damaging policy shift was the move to the composite method of scoring timed writings. In my view, it misrepresented student achievement and did not reflect real-world expectations. It felt more like a mechanism to obscure performance than to measure it meaningfully. As a student preparing to enter the business world, I expected a more transparent and industry-aligned approach.

It also became clear to me that Kendra Howard is not well suited to her role. Her lack of organizational clarity and ineffective leadership negatively affected both staff and students. Complaints about Nicole Barr's behaviour were ignored, despite repeated issues. Nicole was often late or absent, and when present, treated students with open hostility. I witnessed classmates leave class in tears. Her inconsistent marking practices created a culture of fear, not learning. It seemed as though her grading could be used to penalize rather than assess. That is unacceptable.

Despite multiple concerns raised by students, there was no accountability. The environment became disheartening. After this experience, I would not recommend Hillside College to others. As a taxpayer, I find it deeply troubling to see public funds supporting such dysfunction.

I urge you to investigate the situation at Hillside to ensure future students receive the standard of education they deserve.

Sincerely,

Susan Kidd

Verity lowered the paper, stunned. For the first time in days, a small sense of strength returned. Someone had seen. Someone still cared.

Maybe it would take hearing from the students themselves to spark real change.

"Susan, this is a strong letter, and I'm glad you took the time to write it. May I offer one suggestion?"

"Yes, please."

"I suggest you address it to the Principal, Dr. Farmer, at the main campus. You might also copy the College Board—I can give you the correct addresses—and include a copy for Jared as well."

∾

Needing to retrieve her *Office Procedures* textbook from the staffroom, Verity planned to be in and out quickly, hoping to avoid running into anyone. But when she caught sight of Joe at his desk—alone—she couldn't resist approaching. He'd sat on the Selection Committee that chose her replacement.

Before she had the chance to speak, Joe looked up and offered what he seemed to think was consolation. "Gina edged you out by just a little—really, just a little. There was another candidate, Beth, who ranked number one overall. You've been here close to a year, I think, and Gina only a few months, so... don't ask me why they hired someone from outside."

Verity appreciated the gesture. She would have liked to talk longer, but the ache in her chest made it hard to stand there. She gave him a half-smile, thanked him for the information, and hurried away.

Since Joe had already opened the door to communication, Verity felt comfortable writing him a note later that evening from her apartment. She included Susan, another committee member and head of the typing program, someone she had worked closely with.

. . .

I WANT *you to know I'm struggling to understand why I wasn't selected for either of the two positions in the recent competition. I am aware that both of you were on the Selection Committee.*

Please know this isn't a case of 'sour grapes'—you both know how my analytical mind works. I'm simply trying to make sense of it.

Would you be willing to help clarify a few things for me?

– Were the selection criteria explained to all members of the Committee?

– Were those criteria consistently applied?

– What criteria did you personally rely on?

I appreciate your understanding, and I'd be grateful for any insight you're willing to share."

NO REPLY.

SINKING

By Wednesday, March 27, Verity was feeling a bit stronger. Some steadiness had returned, and she began to wonder if she might still hold any influence with Jared. She decided to skip the lunch club meeting and instead booked an appointment to see him during the break.

Jared's secretary let her know he could meet briefly at 12:10 that afternoon.

When Verity stepped into his large office at the main campus, the afternoon sun stretched in long lines across the floor. Jared stood as she entered, seeming even taller than she remembered.

"Jared, I just want to apologise for my behaviour at the staff meeting," she began. "I gave my best effort, along with most of my colleagues, to help you understand what we saw as the root of many of the problems at Hillside. And I wish I'd left it at that. I shouldn't have gone to that second meeting. I was exhausted by then."

Jared nodded, his face unreadable. "Yes, it was unfortunate, Verity. But you can't take back what's already been said."

Verity wanted to sit, but Jared hadn't offered a chair, and he barely met her gaze.

Instinctively, she reached out and touched his arm—just for a second, just long enough to make him notice. "I was hoping we could talk—just the two of us—with cool heads, without the influence of other staff."

"You're asking for special attention, Verity, but frankly, it's a bit late." Jared turned toward his desk. "I have another meeting in five minutes, so I'm out of time."

"Just tell me one thing. Did I lose the contract because of my stance on Kendra?"

Jared didn't pause. "The successful candidates had an edge in terms of teaching and field experience."

"Well, that's interesting," Verity said, her voice low but steady. "Because I know what Gina's qualifications are. We talked after she joined in January—she told me herself she had zero experience teaching at the college level."

Jared exhaled. "You know what? I wish you the best, Verity, but my 2:45 is here now." He opened the door and gestured for her to leave.

As Verity walked away, the sound of her footsteps echoed down the hall, down the stairs, and out through the front doors.

TOWARD THE END of her Typing 181 class that same afternoon, several students approached Verity, asking how they could help. The grapevine had reached the student body, and it had undoubtedly noticed her attempts to keep up appearances.

Maureen led a group of five to Verity's desk. "We just want you to know we're all upset about you leaving, and we'd like to help... maybe talk to Kendra, or write a letter. We're just not sure what would make a difference."

As the others nodded in agreement or looked on with wide, earnest eyes, Verity felt a wave of warmth at their support.

For most of her career, Verity's strong ethical compass had kept her from ever involving students in administrative matters. But now, with pressure mounting and every other avenue seemingly exhausted, she felt herself crossing a line she never thought she would.

"I'm very touched by your kind support." She paused for a moment to be sure of her decision, then continued, "If you're willing, I can include each of your names in a letter I'm preparing for Dr. Farmer. I'll let him know that you'll be submitting statements about your experiences here."

She looked across the five young faces, searching for any hesitation.

"Does that sound like something you'd like me to do?"

They nodded, or gave other small signs of agreement, then quietly returned to their workstations. As they walked away, Verity added, "If you're able to finish them by the end of today, I can include them with my letter."

IN HER LETTER to the college principal, copied to both the college chair and to Jared, she added this paragraph:

These students have asked me to provide statements regarding their experiences at Hillside: Eileen Dampier, Georgina Evans, Helen Hampshire, Maureen McCullough, and Cassie Roland.

74-03-28

Dear Dr. Farmer

AFTER SERVING *eight months on short-term contracts in the Business Division at the Hillside campus, I was denied a two-year probationary contract for one of the two vacancies posted in March this year. The reason given to me by Jared Sinclair was that other candidates were more highly qualified. The Program Coordinator, Kendra Howard, however, told me that I lost on "attitude".*

One of the candidates, Gina, was brought in on a temporary contract before my position was even posted. Through our conversations, I came to understand that my qualifications aligned more closely with the job requirements.

As background, there are some details you may find of interest.

My first meeting with Jared took place during an interview following my initial application for an instructor position at Hillside in July 1973.

During my first interview with Jared, he asked whether I would consider acting as an informant if I were offered a teaching contract at Hillside. The goal, he said, was to help identify the "troublemakers" behind the ongoing "problems" in the Division.

Beyond the Director's inappropriate conduct, I am convinced that the Selection Committee failed to follow proper procedures in the competition for my position. I would be grateful for the opportunity to outline the specifics for you.

I believe I was treated unjustly and respectfully ask that you look into this matter on my behalf.

Verity Child

VERITY FINISHED her last two days at Hillside feeling flat, despite the lunch club's efforts to lift her spirits.

"And, please," she told Janet and Angie, "if there are any plans for a farewell gathering of any kind, can you let everyone know that I appreciate the thought—but I'm just not up for socializing, all things considered."

Janet was the first to respond. "Understood, Verity. People will be disappointed, but I'm sure they'll understand."

Angie offered a gentler alternative. "Then we'll take a rain check on the farewell dinner. Just you, me, and Janet when the dust settles. Okay?"

"Sure," Verity said. "But I'm not saying goodbye to you two."

RICK

On Stella's urging, Verity wrote to the President of the Faculty Association, Rick Murdock:

"...There were two positions vacant. One reportedly went to a more highly qualified candidate, the other to someone less qualified.

Since I know the qualifications of one of those two candidates, I feel compelled to ask: What is the definition of 'qualifications'? Does the committee consider a combination of education and field experience?

Kendra told me I lost on 'attitude.' If this is true, I believe I have been discriminated against—and I feel this warrants further investigation..."

VERITY WAS INVITED to meet with Rick in his office on Monday morning, March 25. With a friendly, matter-of-fact tone, Rick said, "The teaching contract is a legal document. The association defends staff members, but unfortunately, Mrs. Child, you're not a member anymore." He added, "The Faculty Association deals with personnel problems."

Verity replied, "There certainly are personnel problems at the

Hillside campus, but for some reason I don't understand, teachers have said they were waiting to be asked if there were problems."

"There's nothing we know about that would allow us to ask," Rick clarified.

"Well, I can tell you for certain that the majority of instructors believe Kendra needs to be made to realize that teachers are not her servants who can be dismissed at will."

Since Rick seemed amenable to listening, Verity continued. "If I may give you a recent example involving the shoddy treatment of one of the new instructors—Christie. She told me she declined the new short-term contract because of the poor relationship between staff and management at Hillside.

"As a new teacher, she expected some direction but received none. Instead, she was shifted into a variety of courses without any time to prepare. When things didn't go well in the classroom, Kendra told Christie she wasn't cut out to be a teacher."

Rick did not change the impartial expression on his face. Still, there was something about his steady presence that invited honesty. Verity wanted to get something else off her mind, and Rick appeared to be a good listener.

"You may be interested in this, Rick, and I know it sounds crazy, but during my first job interview with Jared, he asked if I would be interested in being an informant."

Rick's eyes revealed a flicker of interest in Verity's story.

"He said there's been a long history of problems in the Division."

"What kind of problems?"

"He didn't specify. He seemed so reluctant to give any details that I stopped trying to ferret them out."

"Odd. So, what exactly did he expect you to do in the role of the informant?"

"He wanted me to remain neutral—not forming any real alliances with my colleagues—while trying to figure out who the 'troublemakers' were."

She finished with a rhetorical question. "What does that say about Jared's faith in Kendra and, more importantly, about his ability as the director?"

After taking it all in, Rick informed Verity that the issue was outside the jurisdiction of the Faculty Association, against the administrative purposes of the Association, and that it wasn't possible to override the principal's decision—that would go against the constitution.

"Selection procedures are public information on file in the management area. Candidates are ranked on education and experience."

Verity pondered this. *If I have less working experience, it's probably because I was busy getting my degree—as well as actual teacher training. And Nicole wouldn't have ranked high on either education or experience.*

Rick let her know the actual ranking. Contrary to what Joe had told her, Gina ranked first, Beth second, and Verity third.

Rick added that Selection Committee members are expected to be as objective as possible. And then there was this: "It is thought that the coordinator is best qualified to judge, and therefore her vote bears more weight," Rick said—rather sheepishly, Verity thought.

Verity's heart sank at the confirmation. If the voting imbalance was sanctioned as acceptable protocol, then she had wasted a lot of time, effort, and emotional energy trying to fight the battle.

In that moment, she felt depleted. Like a high-wire artist losing her footing, all she could hope for now was that the safety net was in place.

As she'd suspected, the Selection Committee routine was a complete fraud. She thought of how Nicole's subjective marking scheme had allowed her to throw her axe at any student she didn't want to succeed. How was this any different? *At least in a real circus act, the victim always survived.*

"I think that the director asks for input from each committee member and uses their input to compile the criteria," said Rick. "But was the criteria made clear to all of the members before the meeting? I'll phone and ask, but I don't know if it'd stand up in court to say what criteria they used."

Verity got the impression that Rick was a decent guy, sincere and forthright in his approach. He advised her to "access the information with a lawyer, but run it by Dr. Farmer first, and try to determine whether legitimate procedures were followed. Selection Committee files would bring a stronger case," he said.

Verity paused for a moment, knowing that what she was about to say had the potential to make her sound unstable. "There's something else that I've been concerned about, Rick, and that's the number of illnesses that occurred in the eight months I worked at Hillside. And I know it sounds crazy, but I'm not yet ready to share perhaps the most shocking thing about the Kendra–Jared–Nicole team."

Rick sat motionless, staring at Verity.

"I'm sure you know about Nicole being carried away on a stretcher in January," Verity persisted.

"Yes. So, did you think it might have been food poisoning?" asked Rick.

"I thought that was a possibility, yes, but no one seems to know anything further — or at least they're not saying. I heard she'd been in the hospital, and I heard that Stella was being questioned for bringing a peanut butter sandwich to school, but if she did, it doesn't necessarily follow that she brought it into the building. I saw her eating a peanut butter sandwich myself, but she was outside, on her way to her car."

Verity continued, as Rick seemed to be listening intensely. "I never saw Nicole again, even though there was a rumour that she was expected to return. And another rumour that she was in hospital having a hysterectomy." Verity shook her head. "So, in short, I have no idea — they're all just rumours to me, and there may not be any truth in any of it."

Rick picked up a thread from Verity's remarks. "Well, that's a lot to wrap my head around right now, I have to say. If you decide to share what you know about the relationship between Jared, Kendra, and Nicole, maybe we can help you further. But for now, that's all I can offer.

What he said next surprised Verity. "I'm not certain the Selection Committee followed the correct procedures."

Verity's ears perked up.

"Considering that you are no longer a member of the Faculty Association, and accepting everything you've told me — including Jared wanting to hire you as an informant, which is highly inappropriate — I can see that you now have a few options without resorting to costly legal action, where success isn't guaranteed. Frankly, the solution might be to revolt."

This statement came out of the blue for Verity, and she could hardly believe her ears.

"Revolt? In what way?" she asked.

"I'd start by meeting with Dr. Farmer, if I were you," Rick replied.

Verity left his office feeling somewhat validated. She couldn't wait to share the news with Angela.

IN THE QUIET of her apartment that Wednesday evening, Verity continued writing reports and making notes. This had become her new job. She would let nothing slide.

Having downed a full supper of nearly blue steak, fried potatoes, and mixed vegetables, Verity sat at her kitchen table, freshly brewed coffee at hand, ready to fire off her thoughts.

"...as a private citizen and taxpayer, I am appalled by the human potential wasted at the hands of an incompetent coordinator."

"...I think it is important to ask why the standards have been so greatly lowered from 1973 to 1974."

"...we believe this is an attempt to hide the real source of the problem, i.e., the incompetence of the Coordinator, Kendra Howard."

At that statement, Verity stopped short. *Why am I still hiding the whole story?*

CRAZED

Interrupting her flow of energy, the phone rang in Verity's apartment on the evening of April 8, 1974.

"Hi Angie, I'm glad you called. I was just about to draft a letter to my students—the ones who rallied to offer support when they learned I was leaving."

"Oh, I wouldn't involve the students, Verity. How would you even get their addresses?"

"They gave me a farewell gift, so I asked for their addresses to send my thanks."

"So, they gave them to you for a different purpose, then."

Angela's words struck Verity's heart like a bullet. Still, she couldn't shake the overwhelming need to make things right—not when she was finally gaining some ground. She knew she was sinking below professional standards, but the unrelenting truth that it was the students themselves who were violated gnawed at her soul. This felt like her last chance. And in that way, she convinced herself it was okay to proceed.

Still, Verity was torn.

Angela continued to relay tidbits of news to her from time to time. "Kendra ran to catch up with me in the hallway," Angela said. "She informed me that Dr. Farmer had sent her a letter saying the Selection Committee had followed all the proper procedures."

Angela and Verity chuckled over Kendra's naivety. Did she think Angela would believe such a story? And, more to the point, did she hope Angela would pass that information along to Verity?

Then Angela delivered news that sparked quiet excitement between them:

Kendra's contract was up for renewal, and Angela had applied for the coordinator position. They both knew that if Angela succeeded, she would hire Verity back.

Angela asked Verity not to mention this to anyone.

"The word from Joe," Angela added, "is that Kendra's afraid you'll take the case to the Department of Education."

Verity thought, *Ah, so they're expecting trouble.*

Angela also reported that Rick had called Joe to investigate the hiring policies. Verity was glad to hear Rick was taking her concerns seriously. Her instincts about him felt right—he'd been sincere and forthright during their meeting, which Verity found refreshing. But there was something deeper, too. To her surprise, she felt drawn to Rick in ways she didn't fully understand. She chalked it up to chemistry.

Joe suggested to Rick that he ask Angela about "the summer uprising." He pointed out that Hillside had experienced a high turnover—not only of staff but of coordinators—roughly one coordinator every year since 1965. This was news to Verity, who began to realize the problems at Hillside likely started long before Kendra and Nicole's tenure.

Joe advised Rick to talk to all the staff who had been let go since 1965. He also shared his opinion that a key issue was the shift in student intake, from monthly to weekly.

Joe told Rick that when he served on the Selection Committee, the criteria he used were field experience and teaching experience in office administration.

Rick said he planned to call Kendra, Susan, and Teresa to ask what criteria they used. He explained that he wanted to get a "general overview" of what happened and what each member contributed to the evaluation.

Ah, so Rick didn't yet know what criteria, if any, had been used. This man didn't rely on a policy brochure; he sought the truth and went straight to those involved. In these ways, Rick reminded Verity of herself.

Of all the information, the detail that caught both Verity and Angela's attention was Rick's comment: "...it seems as though the Committee did not offer opinions concerning ranking." To them, this pretty much confirmed that the Kendra/Jared team had already chosen the winners before the hiring process even began.

Angela also shared that after Verity left, four of the permanent instructors had asked Jared to investigate the coordinator. To Verity, this was the kind of proactiveness she had hoped to see while she was still teaching at Hillside.

"They were told an investigation had already been done, but no results or conclusions were ever shared," Angela said.

"When Rick heard about this supposed investigation, he remarked, 'This may go all the way back to the top then,'" Angela added.

Rick had told Verity that if there were criteria and they hadn't been followed, she had a case. If they had been followed, then she would not.

Now that Verity was home, having lost touch with the President of the Faculty Association, she decided to call him. They arranged to meet the next day at 10 a.m. in Rick's office.

"Good morning, Verity," Rick said with a smile, motioning toward a more casual seating area away from his desk. "Have a seat."

"Thanks for seeing me, Rick. I just wondered if you had any further information on the case."

"Yes, I think it's becoming clearer to the investigative team that the Selection Committee procedures were not followed."

"That's good to hear. And if that ends up being conclusive, would that change anything for me?"

"I can't say, Verity—meaning I don't know at this stage. And it looks like there's a lot more to dig into than I first thought."

"Rick, there is." Verity paused, debating whether to drop the bombshell. "You know, you've been so decent to deal with from the start, so I want you to be the one who hears something that might explain a lot. I didn't feel the timing was right until now."

"Please. Fire away."

"Okay, brace yourself—this is big."

"Trust me, I've been here for ten years, and I think I've probably heard it all."

"I'm just going to come out with it. During my time at Hillside, Jared, Kendra, and Nicole were... a threesome."

Rick frowned and jerked his head back. "A threesome? You mean like that elite triangle thing, right?" He half-smiled.

"No, the sexual kind." Verity's face was unreadable. She looked directly into his eyes as she said it, then quickly glanced away.

"Okay, you're right—that's big. But tell me, how do you know that's true?"

Rick remained calm, and Verity felt relieved she'd chosen to confide in him. She recounted Teresa's drunken disclosure, then fell silent, letting Rick absorb the news.

"Is it okay if I take this to Dr. Farmer?"

"Of course. I want him to know—if he doesn't already. The investigative team will eventually discover that this corrupt threesome is the real source of the problems at Hillside."

As Verity descended the steps to the lower floor, she noticed a woman approaching.

"Hey, you're that teacher from Hillside, right? We had a brief chat at the teachers' conference in Victoria, remember?"

It took Verity a moment, especially after dropping that heavy news on Rick, but she recognized the woman, along with the embarrassment she'd felt that day.

"Sounds like things are heating up at Hillside, huh?"

Verity wondered what the woman knew.

"Well, actually, I'm not there anymore."

"Oh, we know that. Don't worry. But have you seen the letter a student wrote to Dr. Farmer?"

"No, I haven't. How did you hear about it?"

"Rumors spread like wildfire around here. And as for the letter, I do have a copy—if you want one."

"Yes, please. I guess it just takes someone who knows someone, right?"

Verity was appalled to know that a private letter had been copied and distributed to anyone other than the intended recipients, but her involvement compelled her to take a copy.

BACK HOME IN HER APARTMENT, Verity slipped out of her clothes and ran a hot bath. Pouring in an extra dose of liquid bubbles, she settled in, deciding to read the letter as the warm water washed away the day.

"As a taxpayer, I am deeply concerned that the person holding the coordinator position in the Business Office Training Division at the Hillside campus of Everton College is, by any reasonable standard, unqualified for the job.

From what I understand, she was a seamstress before attending Hillside as a student, after which she became a secretary here. Considering the many hurdles individuals face to secure employment, it is beyond my comprehension, both as a former student and a taxpayer, how this person was selected.

Furthermore, during my time as a student, three of the best teachers were suddenly fired. After the last dismissal, students protested for three days, convinced she had been wrongfully let go.

Based on what I have seen of Kendra Howard's abilities, I find it highly unlikely she should be in any position to judge others.

Additionally, my husband works in the federal prison system. After hearing my complaints about Kendra Howard repeatedly, he recognized the name and did some research. He discovered Mrs. Howard has a criminal record.

In the future, I strongly suggest you exercise greater care in screening your employees."

"WHAT?!?" Verity sprang up, stepping out of the tub and hastily drying herself off, a tangle of bubbles and wetness clinging to her skin. She grabbed her terrycloth bathrobe and made a beeline for the bedroom phone. Before dialing, she reread the letter, just to be sure the stress wasn't playing tricks on her.

"Angie, you won't believe this."

SUNDAE

As Verity stepped into the parking lot on her final day at Hillside, she spotted Teresa unlocking her car. One last unanswered question nagged at her.

"Teresa, hold up a sec, please!" Verity called, jogging closer and leaning into the passenger window.

"Do you have a minute?"

"Yes, but not here," Teresa said quickly, glancing around. "I don't want to risk Kendra seeing us together—things are crazy right now."

"Okay. Let's meet at Pixie's Diner—it's on your way home. That work for you?"

"See you there." Teresa slid into her seat and pulled away, with Verity close behind.

Settling into a red vinyl booth, Verity welcomed the change of scene. She ordered a strawberry shake and fries—comfort food after a long, punishing week. Teresa indulged in a chocolate sundae.

"Look at us," Teresa said with a grin. "Kids out of school on a Friday afternoon."

Verity smiled at the joke and sipped her shake through a straw.

"It's been a crazy-stressful week, Teresa, as you can imagine." She chose not to mention her separation from Charlie.

"They say job loss is one of life's biggest stressors."

"No kidding. But I wanted to talk about something else, and I'm guessing you're okay with that."

They both chuckled, silently agreeing they'd had their fill of heavy topics.

"I just wanted to ask you something more about Nicole—if that's all right."

"Jeez, I've already spilled the beans big time," Teresa said, stirring the melting ice cream. "What's a few more cupfuls added to the pile? Besides, you're out the door now, so I guess I don't have to worry about Kendra finding out."

"Don't worry at all, Teresa. Whatever you say stays with me."

"Okay then—but first, I just need to say this sundae is heavenly." She took another bite, scraping chocolate from the sides of the glass with deliberate pleasure.

"It's about Nicole's condition. I'd noticed the fatigue, the shaking hands, her bouts of depression and anxiety, of course."

"Yeah... pregnancy can do that to you, I guess. Well, maybe not the shaking hands—I don't know."

Verity froze mid-bite, a fry suspended halfway to her mouth. "Pregnant? Nicole is pregnant?" Her eyes went wide. Her jaw stayed open around the unbitten fry.

"Indeed. I guess the threesome got careless."

"You're saying Jared's the father?" Verity slowly lowered the fry, staring across the booth.

"Yup."

"How do you know that for sure?"

"I overheard Kendra talking to Nicole on the phone. I stayed late one day to prep a test for my students and needed to ask Kendra if we could use a larger room. When I got to reception, Ethel was gone, and Kendra's office door was ajar."

Verity could picture it clearly and leaned in, listening.

"I heard Kendra exclaim, 'Nicole! Are you sure that Jared is the father?' I tiptoed back a bit, hoping to catch more."

"And?"

"She must've heard me. She ended the call fast. So I went ahead and approached the door anyway. The flushed look on her face wasn't from menopause, let me tell you."

Verity paused. "Well, if I didn't already suspect Nicole might be pregnant—and that Jared might be the father—my analytical brain would be questioning whether you heard what you think you heard."

"What do you mean? I heard it—clear as day."

"But think about it. Imagine another scenario—say Jared got someone else pregnant and Nicole found out. You could imagine Nicole telling Kendra about it, right? Then Kendra responds, 'Nicole! Are you sure that Jared is the father?'"

Verity let that settle, watching Teresa process.

"See what I mean?" she said softly.

Teresa hesitated, then nodded. "Yeah... I do."

Verity shifted gears. "Do you know anything about the muffins in Kendra's office? Or Nicole getting food poisoning?"

"I don't," Teresa said, shaking her head. "And I think if something like that had happened, it would've spread like wildfire in our little group."

CONSEQUENCES

Saturday, March 30, 1974, marked Verity's first official day as an unemployed teacher. She was still in her robe when the phone rang—it was Angie.

As usual, Angie skipped the small talk.

"Fifteen people were interviewed. Each interview lasted about half an hour."

Verity sat up straighter. "How do you know that?"

"Janet asked Stella to meet with her, Joe, and Susan. They wanted to dig into the hiring process—what criteria were used, what input each panel member had, and whether anything was done to make sure bias didn't creep in."

Verity let out a breath. "Sounds like Janet's fingerprints all over that."

"Yes. They found that committee members each offered individual criteria, yet never settled on an overall framework." No surprise there—that's about what you'd expect, given how they were hired."

"What did Kendra and Teresa contribute to the evaluation?" Verity asked.

"Teresa emphasized teaching experience. Kendra didn't contribute anything."

Verity let out a dry laugh. "Well, of course not. She probably knew she'd be picking the winners herself no matter what the others thought."

Angela went on. "It seems the Committee listed a few general considerations, but no one ranked anything. Janet pointed out that it strongly suggests Kendra made the final decision herself, and the Committee was just there to give the appearance of a fair process."

"Sounds about right," Verity said with a heavy sigh.

"Beth, apparently the number one candidate, didn't have any real field experience. Just three years teaching typing at a junior secondary school," Angela reported.

To Verity, the ranking didn't matter. The game had been rigged from the start. "This is all that matters, Angie," she said. "Right out of the gate, it was three against one. Jared and Kendra wanted me out, and Teresa just went along with them. And with no terms of reference for the committee, it was doomed from the beginning."

With nothing more to say on that score, Angela shifted gears. "Want to hear Stella's comment after their fact-finding meeting?"

"My ears are burning," Verity said with dry sarcasm.

Angela chuckled. "With that famous twinkle in her Irish blues, she said, 'This might go back to the top.'"

Verity scoffed. "That's wishful thinking—from someone who prefers staying in the background, giving advice in hopes of furthering her well-being. Stella's version of well-being is hanging on until retirement with the biggest possible payout. Everything else is just entertainment."

As the words left her mouth, Verity paused. *Have I become this bitter?* She didn't want the fallout to erode the core of who she was. *I have to hold on to my ideals,* she told herself. *I can't afford to lose sight of who I am.*

SHATTERED

Sunlight filtering through the edges of her blackout curtains felt like a personal affront. Verity wanted nothing more than to stay cocooned in her bed and let Sunday, March 31, slip by unnoticed. *Why bother getting up? No students, no colleagues—no obligations at all.*

When Charlie called last night, just as she was slipping under the covers, she immediately regretted answering.

"Sweetheart, I've been trying to reach you."

"How hard did you try, Charlie? I've been home every day for the last five days, and it's been two weeks since I found out about your floozy of a girlfriend."

"I thought I'd give you some time to cool off, honey. But I did call you on the 24th—that was my birthday, remember?"

"How strange. I suppose I had better things to do on your birthday than celebrate the day you were born."

"Look, Verity, it's not what you think."

"You're a lawyer, Charlie, or should I say 'liar'? You know I saw the proof—your affair."

Verity lifted her glass of whiskey. "You've shown me you can't be trusted, and that our vows meant nothing." Her voice trembled despite herself.

"Verity, it was a one-time mistake. Tara meant nothing, and we're finished."

"Oh, that's so comforting, Charlie. Sweet dreams await me now that I've heard that."

"I just want to know if I can come over and talk with you. I want you back, Verity; I love you."

"I thought I loved you too," she replied quietly, "but you aren't the man I married."

"I'm still me—flawed, yes, but I'm still your Charlie. Please, just an hour of your time?"

Charlie's plea echoed in the silent room. Verity set down her glass. "You have no idea what I've endured these past weeks. And truth be told, I've grown used to being alone." She pressed "End," and the line went dead.

THAT WAS ONLY one reason Verity remained in bed the next morning. All the relationships she had built through time, care, and diligence lay broken around her.

She felt utterly numb, as if she were a worn-out performer in a circus long past its prime, so accustomed to the crack of the whip that her heart believed there was no coming back. Day after day, nothing changed. Staying under the covers felt safer than facing the world. She tried not to wallow, but motivation eluded her completely.

Eventually, her thoughts drifted back to Hillside. Perhaps her aspirations had been too ambitious for that place—helping students succeed, earning their respect, honing her craft to its fullest. Now it all felt out of reach.

Her ideals lay in ruins. She had believed that by focusing on delivering the best teaching she could, the college would naturally want to keep her. She'd thought that by ignoring office politics and the ineptitude of those in charge, she could still fulfill her goal of being a good teacher. It never occurred to her that, by behaving with integrity, she would instead be seen as a threat, at least by Kendra and Jared.

Verity recalled a secondary-school teacher who urged her students never to surrender their ideals. That teacher often quoted Anne Frank: *"I keep my ideals because, in spite of everything, I still believe that people are really good at heart."*

As an instructor, Verity had hoped every lesson, every piece of feedback, and every earnest effort in her classroom would stand as proof of her professionalism.

Perhaps people misunderstood my ideals. But if the foundation itself is cracked, it doesn't matter how much steel reinforcement you pack inside the walls above—the whole structure remains at risk.

The person who used to get up an hour earlier than necessary each morning, excited about the day ahead, now felt glued to the bed. All she wanted was darkness and silence.

At the best of times, all Verity could conjure up was the notion that maybe they'd call her back in, recognizing their mistake, eager to make amends. She could re-establish her position.

If she could turn back time, maybe she'd play things differently. Perhaps a high moral ground wasn't worth the pain she felt today.

No matter the calibre of those in charge, what mattered was that they *were* in charge. It was inexperience that led Verity to believe that if she excelled at her job, she would be successful. So confident was she in this belief that she ignored her vulnerability:

Her appointment was strictly temporary, and the college had no obligation to renew it.

That evening, Stella rang Verity's apartment.

Perhaps relieved that Verity was no longer on staff, Stella didn't hold back.

"Nicole reminds me of T.S. Eliot's *The Hollow Men*—'They base their premises upon shadows rather than substances.' She dazzles everyone with her jewellery, but she's utterly hollow."

Verity gripped the phone tighter as Stella pressed on.

"Kendra's plain. I decided long ago to keep my distance from anyone who stirs up trouble. Last July, I got three calls from students —I sent them straight to Kendra. I'm not cleaning up other people's messes."

So that's why Stella lurks in the background—she never has to take responsibility, Verity thought. *Does she pat herself on the back for staying silent when she could have helped? I wonder if she knows Edmund Burke's line: 'All that is necessary for the triumph of evil is that good men do nothing.'*

Verity cut in. "Kendra affects a lot of lives—and not for the better. Listen, Stella, I need to ask you something."

"Fire away," Stella replied.

"It's no secret you have connections with the college's decision-makers," Verity said.

Stella chuckled. "I know a few people, that's true."

"Have you kept any of them informed about what's been happening at Hillside—especially regarding our philandering director?"

A long pause followed. Verity worried the line had gone dead. Finally, Stella spoke. "Oh, I'm sure some of them know about Jared's indiscretions." Then, almost too quickly, she shifted gears. "Anyway, I've got to run—but I want to urge you to go all the way in seeking justice for how you were treated."

Verity listened as Stella continued. "I know a lawyer who specialises in employee–employer disputes. Others burned by Kendra have gone to him. As a former Deputy Attorney General for the NDP, he'd be a fighter."

~

THAT EVENING, Stella phoned again—and didn't even say hello before launching in.

"The college exists for management, not for students."

When Verity remained silent, Stella pressed on.

"My concern has always been for your approach to adult learners. Students talk—teaching is a privilege. From the moment I met you, I recognised the qualities of a great instructor. You have my full support."

Verity's patience snapped. "Stella, I'm tired of your belated support. You weren't there when we needed you, so don't waste my time now that I'm gone." She slammed down the receiver.

A surge of pride warmed her. In the past, she'd have nodded politely and gone along. Now, she refused to be placated.

KNEE-JERK

The phone rang at 7 a.m. on Saturday, April 6, and Verity chose to answer the call.

"Hello?"

"Verity, is that you?"

"Aunt Lucy! It's so good to hear your voice!"

"Well, dear, I've been missing you, so I thought I'd give a call and see how you're doing."

Verity hesitated before answering. She'd shielded her beloved ninety-three–year-old aunt from every upheaval—workplace betrayals, marital strife—sending only sunny letters and cheerful bouquets. Best to keep it that way.

"Oh, thank you, Aunt Lucy. I'm doing quite well. And how are you?"

They spoke for about an hour, and Verity found comfort in reconnecting with a world that felt wholly good.

She carefully dodged questions about work and Charlie, determined that her beloved aunt should sense nothing amiss. Yet talking with Aunt Lucy, just like old times, renewed her resolve to try and rebuild her life.

I can't let Aunt Lucy down—and I won't let myself down.

Verity had been mostly confined to her bed for five days, rising only to scramble a few eggs, toast bread, fetch water, shower, and then retreat again. Time lost all meaning; at 3 a.m., the ticking clock felt entirely irrelevant.

But after Aunt Lucy's call, Verity realised she faced a choice: keep spiralling down or take even the smallest steps forward. Still capable of choosing, she resolved to move ahead, however haltingly.

THE FOLLOWING MORNING, around ten, her birth mother rang. "I'm so sorry, Verity," she said, her voice trembling. "Aunt Lucy passed away last night." Verity sat frozen. "She died peacefully in her sleep," her mother continued softly, pausing to let the words settle. "And, that's the best any of us can hope for, isn't it?"

Verity's eyes filled with tears. "Oh, Mom, she called me just yesterday. We had such a lovely chat—like always." Her voice caught as she tried to steady it. "I can't believe she's gone. I loved Aunt Lucy so much."

Tears spilled freely down her cheeks as the truth settled in: she would never again hear her aunt's warm voice or see her gentle smile. It didn't matter that she was ninety-three. The loss hit with the weight of losing a parent, an anchor.

A heavy darkness seemed to fold around Verity, and she wasn't sure she'd ever find her way back to the light.

Angie had checked in almost every day since Verity was let go. With her friend's encouragement—and a growing resolve to move forward—Verity finally launched into a flurry of actions, hoping they might bring clarity or even resolution.

To focus her thoughts and pick up the trail, she turned to her notes and reviewed what had already come to light:

"There was a threesome—Jared, Nicole, and Kendra.

Management of the BOT Division operated on whatever ensured

their survival. That included a watered-down evaluation system to help students graduate easily and an aggressive enrollment push that made the college look good on paper.

Nicole was pregnant, and Jared was likely the father.

Nicole became ill, supposedly, and vanished from Hillside. Rumor had it she was in the hospital. That still seems odd to me.

When Nicole left the picture, was Jared looking for a replacement? Was he still seeking a spy? Did he suspect Stella was feeding information to the higher-ups?

What incentives kept Nicole and Kendra in the threesome? And how far would they go to protect it?"

Verity decided to pour all her efforts into answering those questions. She'd already invested so much—and paid dearly for it. There was no turning back now.

She wrote to Jared, requesting a letter of recommendation.

It was her turn to lie.

74-04-08

Dear Jared

Please provide me with a letter of recommendation to be used in my current search for employment outside the college. In the meantime, should a teaching vacancy arise within the Business Division at the Hillside campus, I would be grateful for the opportunity to apply.

Thank you for permitting me to attain my recent six months of teaching experience, a period I found rewarding both personally and professionally.

Verity Child

. . .

JARED'S REPLY arrived two days later, on Wednesday, April 10.

To Whom It May Concern:

MRS. CHILD'S B.A. in Office Management and her teaching experience at Toronto Community College fit her well for her position at Everton Community College. She faced a difficult challenge in starting mid-stream and handled herself very well indeed.

Jared Sinclair, Director
Business Office Training Division
Everton College

Verity made plans to contact other teachers who had suffered similar treatment at Hillside. She occasionally joined the lunch club at Riley's, and on Wednesday, April 17, they began to strategize.

Janet offered practical advice. "Talk to all the instructors who've been laid off since Kendra took power. Give Rick their phone numbers—he's Head of the Faculty Association, so it makes more sense for him to reach out."

Angela leaned in, a spark of energy in her voice. "Ask him to check the records. How many coordinators were terminated during Jared's reign? And how many instructors during Kendra's?"

Janet nodded. "Exactly. I bet most of them were people who either refused to play along with the threesome or tried to make real improvements at the college."

Verity was adamant. "And I want to know if any other instructors were invited to play the role of spy. And if so, were they given any reason other than *problems at the campus*?" Her eyeballs hardened.

"And let's find out if any of those people suffered any serious illnesses during their time at Hillside," added Verity.

STALK

ack in her apartment that evening, a sense of unease gnawed at Verity. The more she tried to piece together who Kendra really was—and what her true motivations might be—the more compelled she felt to see where Kendra lived.

Kendra had always put on airs about her life in an upscale suburban neighborhood. Verity already knew her home phone number and her husband's name, which made the address easy to track down.

She rummaged around for a disguise. Wrapping a dark blue scarf around her head like a turban, she planned to pull the hood of her black sweatshirt over it, completely covering her hair. From an old Halloween costume box, she fished out a pair of faux eyeglasses with heavy, dark frames. When she caught a glimpse of herself in the mirror, she laughed.

On her way out the door, she grabbed a book—just in case she needed to look like she was simply out reading.

FAR FROM THE exclusive waterfront Kendra had always implied, the house sat well inland, tucked on a small lot along an inner street. Driving slowly, Verity studied the old stucco home, white with rust-colored trim, clearly built in the 1950s. She knew the type well: modest rooms, plaster walls, and low ceilings that always struck her as cold and uninspiring.

Kendra lived there with her husband, Norm. Their children had long since flown the nest.

The front yard was neat, with evenly trimmed evergreen shrubs flanking the concrete steps that led to the front door. A bright, spring-green lawn added a cheerful contrast to the house's dated trim.

Just inside a black wrought-iron fence stood a small greenhouse, and beside it, a cluster of plants under a clear plastic tent. Something about the setup caught Verity's attention. She pulled over, stepped out of the car, and approached the fence for a closer look.

Peering into the tent, she immediately recognized the plant: *Zigadenus venenosus*, commonly known as Death Camas. Her horticulturist parents had drilled its identity into her memory. Every part of the lily was toxic—sometimes fatally so.

Verity recalled that the deadly species grew wild in the Sooke Hills on Vancouver Island, and she couldn't imagine why anyone would deliberately plant it in their front yard. Maybe Kendra had mistaken it for the Common or Great Camas Lily. Verity knew how easy it was to confuse the onion-like bulbs—one nourishing, the other lethal.

Sliding back into her car, Verity resumed the slow crawl past the house. The curtains were all drawn, preventing any view inside.

So focused on studying the property and scanning for a glimpse of Kendra, she didn't see the speed bump ahead. Her body jolted forward as the tires thumped over it. *Okay, I need to pay more attention to what I'm doing.*

She pulled over to the curb, careful not to stop directly in front of the house. Choosing a spot partially hidden from the nearest street-lamp, Verity cut the engine. The car was in shadow, her disguise intact. Satisfied she wouldn't be easily recognized, she settled in to wait.

She sat there, staring at the house, imagining what might be going on inside. Nearly half an hour passed with no movement, not a single light on, nothing to suggest life within. Verity reached for the key, ready to call it a night.

But just as she turned in her seat, the automatic garage door began to rise.

She froze.

The door revealed Kendra's Chrysler LeBaron, its chrome catching the garage light. Verity's car was too far for a clear view, so she slipped out and walked along the far side of the street, careful to keep her head down and her pace steady.

Her heart pounded. She held her breath.

Inside the brightly lit garage, she saw Kendra step toward the trunk of the car. Her gloved hands carried a flat, rectangular package —something about the size and shape of a pizza box. She opened the trunk, placed it carefully inside, then turned and disappeared through the interior door leading back into the house. A moment later, the garage door descended, closing her off from view.

Verity remained rooted to the sidewalk. The air was cool, but she barely noticed. She stared at the quiet house, trying to make sense of what she'd just seen—why the gloves? What was in the box? And why did it feel like a secret?

She didn't know how long she stood there, unable—or unwilling —to move.

WESTMINSTER CHIMES

After about a week's grace, Verity's team continued to offer advice. They urged her to go to the College Board of Directors and the Principal, Dr. Farmer. Without their support, Verity would not likely have continued the fight.

It was Wednesday, April 24, and Verity joined a meeting of the lunch club.

Angela was in deep thought.

"Do we know why Jared wanted to hire you as a spy, Verity?"

"Uh, I've been thinking that maybe he hoped that I would focus on Nicole as the main troublemaker."

"Why do you think that?"

Verity hesitated, sorting through her thoughts. "Well… Jared never directly said it, but sometimes when we talked, he'd steer the conversation toward Nicole. Her absences. Her 'poor attitude.' He even once asked if I thought she was undermining the department."

"And, when I think about how things evolved—once Nicole got pregnant, she became a liability. So, if I found evidence to prove that she didn't have the best interests of the college at heart, or something like that, then maybe that would provide reasons for not renewing her contract."

Janet picked up the thread. "Yes, but Nicole had the upper hand. She knew about the threesome."

"So do we," Verity said, but we've all said that it's not easy to prove that it existed."

Angela frowned. "So he wanted to control the narrative. Make Nicole the scapegoat."

"That's how it felt," Verity said. "I think he wanted me to gather just enough to make a case against her—but nothing that would touch him or Kendra."

Janet leaned forward. "And when you didn't bite?"

Verity gave a small, tight smile. "I became the liability. He wanted control, not clarity."

Janet gave a low whistle. "It's time the board hears all of this. Every word."

Angela was thinking hard about the dilemma. "Maybe someone was working behind the scenes to silence her another way."

The three fell silent.

"Um, well, I have to say—I can't get that scene out of my mind," Verity said. "It just keeps playing over and over in my head."

"You mean the one with Nicole on the stretcher, right?" Angela jumped in.

"That very one. Yes," Verity nodded.

Janet joined in, a puzzled frown on her brow. "Why do you think your mind keeps going back to that?"

She stabbed a piece of cucumber with her fork.

"Well…" Verity hesitated. "I didn't share this with you before because, at the time, it didn't seem significant."

Angela set her coffee cup down slowly, as though it might help her listen more closely. Janet's eyes widened; she looked up from her salad, fork still poised midair.

"On Monday night," Verity continued, "I decided to drive past Kendra's house. Just to see where she lived."

Janet and Angela went quiet.

"Now, I don't remember if I told you this, but I'm pretty good at identifying plants—herbs, trees, shrubs, all of it. Both my parents were horticulturists, and they taught me the common and botanical names from a young age."

Janet nodded. "Ah, yes—I've noticed you seem to rhyme off the names of flowers and things pretty easily."

Verity leaned in slightly. "Here's what might be significant—or maybe it's nothing. I don't know."

She went on to describe her discovery.

"There's a small greenhouse just inside the fence by their front gate. On the top shelf, under a plastic tent—kind of like a mini-greenhouse—was a clump of flowers set apart from the Canna lilies growing nearby. Curious to see what had been set aside from the other plants, I walked close and peered at the plastic tent."

She paused.

"And the moment I saw them, I recognized them. A clump of *Zigadenus venenosus*—commonly known as Death Lily. My parents drilled it into me how dangerous it is. All parts of the plant are poisonous."

Janet drew in a sharp breath and turned to Angela.

"So, it's called 'Death Lily' because it... causes death?" Angela asked.

Verity nodded. "Yes. It can be lethal to humans. Even small amounts."

Janet looked between Verity and Angela. "Do you two think Kendra is growing Death Lily for... suspicious reasons?"

Verity hesitated. "I have no proof. But I can't stop connecting what I saw with Nicole on that stretcher—and the deathly paleness of her face."

The others fell silent.

After a few moments, Janet asked, "Did you see anything else that seemed off?"

"I don't know if you'd call it *suspicious*, but just as I was about to leave, the garage door opened. I watched from across the street as Kendra walked to her car and opened the trunk. She was holding something—flat, rectangular—that resembled a pizza box. She placed it inside and went back in."

Angela gave a dry chuckle. "Let's hope she doesn't show up at the college tomorrow with pizza."

Verity didn't smile. "I'm serious. Now that you both know, I want you to be careful—don't take any food Kendra offers. And watch out if you see her giving anything to someone else."

She paused, then added, "Now the big question is—how can we find out if Nicole was poisoned?"

"Does anyone know where she lives? Or any of her friends—if she has any?" Janet asked.

Angela, who seemed to know everyone and everyone's business, spoke up. "I know where she lives. It's near the university. I was heading over to visit my mentor a while back and saw her pull into a driveway—I assumed it was hers."

Verity leaned in, intrigued. "Do you remember exactly which house it was?"

"Oh, I remember. It's right on the main road to the university. I pass it every day."

Verity's eyes lit up. "Okay, Angela, how would you feel about knocking on her door one day—if she's out of the hospital—and paying her a little visit?"

Angela gave a noncommittal shrug. "I'll think about it. I might be the best option since we never had a direct working relationship. The few times we talked, it was friendly enough."

"Fair point," Janet said. "But don't you think she might be a little suspicious if you suddenly showed up?"

"Maybe," Angela admitted.

"What about this?" Verity suggested. "You knock on her door with a bouquet in hand. Say it's from the staff—a Get Well Soon gesture."

"Not a bad idea," Angela said. "Hard to turn down flowers. Though she might not answer the door."

"True," Janet said. "It'd be better if you could phone first. Leave it with me—I'll try to track down her number."

As that plan took shape, Angela dropped by Verity's apartment that evening to deliver her notes and a few suggestions.

Point #3 in Angie's notes read: *Verity publicly criticized Nicole, stating that she "couldn't work with her."*

"I said no such thing," Verity snapped. "That was one of Jared's fabrications."

Angela listened as Verity went on. "Do you see? Jared needed a rationale for not renewing my contract, just like he needed one for getting rid of Nicole."

"And he hoped you'd give him that rationale," Angela said slowly. "You could be right, Verity."

"Yes, and honestly, I think you can find a reason to fire anyone if you're determined enough," Verity said. She paused, making sure she had Angie's full attention.

"And you know what else?" Verity continued. "Once I criticized Kendra's competency, Jared would've known she'd refuse to work with me again. And how can you have a threesome when one of the players is missing?"

Angie's mouth dropped open. "Wait—what? Were you considering being part of their *new* threesome?"

Verity gave a crooked smile. "I can't say the thought didn't cross my mind... strictly in the interest of amateur sleuthing, of course."

"Your dedication is extreme. You *do* know that, don't you?"

"I know, Ange. I'm working on it."

On the afternoon of Tuesday, April 30, Verity collected her mail from the locked boxes in the foyer and climbed the steps to her apartment. One envelope caught her attention—it was from the lawyer she'd consulted on Stella's recommendation. Seated at her kitchen table, she opened that one first.

April 30, 1974

...I have now had an opportunity to consider the legislation and, in my opinion, there is nothing in it of assistance to your case...

Her shoulders slumped. Disheartened, she reached for the other envelope, this one from the Chair of the College Board, and tore it open.

74-04-30

Dear Mrs. Child

I apologize for the delay in responding to your letter of 74-03-27, and I want to let you know that the BOT Division is currently under investigation

Thank you for taking the time to bring your concerns to the attention of the Board.

Sincerely,

Gillian Mosley
Chair, Everton College

∾

As Angela's car neared Nicole's house on the afternoon of Wednesday, May 1, she spotted Nicole's BMW in the driveway. Encouraged, she parked behind it, picked up the bouquet of alstroemeria from the passenger seat, and slowly walked up the three steps.

Even though they'd arranged the visit by phone, Angela still wasn't entirely sure Nicole would be home—or would answer the door. She rang the bell. Through the open window, the familiar notes of "Westminster Chimes" drifted out.

When the door opened, Nicole raised her brows at the sight of Angela holding a bouquet. "Hi, Angela. Come in if you want." Her smile was faint, and she looked nothing like the smartly dressed, confident woman their colleagues were used to seeing. At two in the afternoon, she was still in a navy-blue flannel robe and slippers.

Angela handed her the flowers. "This is from all of us. I hope you like alstroemerias."

Nicole smiled. "Thanks, they're beautiful. I'll put them in some water." She nodded toward the living room. "Come in and sit for a while."

Angela followed her into the house and settled on the sofa. Nicole returned a moment later with the flowers arranged in a vase, which she placed on the coffee table before sitting beside Angela.

Angela broke the silence. "I haven't seen you since your sudden departure in January. I remember the date—it was the day before that big blow-up meeting, the one that led to yet another shake-up at the college."

"Oh, yeah. Kendra told me about that."

Angela tilted her head. "I didn't know you two were still friends."

"Ha. Friends?" Nicole let out a dry laugh. "I haven't seen her. She just called me when I was in the hospital—to check if I was okay."

Angela hesitated, then said gently, "We were a bit puzzled about why you were hospitalized. Someone mentioned you'd had a hysterectomy."

Nicole fell quiet for a moment. Then, in the frank tone she used to be known for at Hillside, she said, "Food poisoning. It triggered a miscarriage. I was sick for about a month and a half after I left Hillside."

Angela's face softened. "Nicole, I'm so sorry. I didn't realize you were pregnant."

"Most people didn't."

"And the food poisoning," Angela continued. "What had you eaten, do you know?"

"Oh, yes, the lab report said that I was poisoned from parts of a lily called Death Camas."

Angela feigned surprise, raising her brows before her expression shifted to a deep frown. "Wow! I don't get it—where would you have eaten parts of a lily?"

"Nowhere that I know of. I mean, it was hardly on purpose. But the doctor said it's highly poisonous — that I could have brushed by the plant without even realizing it."

Tears of sadness welled up in Nicole's eyes — a side of her Angela hadn't seen before.

Angela reached out, gently placing her hand on Nicole's left shoulder in a gesture of compassion.

Wiping her eyes with her hands, Nicole tried to lighten the mood. "When they asked me what I'd eaten that day, Lily wasn't on the list."

Angela offered a faint smile, then leaned forward slightly. "Nicole, would you mind if I made a copy of that lab report? I can't say much yet, but it might eventually be useful to you."

Nicole copied the report on her home copier. As she handed it to Angela, she said quietly, "I've never been so sick in my life. They said I could have died."

AN UNEXPECTED KNOCK came at Verity's apartment door that night. Peering through the spyhole, she was stunned to see Kendra standing there, holding what looked like a pizza box. Her heart jumped—not from seeing Kendra, but at the sight of the pizza. Still, curiosity overruled caution, and she opened the door.

"Verity, I know it's late and I didn't call, but I picked up a pizza on my way home from work and thought I'd take a chance that you were in." Kendra's saccharine smile reminded Verity of the day they met.

"You're the last person I expected to see at my door, Kendra. We didn't exactly part on friendly terms."

"I know, Verity, and I'm not proud of that. Do you mind if I come in?"

"I don't have time to visit right now, Kendra, but I appreciate your bringing food to my door." Verity worked to keep her tone neutral, accepting the pizza with care, doing her best not to betray any suspicion.

"Oh. Well, that's what I get for not calling ahead," Kendra said with a strained laugh. She blinked, holding her eyes shut just a second too long.

"Verity, I know it might seem strange, me just dropping by like this, but I wanted to make amends. You're a good person who tries to do the right thing, and I know losing your job hit you hard."

Verity didn't budge. "Right." She offered her own syrupy smile, matching Kendra's tone beat for beat, and reached for the box.

"Thanks for dinner. I'm sure it's delicious—it'll make a fine midnight snack."

She shut the door slowly but firmly, the click of the lock deliberate. Without lifting the lid, Verity set the box on the counter. First thing in the morning, she'd take it straight to the lab.

On Monday morning, Verity received the lab results confirming the pizza was laced with fragments of Death Lily. She called Angela at work and arranged to pick up a copy of Nicole's lab report that night.

"Your suspicions were correct," Angela said, "and, Verity, I can't tell you how happy I am that you are alive and well."

"We can celebrate at your place tonight," said Verity.

Before hanging up, Angela said one more thing.

FAMILY MAN

"Guess who Jared brought to the college today?" Angela asked Verity.

"Oh, I don't know—another hopeful for the three-some?" Verity said, only half-joking.

"His nephew. Robert. He's visiting from Toronto, apparently planning to study dentistry at U of T."

"I never pictured Jared as the family type," Verity said. Angela gave a dry little laugh.

"Well, he brought him into the staffroom and introduced him to anyone present. He's clearly proud of the kid," said Angela.

"I suppose Uncle Jared wanted to show off—Director of BS and all," Verity said, her tone flat. She had no kind thoughts for Jared.

Angela nodded. "And Ethel says Kendra's bringing in a birthday cake for him at lunch."

Verity stopped suddenly, her face draining of color.

"Angie," she said, voice sharp, "call the police. Tell them to meet me at the college. I'm on my way."

Grabbing her purse and keys, Verity raced out the door, not bothering to lock it. Hillside was twenty minutes away. She glanced at her watch—11:30. If all went well, she'd make it to the college ten minutes before the lunch break.

Her heart pounded in her chest as she gripped the wheel, trying to breathe, trying to focus on the road. Her knees felt weak; thank goodness she was sitting.

Ahead, red brake lights flared. Verity eased off the gas and hit the brakes. Just then, something in her peripheral vision caught her eye —a deer bounding left across the road, straight into oncoming traffic. It missed a collision by inches.

She barely had time to register it when her head snapped forward, then slammed back against the headrest. The crunch of metal followed—first from the vehicle behind her, then another crashing into it. A chain reaction. A multi-vehicle collision.

"Not now," Verity fretted, knowing she wouldn't make it to the college in time. She rubbed her neck and quickly checked for injuries. Then she sat frozen, unsure of what to do next. She couldn't just leave the scene of an accident, but what she had to do felt far more urgent than a fender-bender.

In her rearview mirror, she saw the driver of the car behind her approaching. Verity rolled down her window.

"I'm so sorry, Miss. I couldn't stop in time... Are you hurt?"

"It was unavoidable—I barely managed to stop myself," Verity said, cutting the small talk. She opened the glove compartment, pulled out a pen and paper, and they exchanged names, phone numbers, and driver's license details.

Desperate to get moving, Verity drove off as soon as it was safe. It was 11:45. She pressed the gas a little harder than usual, stealing anxious glances in the rearview mirror for any sign of police.

As she swung onto the gravel driveway leading to the parking lot, Verity pulled over to the side, shutting off the engine without wasting time hunting for a parking spot.

Grabbing her purse, she hurried up the steps, but halfway up, her lax ankle ligaments betrayed her. A sharp, familiar tear shot through her ankle. Grasping the stair rail, she cried out, "Ouch, ouch, oh no," then whispered, "Please, not now."

"Are you okay?" asked a young woman who had just opened the front door as the lunch bell released students from their classes.

Verity tried to stand but couldn't bear weight on her right ankle. "I'm afraid I've sprained it," she said, looking up at the kind woman. "Please, could you help me to the front office? It's urgent. I wouldn't ask if it weren't a true emergency."

"Of course." The woman offered her arm. "Just put your left arm around my shoulders, and we'll get you inside." She called out to an onlooker to carry Verity's purse.

Verity pictured the lab reports in her mind but let the thought go. This was the best way forward.

With as little weight as she could manage on her foot, Verity's heart pounded as she counted the seconds it would take to hobble down the long hallway to Kendra's office—with help.

At last, the front office came into view. Ethel was shuffling papers at her desk. She looked up, surprised to see Verity, clearly struggling and being supported by two students. Kendra's door was closed, the *Do Not Disturb* sign hanging prominently.

Verity forced herself to stay calm despite the knot tightening in her stomach. She urgently asked Ethel, "Where's Kendra?"

"Oh, she's with Jared and his nephew Robert—it's a private birthday celebration."

Hearing that, Verity had no choice but to steer the kind woman supporting her toward Kendra's door. Without hesitation, she slipped free from the student's arm, reached out with her left hand, turned the knob, and swung the door open.

Turning to the other student who handed back her purse, Verity said, "Thank you both so much. Now please, get out of here—it's not safe."

The students hesitated, glancing back as they left slowly. Ethel stared, bewildered.

∼

ALL THREE PEOPLE gathered around Kendra's desk looked startled by Verity's sudden intrusion. As she crossed the threshold, her eyes locked on the young man sitting with them. Panic surged through her—had he eaten, or even touched, the cake?

Riley's iconic pink cake box sat unopened in the center of the table. A cutting knife, dessert plates, forks, and paper napkins were neatly arranged, untouched—proof they hadn't started.

"Stop!" Verity shouted, pointing a finger at Kendra, who had risen from her chair.

She glanced back toward Ethel, frozen just outside the door, and commanded, "Call the police."

Jared slammed the door shut, cutting them off from any outside help.

"Verity, what do you think you're doing, barging in like this?" Kendra shouted, her face flushed with anger. "Get out—or I'll call the police myself."

"The police are on their way, Kendra." Verity wasn't backing down—surprising even herself—as she stood her ground with unwavering determination. Still, she couldn't be certain Angela had gotten through, or if the police would even show. She guessed Ethel was probably still frozen in inaction.

Kendra sank back into her chair. "Jared, can you get this woman out of here?" Her voice faltered as she pleaded for Jared's help, trapped behind her desk with Robert seated to her left and the filing cabinet to her right.

Verity shifted awkwardly, putting most of her weight on her left foot, gripping the desktop for support as she blocked the door as best she could. Her unzipped purse lay on the desktop, a roll of white paper placed on top for easy access.

Robert remained silent, studying the players as the scene flipped from a pleasant afternoon tea to an intense crime scene.

Jared sat back down, seemingly forcing calm. Tilting his head, he asked in a deep voice, "Look, Verity, what's this about?"

Verity opened her purse, pulled out her copy of the lab report, and handed it to Jared as she turned to Kendra.

"That cake is poisonous. You're trying to poison Jared—just like you did Nicole." Her voice rose, raw and accusing.

Robert stood abruptly, folded his arms, and took a cautious step back from Kendra.

"That's outrageous!" Kendra cried, desperation creeping into her voice. "She's a madwoman, Jared—please, get her out of here."

Jared glanced at his nephew. "Robert, wait in the car for me, please." Verity stepped aside as he opened the door.

Relieved that Robert was now safely out of the room, Verity stayed alert, watching Kendra closely in case she tried to bolt.

Jared unfolded the lab report and read aloud, "Zigadenus Venenosus—Meadow Death Camas. I don't get it. What are you trying to say, Verity? What does this lab report mean?"

"It means the pizza your coordinator so graciously delivered to me two nights ago tested positive for bits of Death Lily," Verity said sharply.

Jared stared at Kendra, who stood firm. "That's nonsense," she shot back. Then, turning to Verity, "I can't believe you'd stoop so low as to make up stories just to get your job back." Her eyes flicked toward the door, as if plotting an escape.

"This cake came from a bakery," Kendra insisted. "Any fool can see this is a Riley's cake box."

"Yeah?" Verity challenged. "Then let's see you open it and try a piece yourself, Kendra."

Kendra's hands trembled as she grasped the sides of the box, struggling to lift the lid. "Jared, can you help me?"

Verity's breath caught. She knew even the slightest contact with the lily could be deadly. "I wouldn't do that, Jared."

But Jared's hands were already on the box. As he eased it open, Kendra swiped her finger over the icing and licked it.

"There," Kendra said triumphantly. "This is not a poisonous cake —it's a bakery cake. And you've ruined Jared's birthday celebration."

Jared looked at Verity and blurted, "What does this have to do with Nicole?"

"She got the same lab report," Verity said. "The day she was taken out of here on a stretcher. Everyone assumed it was her nut allergy—but it was Kendra's so-called bakery cake."

Jared's face drained of color. "How do you know that?"

"You're a liar!" Kendra screamed, lunging for the door.

Verity was blocking the doorknob, so Kendra attempted to shove her aside, but Verity stood firm. "Get your hands off me, Kendra," she said, driving her elbow hard into Kendra's face.

Kendra reeled back just as the door burst open and a police officer rushed in, knocking both women off balance. Jared stood frozen, dismayed by the chaos. Through the open door, Verity caught a glimpse of Ethel, one hand clamped over her mouth, as though in shock.

"What's going on here?" the officer demanded as he stepped inside, followed closely by a second officer, who shut the door behind them.

"Everyone, sit down," the first officer ordered.

Kendra backed toward her desk but didn't sit. Instead, she bent low and reached into the bottom drawer of her filing cabinet.

"Stop right there!" the officer barked.

In a flash, he was behind her. The second officer drew his weapon. The first officer seized Kendra's right arm, twisted it behind her back, then grabbed her left and snapped the handcuffs into place with practiced ease.

Verity exhaled, long and slow. She covered her face with one hand, letting herself breathe—truly breathe—for the first time in days. The worst was over. Her job was done.

As one police officer led Kendra away, Verity cautioned the other not to touch the cake box without protection.

"Don't worry, we were prepared for this," he said, unfurling a large white evidence bag. With practiced care, he placed the pink cake box and its contents inside, sealing it tightly to prevent contamination.

When the last officer left, Jared quietly closed the door, leaving the office still and heavy with the aftermath. He turned to Verity.

"I..." he began, then faltered. "I'm really... speechless, Verity."

He lowered his head, visibly shaken. "Thank you for saving my life. And Robert's, too. Even if this doesn't prove to be poison, I know what you were trying to do."

Verity saw something shift in his expression—a crack in the polished surface, something softer, more human. Jared looked away, his brow furrowed as if working through the weight of what had just unfolded. When he finally turned back to her, his voice was quieter.

"Why would Kendra want to kill Nicole?"

For a moment, Verity hesitated. A part of her—the part that had doubted herself for too long—felt a quiet triumph at seeing this more vulnerable side of Jared.

"Well," she said gently, "I can think of a few reasons, Jared. First of all... she was pregnant with your baby."

Jared turned away again, silent.

"And maybe," Verity continued, "she wanted to make sure Nicole wouldn't be coming back to Hillside."

"But Nicole played an important role here—one that was immensely helpful to both Kendra and me," Jared said, still grasping for an explanation that made sense.

"Well, I'm just speculating," Verity said, "but maybe she saw Nicole as a threat. The same way she saw anyone who, in her mind, was gaining ground."

Then Verity let herself have a little fun—Jared was right where she wanted him now.

"Maybe she was jealous of that emerald necklace Nicole loved to flaunt. Maybe you took Nicole out to dinner more often. Maybe she got tired of sharing you. Maybe she didn't like the way Nicole flirted with you. Or maybe"—Verity leaned forward—"she was just sick of all the cover-ups."

Jared sank back into the chair, his face pale, a grayish tone settling beneath his skin. Verity noticed—but didn't care.

"Don't you see, Jared?" she said. "Kendra never wanted to share power. She wanted it all."

Jared's eyes widened, stunned by the implications Verity laid out so plainly.

Visualizing Kendra and her husband holding hands, Verity added, "And maybe Kendra loathed the threesome." To her surprise, saying it brought a small surge of satisfaction.

Jared considered Verity's words, and then, as if he suddenly allowed the naked truth to reveal itself, he said, "So she wanted even me out of the way." Jared stared into space. Then, barring his teeth, he added, "She never would've had this job if it wasn't for me."

Verity was having none of that. "Don't paint yourself as a hero, Jared. We all know how Kendra got this job in the first place—the same as Nicole. And your dirty little threesome and your secret penthouse apartment... your cover is blown, Jared, so quit pretending."

It appeared as though Jared hadn't even heard Verity, as he seemed to be lost in his thoughts. After a few moments, he turned to her and said, "She wanted me out of her way so badly that she was willing to kill me and my nephew." He mouthed the words, incredulous, even though he was standing in the very scene of the intended crime.

"Yes," Verity added, "isn't it amazing to what extent some people will go to try and satisfy their ideals?"

Jared helped Verity back to Ethel's desk and quickly walked away, out of sight. Ethel found an ice pack in the first-aid room.

Verity felt relief as the coldness helped ease the pain in her ankle. Ten minutes after icing, Ethel fitted a support sleeve over Verity's ankle, enabling her to walk, unaided, away from the scene.

SHE DESCENDED the steps of Hillside College, breathing in the crisp, fresh air. It felt like ages since she'd raced up those same steps, not knowing what she would find. Now, as she gazed out over the field behind the school, Verity pictured herself taking a long, cleansing walk. She imagined the sweet scent of grass, the way the tall strands would brush against her jogging pants as she wandered through the open space. Only then did she notice what she'd thrown on in her rush to get to Hillside.

Feeling grounded enough to drive, she made her way toward Angela's place, eager to share the stunning update to the mystery that had haunted Hillside College for over three years. As she turned the key in the ignition, Verity paused for a moment, letting the weight of it all settle in.

A wide grin spread across her face, and she shouted, "Yahoooooooo!" alone in the car. "Good on yuh, girl!" she added, throwing her head back against the headrest and laughing out loud, unbothered by the thought of anyone watching.

VERITY KNEW it would take a while before she could truly wrap her head around everything she'd just uncovered. Debriefing with Angela and Janet—and maybe even Stella—would be a good place to start. And she couldn't wait to tell Rick.

As she walked down the stepping stones toward Angela's apartment, Verity felt like she was ten feet tall. But her very first call was to Rick.

"Rick, I've got one more piece of the puzzle for you. If you thought the last one was startling, well... let's just say I'm glad I'm alive to make this call today."

After hearing about the attempted poisoning—and the actual poisoning of Nicole—Rick suggested they go for a walk to ease Verity's stress.

They strolled along the seawall, breathing in the fresh sea air. When they reached a bench facing English Bay, they sat down.

Verity turned to Rick and said, "You know, it's ironic that Jared hired me to be a spy, but I turned out to be the biggest troublemaker for him, threatening to upset the status quo."

"Ironic, indeed," said Rick, and then he asked, "Do you think that both Jared and Kendra plotted to poison Nicole?"

"No. I think Jared planned to get rid of her by not renewing her contract. He just needed a good reason, and he hoped I could dig up something to justify letting her go."

"So, you believe Kendra was the mastermind behind the poison plot?"

"I do."

"And why was she so determined to get rid of Nicole, who seemed like her best friend at Hillside?"

"Because she wanted Jared all to herself. She was after the power and the glory."

"So, she wanted to turn the threesome into a twosome."

"Absolutely. But I suspect Jared was hoping to find a new member for the team. Believe it or not, he made a pass at me."

"So, the spy role could have been a stepping stone to joining the threesome?"

"Could have been—if I'd let it."

"This is heavy stuff, for sure," said Rick. "When I think about motivations, it's clear Kendra would do almost anything to keep her power. But what about Nicole? What drove her?"

"She wanted job security, and because of her influence, she could get away with bad behavior—strange as that sounds. But there was a bigger motivation."

"What was that?"

"Gold and sparkling jewels, for starters. Maybe trips to Hawaii, like Kendra had. I'm not sure. And then, of course, there was the baby."

HAVING UNRAVELED the bizarre events that once seemed such a mystery, both Verity and Rick felt ready to head home. As they stood up from the bench and began their walk back to Everton, Rick glanced at Verity and said, "You know, Verity, I hope this isn't too forward, but would you like to have dinner with me sometime?"

EPILOGUE

Kendra was sentenced to seventeen years in prison— five years for each attempted murder charge, plus an additional two years because of a prior criminal record for theft many years before.

After a thorough investigation into Jared's possible involvement in Nicole's poisoning, he was cleared of all suspicion. The College Board encouraged him to take early retirement, which he accepted. Jared passed away shortly thereafter.

Nicole moved to Victoria and accepted a teaching position at Victoria Community College, this time with no strings attached.

Stella retired comfortably, enjoying her full benefits.

After divorcing Charlie, Verity began dating Rick. When the College offered her Kendra's former position, she declined. All good things come at a cost, and she knew the price of moving forward was healing herself first.

Now, Verity is a millionaire, having inherited a fortune from Aunt Lucy.

ACKNOWLEDGMENTS

Writing this novel has been a journey—one filled with reflection, discovery, and the realization that the past, no matter how distant, always leaves its mark.

To the women who have shared their stories, knowingly or unknowingly shaping this one—thank you. Our experiences, our choices, and the lessons we carry forward are what make us strong, resilient, and beautifully imperfect. This book is for you.

THE VERITY CHILD TRILOGY

Two women. Two lives shattered. One truth waiting to be exposed.

Nicole leaves her small-town life, desperate for something more—until an intoxicating romance takes a sinister turn.

Verity dedicates herself to her career, believing in the power of education and her ability to make a difference. But when she uncovers the corruption festering beneath the surface, she risks everything—her job, her reputation, and her safety—to reveal the truth.

As betrayal and deception unfold, one man's choices unleash a dangerous trio—and a woman whose ruthless acts threaten to destroy everything.

In the aftermath, Verity flees to the Bahamas, where love beckons—but trust is no longer something she gives freely.

This genre-bending trilogy blends coming-of-age thriller, gripping mystery, and pulse-quickening romance into an unforgettable, high-stakes journey of self-discovery and transformation.

Layered and emotionally rich, this series breaks traditional molds, crossing genres, balancing literary depth with commercial appeal, and tackling complex themes.

Get swept up in a trilogy that defies expectations and dares you to look deeper—because every truth comes at a cost.

Trigger warning for Nicole: Includes depictions of physical violence, an attempted sexual assault, and themes of BDSM. While it does not include explicit sex scenes, it explores intimate power dynamics that may be distressing to some readers.

If you enjoyed this book, please consider leaving a review or star rating.
Thank you so much.

ABOUT THE AUTHOR

<u>Maren Hill</u>

Captivated by the intrigue of everyday life, Maren Hill writes heartfelt, emotional stories that celebrate women and the relationships that shape their lives.

Quirky, good-hearted characters you'd love to know, and stories laced with romance, humor, compassion, and inspiration are trademarks of Maren Hill's books.

<u>J.D. Monk</u>

Written by children's book author JD Monk, *Slimy Slick* appeals to children and adults alike with fascinating facts about banana slugs.

"If you enjoy my books, please leave a review. There's nothing more motivational than positive reviews. Thank you!"

ALSO BY MAREN HILL

Cliffhouse Footprints

Cliffhouse by the Sea

Sunrise Island Sisters

Sunrise Island Christmas

Sunrise Island Celebrations

Nicole

The Troublemakers

Our Forever Place

Make a Spectacular Seashell Lamp

Sealed with a Kiss

BY J.D. MONK

Slimy Slick

The Nighttime Adventures of a Banana Slug

"I thoroughly enjoyed ... Cliffhouse by the Sea... kept me wanting to know what would happen next."

"Maren Hill has done it again! Love this book. Would definitely read more by her."

"This story with Alexa and Kyla was riveting. I really enjoyed the dynamics of these two sisters. This is a great story."

"Beautifully done and exceptionally entertaining, heart-wrenching and delightful.

"Gorgeous writing! I love the author's rich descriptions of characters, scenes and situations - I felt like I was living it."

"JD Monk writes with a simplicity that pulls kids into the story immediately, but also with an underlying complexity and intelligence that allows the ideas in Slimy Slick to stay with them long after the tale ends. Well done!"

"This is a great story. Congratulations to the author for bringing awareness to these little creatures who are often misunderstood and undervalued. I love the education/entertainment combo. The illustrations are engaging and hilarious."

"Beautifully written and illustrated -- this is a wonderful bedtime story! Not only do we learn about the importance of banana slugs in our ecosystem in this story, but we're introduced to lovely language to increase the richness of our vocabulary. This is an awesome gift for children (and their parents) who are curious about their environment!"

"What a wonderful read! It was extremely informative about Banana Slugs; a very misunderstood creature. I learned a lot! The graphics are very well done! Definitely a must buy this Holiday Season for the little ones in the family!"

"Loved this book! Very well written, easy to understand and follow for children! Super informative as well, I had no idea slugs were this unique!"

"I have a whole new appreciation for slugs...The kids love it."

"... full of amazing facts about slugs... Completely recommend for curious kids who love nature."

"The fun facts were marvelous and very informative. 5 stars to the author. Highly recommend."

"Great book, full of lots of interesting slug facts. I recommend this for all young and young-at-heart bug lovers."

"Perfect for storytime and a wonderful way to explore nature!"

SLIMY SLICK—NOT
JUST FOR KIDS

The Nighttime Adventures of a Banana Slug

This captivating picture book appeals to kids and adults through multiple reads and is jam-packed with suspense, slime, and fun facts.

Join Slimy Slick on his exciting nighttime adventure through the countryside as he glides toward the tasty treat of his dreams. He encounters an earthworm and a shrew, but the real danger lies ahead. Will Slick's journey come to an abrupt end at the hands of a well-meaning boy whose mission is to capture and eliminate? Does he not understand Slick's important role in the ecosystem?

Readers learn about the clever design of the banana slug and how Slick uses his natural gifts to protect himself and navigate life in the wild.

Discover the world of Slimy Slick through a rainforest adventure that educates and entertains, emphasizing the importance of these fascinating creatures to our planet.

Perfect for:

• Parents and grandparents, science teachers, librarians, educators

• Gifts for kids who love nature, rainforest animals, and learning more about the natural world and zoology

• Read-aloud family sharing

• Gaining environmental wisdom

• Understanding empathy and collaboration

9 781777 489144